Talking it Over with Genghis Khan

HEATHER REYES

Published by Oxygen Books Ltd, 2015

Copyright © Heather Reyes 2015

All rights reserved.

No part of this publication may be reproduced, stored in a retrieval system, or transmitted in any form or by any means, without the prior permission in writing of the publisher, nor be otherwise circulated in any form of binding or cover other than that in which it is published and without a similar condition including this condition being imposed on the subsequent purchaser.

A CIP catalogue record for this book is available from the British Library.

ISBN 978 099263649 4

Typeset in Sabon by Bookcraft Limited, Stroud, Gloucestershire

For Ed, Jo and Catriona

ACKNOWLEDGEMENTS

'Talking it over with Genghis Khan'
　　　　　　　　　　first appeared in *Chapman* (Scotland)
'The colour of 33' first appeared in *Ambit*
'After uranium' first appeared in *Staple New Writing*
'Terrible tales of time and tide'
　　　　　　　　　　first appeared in *Fiction International* (USA)
'One magenta sock' first appeared in *Mslexia*
'Kant's day off' first appeared in *Philosophy Now*
'Feathers' was shortlisted for an Asham Award
'Speak, Gargoyle' first appeared in *Chimera*
'I liked my Bible because it had a lilac cover'
　　　　　　　　　　　　　　first appeared in *Fire*
'In the bruise-coloured night' first appeared in *Fire*
'Come back Lapis Lazuli, all is forgiven'
　　　　　　　　　　first appeared in *Fiction International* (USA)
'The hidden life of carmine' first appeared in *Chimera*
'Campaign for more topaz' first appeared in *Chimera*

CONTENTS

I

Talking it over with Genghis Khan 9
The colour of '33 17
After uranium 21
Do kittens dream in primrose? 32
A grandmother's green should be reseda 37
Terrible tales of time and tide 46
One magenta sock. 53
Kant's day off 58
Big. 68
'Say "Hello" to the fairies, Karl' 73
Nietzsche, my darling 78
Feathers. 89
Pictures for an exhibition 101
Looking for Little Miss Universe. 118
Mr Davidsbündler comes to call
    (or 'If on an autumn morn a traveller') 130
Pink. 139
Speak, Gargoyle 147
The Big 'D' Gang (or 'The Case of the Double Quincunx') . 157

II

I liked my Bible because it had a lilac cover. 183
Where did you put my khaki shorts?. 186
Hello, indigo. 189
The meaning of geranium 190
In the bruise-coloured night 194
Come back, lapis lazuli, all is forgiven. 196

The hidden life of carmine. 200
Remembering saffron 203
The shock of pink grapefruit. 205
The lavender bride 209
Cerise: yes. 210
Campaign for more topaz 214
But is it *periwinkle*?. 218
A moth-coloured nap 220
Reasons to be purple. 222

Interview with the author 225

I

TALKING IT OVER WITH GENGHIS KHAN

When Eva first learned about wars and things, she thought she'd better start going to church – just in case. If you prayed hard enough, you were supposed to get your own way – apparently. Like 'no more wars'. If that was the case, it seemed a pity that not enough people in the past had bothered.

To one side of the chapel of Our Lady of the Immaculate Conception, Jesus pointed to a sort of Valentine's card on his chest – a big red heart with different length sun-rays coming out of it. But he didn't look particularly pleased about getting the card. A bit sad, really. On the opposite side, a lady in blue and white smiled down sweetly at the snake she'd trodden on and the candles around her were crying themselves away. Between the two, above the altar, yellowy white and hanging heavily from the nails was the awful body. The vermillion droplets painted on it, so red and so many, made her think of nosebleeds, and then of a procession of footballers across old snow. But the red shirts of the footballers burst into machine-gun fire, and then turned back to blood as soldiers died in the snow. And all the suffering people began pouring out of the wound in Christ's side. No wonder the other Jesus didn't look too impressed with the Valentine's card: there wasn't really much love about at all, to judge from what was coming out of His side.

If you waited in the quiet of the empty church, waited, and watched the great wound under the ribs, Time ran backwards and you saw nearly two thousand years of tortured, suffering people trailing out of it like a ragged column of damaged ants. And if you waited and waited, in the end you'd see Him stagger out of His own side, stumbling under the great cross – only it would be little, all the people very little, seen from a long way off so the particularities of their wounds and sadnesses were reduced by Time and not so upsetting, like turning the telescope round and looking through the wrong end to push everything far, far into the miniscule distance. But, even at that remove, she could see them stretching out their tiny arms to her.

Then a sudden close-up. People dragging themselves out of the mud – like in that film she'd seen – torn, rotting, showing a piece of cheekbone, the bloodied knob of a shoulder-joint, red trickling from what was once a mouth and from the nose-spaces. They crawled towards her, dragging themselves forward for her to heal and mend and soothe, and to have her tell them it didn't really happen, that History was only a bad dream that all the world had dreamt at the same time.

She started with the soldiers, working the shreds of flesh back onto the faces like a sculptor pressing globs of clay on to build up a head, sucking out the bullets like mammoth bee-stings, and sending them all home to their wives and mothers and children whose black clothes she took off, dressing them instead for a celebration and putting flowers everywhere.

It took a lot of time and concentration to do all that. They couldn't make out why she'd turned so quiet and strange at home. They suspected it was something to do with this going to church business. And it was exhausting work, too, persuading Herod not to kill all those babies, calming Genghis Khan down, and trying to convince Hitler, 'Look, you're not going to win, you know.' It meant hours and hours in your own room, growing paler and paler – except beneath the eyes.

She began to develop her own theory that the thugs of History were really all the same person reborn at different times. Well, they all seemed to have moustaches. Obviously thought they were 'real men' – or suspected they weren't and were trying to ... Anyway, whichever one you were trying to reason with, it felt like the same as all the others – except Genghis Khan's clothes were more interesting. If they *were* all the same person, then she could just choose one manifestation and try talking it over with *him* – all the dead babies, the Jews ... everything. She'd choose Genghis, of course; more interesting to look at if that picture in the encyclopaedia was anything to go by. Better than just a Charlie Chaplin in uniform.

She had him sitting there for hours, cross-legged on her bed, while she paced up and down the pink fluffy carpet, and him having to take his furs off because of the central heating so that all his gold chains and stuff hung on his ever-so-hairy chest and his purple and orange baggy trousers clashed with the pink bedspread.

'Don't you understand? People are going to hate you for *ever*. History will ... '

And sometimes, try as she might to keep him Genghis, his flying moustachios would shrink and he'd become jerky, beady-eyed little Hitler.

'How *could* you ... ?!'

Once she made *him* – yes, Adolph himself – sit there while she read the whole of *Anne Frank's Diary* to him, even though it took until two in the morning and she dozed off during Maths the next day. She'd begun to believe she was getting somewhere with him – them – though you couldn't be sure, of course. But anything was worth a try.

Sometimes she looked around the class and wondered if anyone else was talking to Genghis Khan or any of them, and whether she could ask for help with mending the soldiers. Even if she managed one a day for the rest of her life, she'd never get through a fraction of those poppy petals falling from the roof of the Albert Hall. And that was just for a *couple* of wars. But she realised there wasn't much chance, not in that class, anyway. You only had to listen to them talk.

The thing she found most difficult to understand was how, after the Renaissance and the Enlightenment and the other big ideas clever Miss Wheatcroft went on about, there could still be people killed for their colour, their religion, or what they did with words. So many hurt bodies. Each of us living on a hill of hurt bodies. Let alone minds. But that was to come ...

As she walked to church early on Easter morning – grey, dank, and not at all hopeful, crows circling the still bare tree-tops – she wondered if many people got muddled up between Renaissance and Resurrection, like Nancy Goodrich always did ('always' meaning twice, really). Renaissance was a nicer word. Prettier clothes went with it – rich-coloured velvets, pearls, ruffs, embroidery, gold thread. Resurrection didn't have much more than grubby old sheet-things draped around the people (if the pictures in her Bible were anything to go by). There'd probably be old blood-stains or something, too. And all that dust in the creases. In Religious Instruction, Mrs Legg had talked about the rebirth of Nature and Hope in the Spring and how it was no coincidence that Easter came at this time of year. Eva thought of asking about Australia, where it was autumn now, then remembered that Christians hadn't started down there so it probably didn't count.

She also wondered why you didn't use Renaissance about Nature, only boring old 'rebirth'. Of course, Renaissance was supposed to be all painting and old books and stuff like that (as well as the fancy clothes). But it was such a lovely word, Eva decided to start a fashion for using it about the bulbs coming up again so miraculously, and pink bursting from dead-looking apple-tree twigs ... or any other time you'd usually want the word 'rebirth'.

By this time, her way to church was taking her past the park with the playground where she'd fallen off the slide when she was seven. But it had gone now. So had the old green-slatted roundabout with the huge, red-painted knob in the middle that was too hot to hold onto in the summer and so hand-hurtingly cold in the winter. The park was being remodelled, being brought up to date, and having the drainage done, too. There were still several big concrete pipes that hadn't been used.

Then somebody moved in the bushes. Eva looked around, feeling suddenly alone and visible in the grey morning. No-one else was out walking so early. If it was a murderer, she'd have to try one of her Genghis-type conversations on him, persuade him he'd be a lot happier – and so would everyone else – if ...

From the bushes there emerged a rather elderly woman in an old-fashioned green coat. Her hands were clasped across her stomach and a cream plastic handbag hung from her right forearm. The grass was muddy and her heels, though not so very high, kept sinking in, making the woman's walk look clumsy and uncertain.

She reached one of the concrete pipes, stopped, and looked around as if checking she was alone. A crow flew over slowly, as crows do, making a sound like a laugh in slow motion. Eva kept very still. The woman manoeuvred herself onto her knees at the entrance to the pipe, then disappeared inside. Perhaps she was looking for something she'd lost. But how did she know it was in the pipe? She couldn't have dropped it there herself. Women like that didn't go in pipes.

Eva went closer so she could see right in. The woman was on her side, making struggling movements with her arms and legs every now and then. And slowly, very slowly, she was edging her way through the pipe. From time to time she seemed to be looking at her watch.

Eva wondered if she should call an ambulance.

Then the woman was through. She struggled stiffly to her feet and pulled something brown out of her handbag, which she had kept hold of all the time. Unfolding it, she spread the brown thing on the ground, got down on her knees again, then awkwardly manoeuvred herself right down and onto her back.

It was then that the awful crying started – a comedian taking off a baby, but also a man on fire.

Remembering the broken glass that was often all over the playground, Eva ran to bind the old woman's wounds. This was a real woman, real wounds, so it would probably be easier than what she was used to. She only wished she had more than one handkerchief with her.

The woman looked more and more a tortoise on its back, limbs working like a tipped-over clockwork toy. Her face was puckered, her old but lipsticked mouth open wide, and there was a white bulge of flesh between the tops of her old-fashioned stockings and the crotch of her pink knickers.

Eva stood beside her now, looking down. The red mouth snapped shut. The eyes opened, disbelieving, then afraid, and only after the years and years of the five seconds for which they looked at each other in silence did the woman's face dissolve into something like embarrassment.

'Are you all right?' Eva made herself say. The woman eased herself up to a sitting position and reached for the cream handbag (now smeared with mud) that she'd put on the ground beside her when she went down onto her back. 'I thought you'd hurt yourself. There's often broken glass. Sorry if I made you jump.'

'It's all right,' said the woman, struggling ungracefully to her feet. 'You didn't really spoil it. I'd done the main part already.'

'Main part of what?'

'The treatment. I read about it in an old magazine at the dentist's and thought it might help. "Re-living the birth process" they called it. I've had my eye on these pipes for ages. And it had to be ten to eight – that's the time I was born.'

'On Easter Day?'

'No ... October.'

'It doesn't matter about the date, then? – just the time.'

'I'm not sure now you mention it. Perhaps you're right. Perhaps that's why I don't feel different – well, not very.'

'You don't feel better?'

'It might be too soon to tell. These deep things take their time.'

Eva thought of all the hours she'd spent mending soldiers. She scanned the woman's body quickly. It must be internal injuries, then.

'What is it that's wrong with you?'

'They tell me it was the Blitz – being cuddled by a dead mother for a day before they dug me out. They say I've never been quite right in the head because of that. But it's difficult for me to know. I mean, what are other people like in the head? I was only three at the time.' She bent down with an effort, picked up the sheet of brown paper, refolded it and pushed it back into her handbag. 'Didn't want to get my coat dirty,' she said, brushing the skeleton of a last-year's leaf from her sleeve. 'I'll go back now.' But she stood still, looking at the pipe.

After a few moments, Eva thought she'd better remind her about going back, and take the opportunity of using her word, too. She said, 'I hope you feel better ... for your *Renaissance* ... when you get back.'

'Oh – yes – back. Thank you.'

Eva was disappointed. The woman didn't bat an eyelid at the word 'Renaissance'. Never mind. She could try it on someone else – it just seemed such a perfect opportunity.

The woman turned and began to walk away, crookedly, over the oozy grass. There was laughter from the pond: the ducks had woken up.

'So,' thought Eva, 'it's worse than I thought. It's minds as well as bodies. I'm going to give Genghis a real piece of my mind tonight.' She sighed wearily and dragged herself on towards the church.

After the service she knelt there, as usual, looking at the three of them – Jesus of the Valentine, His snake-squashing mummy, and big dead Jesus. A tiny woman in a green coat crawled out from under His ribs, catching her handbag on the edge of the wound.

'I could do with a bit of help,' Eva said. 'It's a bit much expecting me to do it all. I don't mind having a go at things I can see, but I'm not a psychiatrist.'

Jesus stretched, looking surprised to see the Valentine's card in his hand, turned it over curiously, shrugged, and tossed it over His shoulder. Mary said 'Stay!' firmly, to the snake – thought better of it, removed her white veil, popped the half-dead creature in it, tied it up and kicked it into the corner.

Eva stood up.

'We thought you'd never ask,' said Jesus.

'OK, let's get going,' said Mary.

Eva paused and looked hopefully towards the crucifix.

'Not a chance,' said Mary. 'Dead as a door-nail. He can be a reminder, anyway.'

Eva couldn't help wishing their clothes were a bit more striking and their faces less plastery-looking. Would they cut any ice with Genghis Khan?

A passing bag-lady saw a girl and two statues walk out of the church. Eva noticed her and called out, 'Don't worry. Everything'll be all right soon. There's going to be a *Renaissance*!'

The bag-lady paused, broke into a cackling laugh and continued towards the litter-bin she'd spotted on the next lamp-post.

THE COLOUR OF '33

Kandinsky. That sky-candy man with his blues and his rainbows. 'Blue Rider'. 'Blue Mountain'. 'Blue of the Sky'. Some people say his rainbows mean Salvation. Those rainbows! – arcs in the heavens. Geometry of the spirit? – or just geometry? Whatever.

Acts of special intimacy in the presence of strangers: art shows are the sexiest things – don't you find that? Museums too. All that dim lighting and a sense of one's brevity. *Carpe diem.* The best was when we all but came together by paddling palms in front of a half-lit case of Chinese jade. (True, we were familiar lovers and it was Paris – but it felt subversive, insides melting like that just two metres from a Nazi-faced guard.)

You stand there, stripped naked by the picture – bare, forked animal. The irresistible foreplay of the label draws you on with names and titles and little tickles of interpretation and, before you know it, you're right there, in the arms of the painting, giving yourself to it, feeling its entrance as gentle or forced. (Had a friend, once, raped by Munch's scream: took her a long time to get over it.)

At the Kandinsky we started off together. Okay, so I like to spend a little longer on the foreplay than my lover does, but over the years I've learnt to read the labels quickly so I can keep up with him. It wasn't really a problem. I'd also got used to being at his side when his eyes caressed the curves that were not mine and he was led away to the picture's private place to take his pleasure. Fleeting intimacies. I tried not to be jealous. Sometimes he would share his experiences with me – how the picture had touched him and where; whether it was an encounter he would remember. Of those that had satisfied him most – or touched him in some way or place that none other had – I would find postcards pinned to his notice-board or propped against his desk-lamp. I've learnt to accept these passing enthusiasms competing for his attention – apart from my rage that time over the Modigliani nude. It wasn't so much the exquisite, long neck and seductively lowered eyes I minded, but the dark triangle below. 'Should I dye mine black?' I asked him. His laughter reduced me to tears. Us women and our insecurities!

But this was Kandinsky. His arm around me, we stood naked in front of 'Improvisation 27 (Garden of Love)'. I believe they call it troilism: three in a bed. Moistly we went together into the yellow burning at its centre. It had its way with us both and our pleasure was equal. I have no problem with that.

'Composition VII' was a different matter. Still langorously post-coital from the Garden of Love, we ambled towards it. I hadn't even finished reading the label when his arm dropped from my shoulder and he was tearing off his clothes muttering, 'Oh, beautiful, so beautiful ... ' and before I could even say 'Wait for me!', he was in there and wrapped in a rainbow, giving himself to cherry, cobalt, and reseda, entering blindly into the white spaces. He was too far gone for sharing. I'd leave him to it, come back myself in a while. It'd be worth it, judging from the moans of pleasure in his eyes.

I went to another room entirely. What's the big deal with chronology?

The usual orgy was in progress – shameless sensuality in a public place. Optical thrills spilling and quivering on the skin of our dreams. Eyes wide, I loved it.

Across that crowded room I saw my chance for a light encounter – a canvas scattered with tit-bits of charm. But just as I began to slip out of my tee-shirt, two Spanish women beat me to it. They were well away – noisy with it. (Critics, maybe.)

Only one picture touting for attention now: dark and

The colour of '33

different. Small. Silent. Monochrome. Alien and neglected among all that refined promiscuity of rainbows. One haunting old black-and-white photo in an album of jolly-coloured snaps. At least I'd have it to myself.

I went for the foreplay. It wasn't exactly frisky. Title: 'Grim Situation'. Date: 1933.

I was going to get more than I'd bargained for. It tapped depths of depraved knowledge in me that I'd nearly forgotten among all those kaleidoscopic antics, those carnivals of colour. All that sky-candy.

Jack-boots. Whips. Black leather. I cowered in the corner, guessing what would come. A brutal opening. 1933.

Naked and bleeding with History, I was still standing before that dark aberration when a couple of teenagers came up – American. They were holding hands with a Babes-in-the-Wood kind of innocence. I'd have bet my ears they were virgins (in art, at least).

'Hey, it's a funny little potato-man!'

'Or some kinda large bean – a bean with a kinda face on.'

'You mean it's a human bean?'

That seemed to strike them as pretty funny. They were absorbed in laughter for a while – during which she leaned towards him and flicked his ear lightly with the tip of her tongue. I don't think they even saw me there, still trembling from the jack-boots.

'What d'ya think the human bean's supposed to be doing?'

'I dunno. Looks like he's about to fall off the edge of something.'

'Maybe he hasn't noticed where he's at.'

'Maybe he's blind and no-one's told him.'

'D'you think it's maybe some kinda drawing he never got around to colouring in?'

'I dunno. Maybe it says on the ticket.'

I stepped back so she could read the label – though it seemed their mood of happy inconsequentiality was about to be

Talking it over with Genghis Khan

sledge-hammered by a date. 1933.

'What does it say?'

'Just "Grim Situation".'

'Yep – I guess it would be, if you couldn't see where you were going.'

'Doesn't say anything about it not being finished – nothing 'bout the no colour.'

It just came out. 'The date,' I said. 'The date explains it all. 1933.' They looked at each other. I saw their eyes say, 'Loony: let's split' – the way you do when you're young.

They split, leaving me to 1933.

Maybe I was jealous: they'd merely been toyed with and sent on their way with a pat on the buttocks while I was still sore from deep abuse.

And even if their virginal state had've been momentarily fingered by the Grim Situation, they only had to turn away from History and ... 'Look! Here's a rainbow he made earlier!' He was nothing if not merciful, old sky-candy man.

What with the colour of '33 in me and that 'mad woman' look from the young, I searched out my lover to comfort me. But he was heavily into a cute little patch of red when I found him. He didn't even notice me. It was getting very up close and personal and I was in no mood for sharing the colour of blood.

A sudden urge to drag him away at the height of his pleasure and force him to endure that abusive 'Situation' so he'd understand how I was feeling.

But that's not how we are with each other.

I'd have to find my own solution. 'Come on, sky-candy man, help me ... '

Only one thing for it. Blue.

'Blue Mountain' was being stroked and climbed by a whole party of Italians. But there was 'Blue Rider' ... Just what I needed.

Ah – that's better. Now, ride me, Blue Rider, ride me ...

AFTER URANIUM

On the first day at the High School, you had to write about what you wanted to be when you grew up. When she was eight, Alma had wanted to be a ballet dancer, because she'd read the story of Anna Pavlova. When she was nine, she'd wanted to be a missionary, because she'd read the story of Gladys Aylward. When she was ten, she'd wanted to discover uranium, because she'd read the story of Marie Curie. It was a while before it dawned on her that you couldn't discover uranium twice.

And now she didn't know what she wanted to be.

'Why aren't you writing anything?' said the girl with the heavy laburnum bunches who sat next to her.

'I don't know what to put.'

'It doesn't matter. Put any old thing – a nurse or a typist or something. They only want to see what our spelling's like.'

'Then why don't they give us a spelling test?'

A painful jab from the girl's blue-cardiganned elbow warned of the teacher's approach.

'Bring your books and sit over here, Alma, next to Janice. I think you'll be able to work better.'

The laburnum-haired girl kept her eyes on her two lines of spidery writing where variations on 'secritury' had been attempted several times.

So Alma sat at the desk with NH carved by the hole that used to be for the ink in the old days but was full of pencil-sharpenings and the crumbs of old erasers. Janice's desk was joined to hers and had a horse's head scratched into the bottom right-hand corner. 'Midnight' was carved beside it. They decided it was either the name of a horse or an adventurous arrangement to go riding with NH in the thickest dark. If it was the latter, Nancy Howard or Nicola Hills or Ninette Hunter and her friend must have been girls of high spirit; it fitted in with the courage to carve on desks. Janice and Alma agreed it was something they would probably never do.

Janice said Midnight was probably dead by now, and Alma said NH might be married.

Janice said it was a shame animals didn't go to heaven, and Alma said she thought they did.

Janice said she was a Catholic so she knew animals went to Limbo because they didn't have souls, and Alma said she thought they did have souls.

Janice said she *wished* they went to heaven, and Alma said she'd always thought they did … but could be wrong.

Between Algebra and History, between Cookery and Latin, between Music and Biology, they discussed the destiny of the souls of animals.

But it wasn't long before Alma stopped believing in animals going to heaven – or people either. It was Poppa's fault – though not really: he hadn't started the wars he told her about.

She'd never had much to do with Poppa when she was little. He was just the thin, very, very old man who lived in Granny Hardy's house. The front garden smelled of cat's piss and the hallway of old bacon. But in the bathroom sat Poppa – great-grandfather, really – painting his pictures with a six-haired brush for the people's eyes. He painted in the bathroom for the daylight, but under the stairs was a little room without windows where he kept all his painting things. It was called 'the cubby-hole' and smelled of turpentine and linseed oil and varnish. There was lots of paper, too, and a green reading-lamp, because that was where he wrote his stories – stories about somewhere called the Somme.

The first time he took her into the cubby-hole he showed her all the tubes of paint and taught her their tongue-twister names: ultramarine, indigo, vermillion, magenta, aquamarine, verdigris ... She loved the cubby-hole with its smells and magic words and the feeling of being in a secret place.

The next time she went into the cubby-hole, some weeks later, she wanted to please him so she told him there was a girl who wanted to be an artist in the book she was reading. The trouble was, the girl wasn't very nice; her sister was much better and wanted to be a writer. He said it sounded a very interesting book. She told him it was called *Little Women* and that the girls' father was away helping in the American Civil War. And that's what started Poppa off about war.

How could she ever rid herself of the green faces in the green mud and poppies growing out of the blood? What *kind* of green? – slime green? – mould green? – mud green? But they were faces – faces of *people*. He told her they called it the Great War because they thought it would be the last one ever, but then came Mr Hitler and the Jews in the ovens and the burning children of Hiroshima. And when she'd asked him, 'Why did God let it happen?', he'd given her a straight answer. But she didn't like to tell Janice. She didn't tell anyone. Somehow she felt they'd all be cross with Poppa if they knew he'd been telling her all those things about the wars.

Next time they had to write a story, hers was about a giant insect crawling out of the mud and kissing a little girl and turning back into a soldier and marching away over the sea into a pink sky that rained poppies. They were supposed to bring the sea into the story somehow. Janice wrote about a day at the seaside – but then Janice spent a lot of time at the seaside, whole summers in Cornwall with her grandmother. She told Alma how the bungalow was strawberry-ice-cream coloured with royal blue lobelia in the hanging basket by the front door and how the net curtains were prettily gathered into bunches at each side of the window, so that when the invitation came for Alma to go with her, she really wanted to.

Janice said it would be her best summer ever, having Alma there, and perhaps they could write a story about it called *The Summer of Friendship* or something like that. Alma said perhaps.

But it turned out to be the summer of Vanessa.

The three-legged dog was bobbing along the base of the cliff again, a little way in front. They called him Bouncer on account of the funny way he moved, but it couldn't have been his real name because he never came when they called him. It would have been nice to know who he belonged to so they could ask how he was made three-legged. Janice said it was a shame Bouncer would die one day and not go to heaven. They stopped and watched Bouncer with the silent respect of undertakers.

But Bouncer had found a girl lying on the sand – or *in* the sand: you couldn't tell which at first because her limbs were almost the same colour as it. He hopped around her excitedly. They thought they'd found his owner. Then a piece of sand came to life as the girl lifted an arm to shoo the dog away. Bouncer persisted and the hand picked up a stone and threw it at the one back leg.

Her hair was the colour of thickened honey, frizzed and standing out like a lampshade with a segment missing where the face looked out, green-eyed and commanding.

'Call off your dog, can't you.'

'He isn't ours. We thought he was yours. He seemed very excited to see you.'

'I've got my period. They can always tell. That's why I'm not swimming or anything. I'm going to read the whole day. I'll have finished an entire book by tea-time, I expect. It's a love story. You can sit down for a while if you want to. I'm Vanessa and I'm thirteen.'

Alma said she was twelve and Janice was going to be twelve next week, and that they'd both read *Little Women*. She lifted

After uranium

her right buttock and pulled from under it a piece of leathery seaweed with a dried, sharp edge. Janice sat down close to Alma, knees up under her chin, cuddling her own pale legs. They looked along the beach, embarrassed, but obedient to the long-limbed creature who said she was a Vanessa.

Bouncer stood at a distance, wary, but head lowered and nostrils open to the compelling scent.

'What do you think happens to animals when they die?' Janice said.

Vanessa grunted and Alma blushed: it wasn't the kind of question to ask someone you'd just met and who was already getting breasts.

'I bet *she* won't have periods for ages yet.' Vanessa pointed to Janice. 'She looks terribly immature.'

Janice looked down and pretended to be interested in a stone she'd found in the sand.

'What's it like, having periods?' Alma tried to rescue them both from the green-eyed scorn.

'I'll show you, if you like. You can come to tea.' She nodded in the direction of a small wooden building on the cliff-top. 'It'll have to be tomorrow or there won't be much worthwhile. I hope you like brown bread for your sandwiches: we never have that white stuff. And it'll be shrimp paste or gooseberry jam. We finished the crab-apple yesterday.'

Vanessa led them up the wooden steps that zig-zagged from the beach to the top of the cliff. A thin metal pipe, fastened at intervals to weathered wooden supports, made a flimsy hand-rail. Half way up, a section of cliff had slipped away from under the steps so that they were not supported. Alma and Janice hesitated.

'Oh, come on, you babies.' Vanessa rolled her eyes skywards. But Janice kept hold of Alma's skirt. 'It's perfectly safe, you two silly bunnies. It's always been like that. I cross it half a dozen times a day. Even the two little boys next door do it, and they're only about *four*.'

The pale, anxious hand still clung to the skirt and the plain brown eyes in the unexceptional face pleaded with Alma not to go on. But up there, seven steps over nothing, the sun was turning the ends of the honey hair to spun gold and green eyes were ready to shed contempt upon children.

'*Go* back, then. *Don't* come to tea.' She turned away from them and stamped on the steps so that the lower ones vibrated alarmingly. Janice let go of Alma's skirt, turned and, grasping tussocks of coarse grass on one side and the rusty hand-rail on the other, went back down to the beach.

Light-headed and breathing heavily, Alma took the seven steps over nothing and was suddenly close to the navy-blue shorts tight over neat buttocks, and was rewarded.

'I thought *you* wouldn't go back.'

'She's not even twelve yet,' said Alma, trying hard to retain a residue of loyalty.

'I've been thirteen for ages. I have lots of *hair*.'

'I thought so.'

The holiday bungalow was entirely of wood painted a faded primrose. On the covered verandah along the front were two pairs of sand shoes and a pile of sea-shells. Vanessa saw Alma's eyes register the childish collection.

'I didn't get those; they were here when we came. We're here for six weeks, you know, though Daddy's only here for three: he has to get back for his work.'

Head thrown up a little, she pushed abruptly against the ill-fitting door. The panes of glass in the upper half of the door trembled, asking for gentleness.

All the colours were faded – wood, curtains, china – as if they were weary from too much light, too much sunshine, a million sunshines.

Her father was tall, very sun-tanned, with thick curly hair and a bulky blue sweater. His shorts were so brief that when Alma sat down and he stood beside her with the plate of shrimp-paste sandwiches, his bronzed, thickly-haired legs came up to the top of her head.

'The other one couldn't come after all, Mummy.' Vanessa addressed a cream dress sprigged with blue, then turned to Alma. 'But you can tell her what she missed, can't you.'

From the bottom of the steps she saw Janice, still on the beach. From the way she moved, Alma could tell she was looking for perfectly white stones, round or oval, smaller and smoother than birds' eggs. They often did that together on a different part of the beach where there were more stones – looking for the purest and most perfect ones. Janice was pretending not to be waiting.

Alma bent down and picked up an ordinary brown stone, fingering it abstractedly. Janice didn't greet her. In the end she went and stood right beside Janice and said, 'The shrimp paste was awful.'

They both knew they'd never discuss the destiny of dead animals again. And she doubted if even Poppa would know how to mix those colours too much in the sun ... Then, in the midst of those greens, blues, yellows, and browns diluted with light had come the bright white pad with the vivid stain of blackish red – making you think of wounds and soldiers – and the strange odour mixed with sweet talcum powder.

No wonder Bouncer knew.

More than one terrible secret was too much.

Janice didn't ask what happened in the bathroom of the house on the cliff, so Janice told her about Poppa and the cubby-hole stories and the faces in the mud. Alma didn't cry about it anymore. She'd put the faces in a large, dry chamber of horrors along with what men did to ladies and the black child with twig legs, balloon belly and flies crawling in its eyes.

It didn't make Janice cry, either, because she said the 'real' bit of the soldiers would have been in heaven by then, not in the mud.

But before they went to sleep under the identical flowered bed-covers with the tasselled bedside lamp between them, they agreed that war was dreadful, and so was having no food. They said they'd see to it that when they were grown up there wouldn't be any more wars – or try to – and they'd raise lots of money so everyone would have enough to eat.

Janice said they could start raising money for the poor right away. They could collect beautiful stones – quite big ones – paint lovely patterns on them, and sell them as paper-weights. She'd seen it in a magazine.

So they went to the beach to find paper-weights for the poor. But the sea and the sky grew vaster and vaster, and searching among the debris along the base of the towering cliff didn't make you feel any larger in the world, either. And there was no sign of Bouncer ... or Vanessa.

By the time they passed the steps to the faded primrose bungalow, they knew they would never sell paper-weights to save the world.

Janice didn't look at the steps and Alma said it might be easier to make the world better if they were men.

Janice said perhaps they should look for stones with holes in them for a change: they could put them on ribbons and sell them as necklaces. Alma said that would be too difficult: there wouldn't be enough of the right stones.

Down the cliff-steps came a mother with two little boys. Vanessa was right: they didn't mind the steps at all. Janice said, 'I bet Vanessa'll smack her children, the way she threw that stone at Bouncer's leg. I won't smack my children, will you?'

Alma said she wasn't going to have any children, and Janice said why not? Alma said because with sons she'd worry about them having to go to war, and with daughters she'd worry about them having babies.

Janice said Alma worried too much.

They both woke up with the storm that night. Janice put her fingers in her ears and went under the bedclothes. Worse than the thunder was the bush outside the window, creaking in the wind like old floor-boards trodden by ghosts and making shadows on the curtain like a hook-nosed general when the lightning came. Alma listened for the man being swept overboard and the fish laughing and the yellow sou'wester caught in the whale's throat and making it cough.

'It must be dreadful up there – Vanessa's place.'

'I bet the doors are rattling.'

'I bet those little boys are scared.'

'They've probably gone in with their mother. She's probably telling them it's only clouds having a battle.'

'When it thunders she'll say, "There go the big guns again" – though that'll probably make them even more scared, being boys.'

'But I don't suppose they know about war yet – Vanessa said they were only about four – not proper war, like with rotting faces and ovens and stuff.'

'Poor little things,' said Alma. 'I think I'd rather be a girl after all, even if it does mean having periods. But I'm still not having babies.'

But Janice said if God didn't mean her to have babies, He'd have made her be born a boy.

Alma said she thought it was just different chemicals.

In the morning the sky was pale grey all over, the sea darker grey, smooth and thick-looking as oil, with no strength left to make any more waves. The edge of the tide that only last night had roared like a drunk man, smashing everything, dozed against the sand a few yards below the thick straggle of seaweed and rubbish it had thrown at the land during the night.

A little way out, something light brown was floating, inert, with a look of weighty softness that suggested dead flesh of some sort. It drifted slowly with the direction of the current, moving nearly parallel to the beach, but not quite. Making almost imperceptible progress towards the beach, it would be washed up, in the end, some fifty yards or so further along. Was it a small child? – a dog? – a large sea-bird? Janice hadn't noticed it. Alma tried to forget it, but her eyes kept sliding towards its slow, persistent progress towards the beach. She tried to convince herself it was driftwood because she didn't know how she knew it was something dead.

They came level with 'Vanessa's place'.

'You see!' Janice pointed to where the steps ended half-way down the cliff. The lower part of the stairway lay twisted on the beach. They looked up. The two little boys were leaning over the wooden gate at the top of the steps, marooned. The mother appeared and looked as if she were trying to tie up the gate with string.

'I bet they're fed up, not being able to get down to the beach,' Janice said.

'Might be just as well.'

Janice followed Alma's eyes to where the dead thing lolled at the edge of the tide. Alma hoped Janice wouldn't say anything about heaven, whatever the thing was: she didn't want to feel like hitting her.

It was an enormous sea-bird. They were looking straight down at it now, rolling heavily back and forth as the water nudged, then tugged at its weighty wings. No-one else was on the beach and the bird at their feet was the only one in sight. Even the little boys had gone from the cliff-top.

'It's as if something terrible's happened and everything's dead,' said Janice, 'as if there's been an atom bomb or something.'

'Then we'd be dead, too,' said Alma.

'We might not be,' said Janice.

'I don't want to die – ever,' said Alma.

'I wouldn't mind as long as I could be in heaven,' Janice said.

Alma watched her look up. The sky was blank and grey, rather near, with no hint of infinity.

DO KITTENS DREAM IN PRIMROSE?

The story of a question. Of what it led a young woman called Lily to think about. And how this changed her life. (Possibly.)

It wasn't her own kittens she was looking at when the question came to her. She didn't have any. It was someone else's kittens – someone who played at having a special affinity with cats ... just as Lily played at having no affinity with cats. Nor with any other animal, come to that. Not even men. Or, rather, she played the part of someone who knew it wasn't possible to be sure if one *did* have an affinity with animals as you couldn't know what it was like to be them. Not being able to get inside their heads. (That is to say, Lily was a reasonably intelligent young woman.)

'If they don't dream in primrose, then they should.' Those wide, permanently startled eyes probably let in too much sunlight, turning the world to a collage of diluted butter colours.

The colours of the day tinged with moonlight for dreaming. Pale butter, add a drip of silver and there you have it: primrose. The colour of kitten dreams. Perhaps. Dreams of what? Being set among primrose pigeons? Or being let out of a dark bag into the primrose light? The nightmare of a hot, tin primrose roof? The wish for pleasure, the need for freedom, the fear of pain. Common to all living things. Something to do with the pleasure principle, wasn't it? Lily was trying to remember that lesson on Freud.

Remembering Freud reminded her how startled she'd been to discover she was supposed to have wanted a penis, when she was little, and to have wanted to seduce her father. If both these supposed wishes had've been granted, she could've ended up (so to speak) buggering Daddy. And how *could* Freud have thought little girls wanted *giblets* – them so vulnerable, stuck on the front like that. It made you wince to see a man on a bicycle.

Nor did she believe little boys envied girls their wombs. Only those too young to know anything about it could do that. The mere thought of that monthly mess and the terror of having a live animal growing inside you, surely that was quite enough to put them off.

He certainly was a queer fish, Freud – life just a boobs and willies affair for him. Lily thought she probably preferred Jung – though she wasn't sure how viable the idea of a collective unconscious actually was. She asked Angelica what *she* thought of Jung. Angelica was interested in dreaming. (She was the one with the kittens.)

Angelica was fascinating and lovable to Lily. Lily – sharp-featured, ash blonde, exquisitely tapered ankles – loved to be near the rounder, milky flesh and lush auburn hair that was Angelica. Though Lily didn't love her so-called affinity with cats: pretence, she thought it, secretly.

Over the mantelpiece, a large, rectangular mirror showed Lily and Angelica, legs curled under them, on the floor, beside the large, blanket-lined basket where seven Persian blue kittens slept on and by each other and their mother.

'What do I think of Jung?' repeated Angelica. She often did that – repeated a question she'd been asked. It was only slightly irritating. You could tell she did it to give herself more time to think. Angelica was very thoughtful. It was another reason Lily had for loving her.

'His "archetypal images" theory seems quite reasonable to me,' said Angelica (thoughtfully, of course). 'After all, there are certain things all humans on the planet experience – the events of the sky, knowledge of water and fire, fear, the wish to control what seems uncontrollable ... like illness, death, birth ... and for there to be a great and benevolent parent in charge, one you can rely on, utterly. Someone to love you and keep you safe.'

Lily thought this was a good answer. She certainly liked the idea of an uncompromisingly benevolent and reliable – if distant – parent to all the Freud stuff about sex between parents and children. But then it probably depended on what you meant by 'sex'.

Then Lily began to wonder whether animals might also possess archetypes of their own – emerging only in dreams since they could not manifest themselves in religion or a mythology passed down the animal generations as they had no proper language – not the kind for telling stories with. For cats, did 'being chased by dogs' turn itself into an archetypal image? Or the wish to deprive all birds of flight? – or that mice should move more slowly? And if there *were* a special range of cat archetypes, how different would they be from dog archetypes? ... or kangaroo archetypes?

She couldn't help thinking that the *similarities* between creatures of the planet could more or less be taken for granted: it was the *differences* that made them interesting and worthwhile.

At one time, people wanted to read histories of whole nations, of the whole world – wanted to make it one big story, the story of Mankind. Which meant ignoring so much. Including, most often, the breasted half of the world's population. Reducing, eliminating, changing. But things were more sensible now. There were histories of things like fingernails, spoons, or the words used for sex. Just the other day she had seen, in a bookshop window, a history of skin.

The history of cats was not the history of dogs. Difference. Differences.

It was sad to think those kittens, dreaming away there – in primrose, probably – would never know their own history.

'What *is* the history of cats?' she asked Angelica, partly to make Angelica love her more, because Angelica enjoyed telling people things she knew – but without seeming arrogant about it. It was one of the reasons Lily loved her.

Angelica told her about the taming of the African wild cat, *felis lybica*, in Egypt around 3,000 BCE to guard the stores of grain, its progress to special god-status, but how it had been so terribly abused and maligned, too, especially in the Middle Ages. She told her about the Great Cat Massacre and why they were associated with witches. She told her about a minor cat hero, Howel Dda, Prince of South Central Wales, who passed a law, in 936 CE for the protection of cats, and how sad it made her to think of the millions of kittens drowned or thrown against walls or having their tiny necks broken. She was not, she said, sentimental, but such things turned her against men. Most of them could do it so easily, it seemed.

Lily didn't want to think of what happened to kittens ... how their miraculous little lives were snuffed out without a thought – in water, against walls, or hands on the neck. Nearly always by men.

Lily said she supposed the reason she'd never felt anything special for cats was the fact that most of the words beginning with 'cat' seemed to have something negative about them – cataclysm, catacomb, catapult, catarrh, catastrophe, catatonic ...

Angelica smiled. 'So cats must suffer because you didn't learn Greek.'

Lily blushed, indignant. 'I have never hurt a cat in my life.'

'*It is enough for a good man to do nothing in order for evil to ...* '

Lily found she had placed a hand over the quoting lips.

Angelica touched the palm lightly with her tongue.

Lily withdrew her hand as from a small electric shock.

Angelica laughed. Then she touched Lily's burning cheek lightly with the backs of her fingers. It was the same movement Lily had seen her make touching a cat. It was a very bold thing to do, wasn't it? She thought she knew Angelica very well and it wasn't what she expected her to do at all.

She tried telling herself you should never be surprised by what people do because you cannot get inside their heads and everyone sees the world differently. Like watching someone asleep and knowing they are living through a secret dream you cannot see, and longing to be in the dream with them because of the special smile on their face. Perhaps that was why, in love, opposites so often attracted – the wanting to get inside, or encompass, what was different. Man. Woman. Some differences were just too great, though, for Lily. The smaller differences were quite enough. Even those took courage to encounter without flinching.

She shivered slightly with the difference of feeling her skin touched in that way. As if she were a cat. But she sat very still.

Angelica continued to stroke her cheek.

Lily continued to be surprised.

A GRANDMOTHER'S GREEN SHOULD BE RESEDA

One of my grandmothers was the kind people complained about. Sharp-tongued, tending to intolerance, couldn't stand it when neighbours dropped in, uninvited, for a coffee and chat – and stayed two hours. She'd tolerate it once, twice – but her patience didn't run to three times. Possessive, suspicious, I have reason to believe she gave Grandpa a hard time.

She'd kept just one friend from her youth – a tiny, frail lady ('Auntie Cecily') with an impish smile, who didn't take life – or Grandma – too seriously. Impossible to offend – or, if offended, swift to forgive. She was just what Grandma needed. And there was no chance she'd get off with Grandpa: a confirmed spinster, she was safe as a lesbian.

On the days my mother went to work, Grandma met me from school. That wasn't unusual. Quite a few mothers worked, so there were always some grandmas and grandpas at the school gates. They tended to look happier than the proper mums and dads. And they tended, on the whole, to be less embarrassing. I say 'on the whole' because there were days when I wished my grandmother wasn't mine. Those were her emerald days.

On her 'emerald days' she wore 'that frock'. Green as Ireland, green as grasping jealousy, green all over, it shrieked at you right across the playground. And she looked terrible in it.

She did it on purpose, I was sure. How could she *not* see how awful it was, how just ... *not right* at her age to wear something so ... so ... *Robin Hood*. It didn't go with her hair. It didn't go with her eyes. Her skin. Her *age*. If even I, with my nine-year-old eyes, could see that, why, oh why couldn't *she*? I wanted a grandmother who was dignified, dependable-looking. Even a bit boring. But solid. Not this vivid, spring-green apparition.

It wasn't the kind of thing you could tell her to her face – not Grandma. Not even Aunt Cecily could have done that.

The week she'd been emerald three days in a row, I was desperate enough to take my chance. We passed a dress shop on the way from school to her house. By its window, I pretended to have a stone in my shoe and, well, the laces were in *such* a knot it took me ages to sort the problem out. It wasn't *my* fault, was it?

You see, I'd noticed, in the dress-shop window, an outfit that was all green, but not that self-advertising, Saint-Patrick's-Day green. It was ... subtle, subdued – *dignified*. It would be so reassuring to have a grandmother dressed in such clothes. I was convinced that, waiting for me, Grandma would casually glance in the window, spot the outfit, fall in love with it (it was a *kind* of green, after all), and ...

But Grandma was not, in fact, very interested in dress shops. When I sneaked a look up from my 'troublesome' lace, she had her back to the window and was reading the newspaper she'd bought on the way to collect me. It'd have to be the direct approach.

'Oh, look, Grandma. Have you seen that nice green dress in the window there? You like green dresses, don't you. I like that nice sort of palish green, don't you?'

'Reseda,' she said, after the merest glance in the direction of the window.

'What do you mean?' I said.

'That sort of green's called reseda.'

'Reseda,' I repeated. 'Mmm. I think that's a lovely kind of green, don't you?'

'It's all right. A bit ... tame.'

A grandmother's green should be reseda

'I think you'd look really nice in that outfit, Grandma.'
'Not at that price! Your grandpa'ld hit the roof if I went spending that kind of money on clothes. Have you finished fiddling with that shoe yet?'

It wasn't so very long after that – a late October Saturday, I think it was – when we all went to have tea with Grandma and Grandpa. (It might well have been Grandpa's birthday, which was around that time.) My aunt and uncle were there, too, and, as often happened, there was some memory spoken of that Aunt Tessie said they'd got wrong: it was whether someone had been at someone's wedding or not. She said they hadn't: Grandma insisted they had – and that she had a photo somewhere to prove it.

The first two albums failed to turn up any photos of said wedding, so Grandma – determined to prove herself right – went and scrabbled in various cupboards until she came back with an old biscuit tin, saying, 'I've a feeling it's in here, with the loose ones.'

She put the tin on the hearth-rug, eased off the rust-edged lid, her face hardening towards proving her point. (She and Aunt Tess often had such run-ins of the will.)

As well as photographs in the tin, there was a neat little stack of postcards held together with a ribbon. I asked if I could look at them, bored almost silly by the 'difference of opinion' about something the significance of which I didn't understand.

The postcards were very old. Some of them were from when Grandpa was in the navy, before he married Grandma and used to sail away down the Clyde, with the band playing and the flags tugging to escape ... off, off to adventures (the way he'd told it to me so many times). They weren't postcards *to* anybody: they were just postcards. Some had information on the back in handwriting that had not changed significantly in half a century. It was the writing on my birthday cards:

Grandma always left it to him, family things like that.

I thought the first one was black-and-white Paris: it was a nice road of those tall French buildings with long windows and little iron balconies. We'd stayed in a hotel like that only last year. There was a row of Parisian shops – one even said something 'de Paris', clear as anything. Then I noticed a weird white building rising up sneakily behind the French ones. The shape of it was very foreign, with a band of patterns around the top of its glare-white tower. Right above the tower it said ALGER. It wasn't where I thought at all – just *pretending* to be Paris. I turned the card over. In Grandpa's hand was 'Pleasant street, Algiers.'

The next one showed a waterfront. A higgledy-pig of nice little houses. And beneath – 'MITYLENE, TO WHICH THE GREEK ARMY HAS ESCAPED'. The 'has' bothered me: it meant they were still there. And what were they escaping from, anyway? The answer was written right across the back, defying the 'Address Only' instruction. 'Where the Greeks escaped to during the Burning of the City of Smyrna by the Turks in December 1922'. Dreadful, distant things – but the words suggesting they were still going on. 'Has'.

Next, a town half destroyed – lots of rubble, half a small brick bridge over nothing, odd bits of wall not keeping anything up or stopping anyone from going anywhere. And among all this a kind of tent with a dark-faced boy and girl outside. It looked as if something terrible had happened. The girl seemed to be about nine or ten – like me. She didn't have any shoes on. Grandpa's words: 'Chanak, a small port in the Narrows of the Dardanelles which was bombarded by the British Fleet on 5th May 1917.' I could read the words but didn't know what they meant. But you could see from the picture it wasn't very nice.

I looked at my grandfather sitting there, chatting to his son – my father – about redecorating the bedroom. He was so

A grandmother's green should be reseda

familiar and yet ... the places he'd been to, the dreadful things he'd lived through ... Old people, they had so much stuff in their heads they never let on about.

There were lots more of Algiers, one of Madrid, a couple of Lisbon then, right at the bottom, one that was so different from that old black-and-white war stuff that it almost made me gasp.

The front of the card was a panel of fine material exquisitely embroidered with a design of two blue-birds among little gold and white flowers with bright green leaves and some words stitched around the edge of it all: the words were also in bright green and could almost have been taken for more little leaves. I turned it over. It was a card that had been sent through the post from somewhere in England because it had an English stamp (brown with a man's head on it). It was addressed to Miss Elizabeth Hilton, c/o Miss Cecily Smith, and an address I didn't even bother reading. The left side of the card was written in a neat hand, but not Grandpa's. It said, 'I hope to see you very soon. Please read the message in the front of this card. Yours, Edward.'

I turned back to the front of the card and struggled to read the small green letters stitched around the edge. 'Unlike sweet birds ... and flowers ... my ... love ... will never ... die.' The kind of message that made you want to smile and cry at the same time. As I went to turn it over again, my finger found a little loose corner of material. It was a tiny flap, cleverly concealed. I lifted it, and my fingers found a paper pocket under the embroidery. With the curiosity of ordinary childhood, I tried to see if there was anything in the pocket. It was a tiny piece of paper folded-up.

No-one was watching me – they were still bickering about the wedding-guest – so I slipped my little finger carefully inside the pocket and hooked out a miniature letter. The pocket tore a tiny bit at the corner, but not enough to notice once the flap was over it again.

I opened the little folded letter, but the writing was so minute and intricate, I couldn't make out what it said. My mother noticed me holding a small something close to my face and looking puzzled, I suppose, as I tried to read it.

'What have you got there?'

I handed her the Lilliputian letter with, 'What does it say?'

Even my mother had trouble. It came out jerkily, a bit at a time.

'*Dearest ... Bob-bon ...* '

At these words, Grandma – who'd been in mid-sentence (still about that wedding-guest) – fell silent and looked odd. In answer to this 'unrecognisable' expression on her face, everyone else went quiet, too. My mother read on. Busy struggling with the words, she didn't seem to notice how everyone was listening.

'*I cannot ... continue my ... present life ... without ... you. You were wrong about ... men only ... wanting to ... marry vir-* (the end of the word seemed to turn itself into a funny kind of cough from my mother and I couldn't tell what it was supposed to be, but Grandma's face changed colour quite noticeably.) *I want us to ... start a new life away from this ... hypocritical ... little ... island. I have two ... passages booked to ... Australia. If you really love me enough to ... defy your parents, meet me at ... our usual hotel on Friday. We either sail together from ... Southampton next morning, or I go alone. My love always, dearest, dearest Bon-bon. Your Edward.*'

You could have heard a feather drop. But I was the only one looking at Grandma. I had never seen her face so red.

It was one of those moments when time freezes. Five seconds – ten minutes – a year – a life-time ... I couldn't tell you how long the silence lasted before Grandma gave a nervous, grunty little laugh.

A grandmother's green should be reseda

'I always wondered why he upped and went off to Australia, just like that. No word ... '

She gave what I think was supposed to be a smile, but it turned into something that made her face look very odd. Then – even though we'd only just had a cup of tea – Grandma got up and said, 'I'd better put the kettle on. Here's me jawing away and not even giving you a cup of tea.' She seemed blind to the cups and saucers littering the room, so recently used they were probably still warm.

My mother and father were looking at each other strangely across the little sitting-room. A stage whisper from my mother: 'How was *I* supposed to know it was her? I mean, *Bon-bon*!' My father's voice sounded odd, too. 'She didn't find the message. It said the message "in" the front of the card: she must've read it as "on" the front.'

My mother picked up the postcard with its still bright embroidery and read out the vivid green stitchery: '*Unlike sweet birds and flowers ... my love will ... never die.*'

Grandpa had gone over to the window and was staring out into the dimmed October evening. I wondered what he could be finding to look at. No-one said anything to him.

My father told me to collect up the cups and saucers and wash them up for Grandma: she'd need them if she was making more tea. I fetched the tray from the sideboard, piled the cups and saucers sensibly, as I'd been taught to do, and carried them through to the kitchen.

Grandma was at the sink. She was crying in a stifled sort of way.

'I've burnt my finger,' she said, in her unfamiliarly tearful voice.

'Does it hurt very much, Grandma?'

'Yes.'

I thought of the 'Burning of Smyrna' on Grandpa's postcard: if a burnt finger could make someone like *Grandma* cry, the

43

burning of a whole city didn't bear thinking about. The past was a dreadful place.

'Shall I kiss it better for you?'

'Yes,' she whimpered, child-like, and extended the pointing finger of her right hand.

I'd only ever burnt myself once – very slightly – but I knew burns left a red mark. There was no red mark on Grandma's finger. But I kissed it anyway.

And even if there *had*'ve been a real burn, the kissing wouldn't really have made it better. It was just a game you let adults play because you knew they *wanted* to make things better for you. But when I kissed her finger – as gently and as make-it-betterly as I could – she started crying more.

She pulled me to her and held me to her belly in the strangest way. I put my arms around her thick, old-woman's middle and held her to me as much as she held me to her.

After a little while, I thought she'd stopped crying, but still not looking at her oddly altered face I said, 'Why did he call you Bon-bon?'

'French for a sweet.' She tried to put on her information-giving voice – the voice she'd used for 'reseda' that time.

'That's nice. You were his "sweetie".' A misguided attempt to cheer her up. I felt myself pressed even harder to her belly – and she didn't say anything.

Not knowing what to do with her silence, I asked, 'Was he rich?'

'Yes.'

'Rich enough to buy you that reseda dress?'

I felt the slight vibration of what might've been a muffled laugh. 'He would've bought me *ten* of those, if I'd wanted them.'

I was old enough to have taken in the comforting prejudice that rich people aren't usually very nice, so I asked her: 'Was he … nice?'

'He … ' She paused. I looked up at her face, wondering if the silence meant I'd made her cry again. Her mouth was moving as if trying to make words that didn't want to be spoken. I couldn't tell what her eyes were seeing. Then, at last, the words came out.

'He had a wonderful way with a woman.'

My memory of the event ends there – except for the knowledge it buried deep in me: my (… your … our …) utter contingency. A little flap. The difference between 'on' and 'in'. And none of us might have been here at all.

'A wonderful way with a woman.' Of course I didn't know what it meant, so the phrase stuck in my mind which has always hated vacuums in understanding.

It stuck in my mind, uninterpretable, until I was of an age to learn exactly what she meant – after which I could never forget it, anyway.

Though he never called me 'Bon-bon.'

TERRIBLE TALES OF
TIME AND TIDE

... of how they wait for no man, leaving you stranded on the mud-bank, the greyly shallow water running fast past your ankles towards the pebbled shore.

Help!

Little me between the grey water and the grey sky and everything going on forever, space-walking, adrift, whirled without end.

Of course, my father strode laughing through the still-so-shallow (to him) water and lifted me out of my timelessness, dripping feet, oozing eyes, onto his Atlean shoulders, home and dry in time for tea – though the sands of that time had infiltrated the childhood honey of the sandwiches. I ate with my back to the sea, the lostness in the grey water and the grey sky slopping about in my grey matter for ever and ever afterwards: that fearful state tasted out there on the mud-bank with the tide having turned.

Page after page of printed clocks without hands. The instructions: clock (a) 10 minutes to 9; clock (b) half past 3; clock (c) ... '

'Well done!'

That wasn't the problem. I could do *that* quick as a flash in the pan. Tick, tick, tick ...

Got them all right and a golden star, licked by Mrs Wilshire's big red tongue, the gluey side of the star rubbed on the taste of fish-paste sandwiches she breathed over our shoulders in the afternoons. (That tongue! – the absolute opposite of grey nothingness.)

No, that wasn't the problem. I could do *clocks*. It was *Time* that was the problem now. 'Big' Time.

I asked and asked.

ME: But how do we *know* time is passing?

Because the hands of the clock are going round.

ME: But I could close my eyes and not be blind, don't you see?

?

ME: Okay. When was the first tick, then?

What do you mean?

ME: When did it start, this ticking and tocking business.

'When' is an adverb of time: saying *when* it started means it already had.

(I couldn't get my brain around that one – maybe because we hadn't done adverbs then.)

Often I loped off to go and sniff around the heels of Old Father No-Prizes-For-Guessing-Who, my face squashed against the window of the clock shop. Grandaddy pendulums thonking, thonking; little boudoir numbers tit-tit-tittering; respectable ones for sideboards conventional tick-tocking, not rocking any boats; Tempus Fugitting just as fast for the rich; tempers fidgetting to cheap, uncheerful, all-we-can-afford ones; a Wonderland clock for a nursery, the rabbit saying in a ribbon from its mouth, 'I'm late! I'm late!'; modern electric, hands turning to silence. The quiet grey water running past, running fast, though oh so slowly on a Sunday afternoon.

But only sometimes. Depending.

That was the problem. It seemed to *depend*. Sometimes it went faster than others.

'Right. So, there's the world ... ' (Mother doing her best) '... like an orange ... ' Segments. Imaginary lines on the old tin globe with the faded seas. If you could take out a segment, everywhere in it would be the same time – a different time from the segments next to it. It didn't used to be like that. When the sun came up it was morning. But it didn't work out once there were trains and their time-tables. If everywhere along the line was on a different time, how could you be sure not to arrive just to see the back end of the train shrinking into the distance? So, instead of the rhythm of Nature we got the rhythm of Man. Cut and dried. Knew where you were – and when (which is more to the point). And wars, of course. Military time. It made it easier to synchronise watches and ... (She didn't need to say it: splatterings of blood, bone, brain ... boum, boum, boum.)

BUT what about, I said, what about when the old man in the park talked about that old war and was THERE as he talked, and when me being four was so clear in my head still, or when Mrs Wilshire talked about what we'd be doing tomorrow: how could all that be NOW because they were all different times but all sort of there together being lived at once. And she said what I was talking about was just memory and imagination, which could make all times now, or you could get out of the now into all times, through imagination, though only as we thought they were, or would be.

That was it!

THE GREAT ESCAPE!

I didn't have to be in nasty *now* at all. I put that to good use straight away – well, next day, anyway, when Mrs Wilshire read us the story-I-hated-most because it was full of animals talking, which is silly.

It worked. I spent the half hour sailing up the Amazon, discovering lots of new birds with beautiful feathers. So I started taking regular walks across Australia, climbing Mount Everest, and diving in the oceans with the big, magnificent fish, and the shimmering shoals of little coloured ones ... Made friends with a polar bear ... Saved a baby monkey ...

And when it was time for THE SCHOOL REPORT that Alice and Jane and Paul and Joseph were so worried about in case they didn't get a good one and lots of presents for it, my escapes had been duly noted, my progress doubted for day-dreaming, and a change most definitely expected. But Mother-dear shrugged, hugged me, said, 'Dream on, my darling, escape all you can. Don't get trapped in the workings of any mechanical clock.'

'But why,' I said, 'why does it all *depend*? Why's there a ball and chain around Time's ankle for Arithmetic and a wind behind it when I'm turning the pages of my *Bumper Book of Myths and Legends*?'

'That's just Time's winged chariot changing gear,' she said. (Whatever that meant.)

And no easier as I got older.

School days? School *daze*. Standing by the sea, the waves coming and coming, always different ones, always the same. Over and over. Could be last or next week. Same time, same place – and but for the date in the top right-hand corner of the blackboard, who'd know? Standing still, the changing dates running past your ankles, fast to the shore. Is that the future I see before me?

Lines on the hands. Crystal balls. Comets and tea-leaves. That meant there was somewhere where it'd all *already happened*. Some people had the trick of seeing that place, and though they didn't seem to make a fortune out of it if Madame Cabalatska on the sea-front was anything to go by (perhaps slipped to the future on the grease of her hair), it certainly made you stop and take stock of the old tock-tock question. If it's all already ... then ...???

Bye-bye free will. Greetings, O puppet-on-a-string, O me. Born with the script in your head, presumably. Strings. Or maybe mechanical. Wind you up, let you go. Strut out your seven ages. No – no rehearsal. That's it. One performance. And no ad-libbing.

'Think of it like this ... ' (my always-trying-to-explain-things mother) '... This ruler ... ' (holding it up, horizontal) 'is where everything's happened already – all of Time, outside of Time as we know it. This pencil ... ' (holding it up, vertical, the pink-rubbered top in contact with the ruler, then moving it slowly from left to right) 'is us, now, going through Time. Everyone together at the same point in history, moving forward through the already happened but not already experienced. Everything there as a *potentiality*.'

'But is a *potentiality* a *necessity*.' (Me.)

Should've seen her face! 'You're not supposed to say things like that, not at your age.'

I grinned. 'It was in my script, maybe.'

And so I'd arrived (an unexpected guest) entirely under my own steam, at the principle of parallel universes.

It'd come out just as words, the potentiality / necessity business. (But what came first, the concept or the word? – another story.) I sat the words down and started a big interrogation, spotlight in their eyes.

Upshot? This, more or less, is what I worked out. Each of us is born with the potential to kill, given hands that possess the normal degree of strength and that we have average access to other people's necks. It's one of the things we *could do*. But most of us don't because our dutiful teachers and our mummies and daddies make us realise it's 'not a good thing to do'. Therefore, it remains a potential, a perhaps, a could-be but doesn't-have-to-be. Not a necessity. So if the horizontal ruler is everything that *could* happen, the pencil of us, now, might have a tiddly bit of choice in the matter. There's different versions of the script. Okay, so, if you've been given a walk-on part you can hardly play the king, but ...

Think of it as a tree. You climb the trunk. No probs. Straight up. One way. Then comes the great divide. Which branch do you take? That one? Fine – but no going back. If you don't take the other one, you'll never choose between those other sub-branches and twigs and shoots ... *Those* potentials are lost in favour of other potentials. Then you must choose between smaller branches, twigs, shoots, the promise of shoots to come ... But the whole tree there, a potential. All the other branches the might-have-beens, the roads not taken, the parallel universes.

The choosing, O the choosing! The responsibility! Walking about with that tree in your head ... It was enough to give you nostalgia for puppetry.

Could be worse, I suppose. The terror of having to write your own script from scratch, and inventing the language as you go. The comfort of some bounds, at least.

Spilled my own beans on the matter to Emmie Dixon one day. Mistake. Advice: keep deep thoughts to yourself. Emmie was of opinion we were each issued with our own personal plan on entry into the world.

'Suppose you get a rotten plan?' I ventured. 'Suppose your plan involves getting raped and murdered at the age of eight, like the girl in the news last night.' (The photo. She looked a bit like me. It was really upsetting.)

But 'God knows what He's doing' banalled back at me.

'Then I wish He wouldn't do it. Seems He has a real *love* of rotten plans, if you ask me.'

'Nobody did.' (Emmie, whose personal plan had included ownership of a pony for the last five years and a daddy with a *very* big car.)

Trouble is, once you've *seen* something, you can't *un*see it. There it was, vast, grey, shapeless Time – nothing Madame Cabalatska could slip into except by guessing and coincidence – and we 'made' history in it, or out of it, day by day, minute by minute, according to the branches and twigs we each chose. The responsibility was *ours*. *We* turned Time into History. *We* made the world. The evil of it as well as the good. Made you feel quite bowed down and Atlasy.

Terrifying True v. Comfortable Cock-and-Bull.

One last effort to look for evidence of my strings – my puppet-strings. No. Not a sign.

Choice? To run screaming into the sunset – or to sit here and watch it, imagining what could be made of tomorrow.

ONE MAGENTA SOCK

Leila, an old friend, came to stay for the weekend. A poet with no binding attachments – no mortgage, husband, children. Exotic in name and look and prone to thoughtful silences, the children weren't sure what to make of her.

Children like grown-ups to be grown-ups. They feel happy and secure with talk of mortgages and sensible eating and being told to tie their laces. They prefer men shaved and suited. They like the back views of women at sinks. They like their parents' friends to be like this, too. They do not expect them to wear lurex socks, for example.

It was clear Leila didn't do much at sinks.

And all she brought them was the smile in her swarthy eyes. No chocolate buttons, jelly babies, puzzle books.

She seemed unused to children – didn't include them in her conversation, neglected to pass them things at supper, gazing always somewhere a little above their six-and-eight-year-old heads. The only thing she had to offer them was a bedtime story while the proper grown-ups did the washing up.

Edward was cross: they'd left *The Hobbit* at a crucial point the night before and he liked the way his father read it. But Leila said she wouldn't read to them: she liked to tell.

Pink from the bath and clean-pyjamaed, eight and six waited – Emily hoping Leila would bring up that dark cloth bag stitched with all those tiny round mirrors. It had made a lumpy cushion on the window-sill all during supper, the candles and the mirrors playing a secret game with each other while the grown-ups talked about the Government – again.

Leila brought the bag. Emily smiled. Leila smiled back. Edward hardened his eyes against her: a collusion of girls.

Emily: (shyly) Can I look at your bag?

Leila's answer was to place the bag on the bed, in front of Emily, switch on the bedside lamp, and turn off the bright central light.

The little mirrors shone.

Emily: (less shyly) Why does your bag have mirrors on it?

Leila: Because they're where I keep my stories.

Emily: I don't know what you mean.

Leila: Each mirror has a different story in it.

Emily: How do you know which is which? They all look the same.

Leila: If you were to get to know the bag as well as *I* know it, you'd see that each tiny mirror reflects the light a little bit differently, and the way the light's reflected reminds me of which story's in there. That one, for example – it's a bit bigger than the others and it's a bit dull and grey. That's the story about the elephant that forgot something important. That tiny, bright one sewn on with silver thread – that's the story of a star who wanted to be a glow-worm.

Emily: (Six-year finger touching the story bag for the first time.)

Leila: You've touched the one about the chicken who flew to the moon.

Emily: (giggling ...)

Edward: (irritable sighing ...)

Leila: No, sorry – it wasn't a chicken. It was a goose. 'The goose who flew to the moon'.

Edward: That's all 'oo' sounds, that is – 'The g*oo*se who fl*ew* to the m*oo*n' ... (drawing out the 'oo' sounds)

Leila: You've a poet's ear, Edward. A very good thing to have.

Edward: (Thinking: silly woman. Poets' ears are the same as everyone else's.) I s'pose next you're going to say there's a story about a little girl called Emily and a boy called Edward.

Leila: No way. Much too boring. Now, pick a mirror.

One magenta sock

He looked for a damaged one. There weren't any, so he went for one that made the shiny centre of a stitched red flower.

Leila: An interesting choice. And one of my favourites. (Emily hoped she'd have a chance to choose – and that she'd choose one of Leila's favourites, too.) This, Edward, is a very famous story about a picture that changed. It's a little bit scary. Is that all right?'

They both nodded, large eyes listening.

'There was once a man called Mr Gray ... '

(It wasn't quite a scary as they thought it would be. There was only one bit where Emily squeezed her eyes tight and put her hands over her ears. But it all turned out fine in the end.)

Emily chose a mirror about a dandelion whose children all went off and left her, then turned into copies of their mother in the new places they'd spread to – all except one, who ...

But they didn't hear the end because six-and-eight had both fallen asleep by then.

At breakfast, the children were shy with Leila again. Emily looked into the white milk on her cereal and said she'd dreamed yellow. No-one bothered to ask her what she meant. Waiting for toast, Edward swung his legs and looked down – which is when he noticed the socks. In fact, he'd noticed yesterday's socks, too, and had said, 'Why are you wearing silver socks? I've never seen silver socks before. How do they make them silver?'

Leila had been busy feeling the surface of a small African carving at the time, so his mother had explained about a material called lurex, woven with silver threads in it. She expected the socks were made of a kind of lurex, she'd said.

Today was a different matter.

'You're wearing odd socks! You've put the wrong ones on. One's grey and one's ... one's a funny colour.'

Leila: Magenta. Magenta's my favourite colour. There used to be two. They were my favourite socks. But somebody's dog ran off with the other one and chewed it up, and I've never been able to find another pair the same.

Edward: (Momentary vision of himself as the hero searching the world to bring Leila another pair of those funny-coloured socks called magenta. He'd have to take the remaining one with him to match the colour. But supposing he lost it! ... Supposing some other big dog should ... Or even the same one as before, looking for the other half of the pair. Supposing ...) I don't see how you're allowed to wear odd socks like that. I'm not. I'd get told off if I went to school in odd socks.

Leila: Ah – you have to wait till you're grown up to do things like that. Once you're grown up you're free to wear one special magenta sock if you want to, Edward – only not many people do. Except poets.

Edward: (Staring at the socks again. Memorising the colour. His lips making a small 'magenta'. Then ...) That grey one's the same colour as my school socks.

Monday mornings they had to write about what they'd done at the weekend. Edward wrote about Leila and the story bag and the one magenta sock. He put his hand up for the spelling of magenta. Mrs Wilton repeated it as if she might not have hard right. 'Magenta?'

Edward: Yes. It's the colour of someone's sock. (Which possibly increased Mrs Wilton's bafflement.) It's a kind of dark red but sort of purple too.

Mrs Wilton: Yes, I know the colour, Edward. (She wrote the word on the white-board. It annoyed Edward that she chose the green pen, not the red or purple one.)

Chloë: (Looking up from her re-telling of the DVD she'd watched.) What's that funny word on the board?

Mrs Wilton: It says 'magenta', Chloë. It's a colour.

Alfie: What kind of colour?

One magenta sock

Mrs Wilton: A deep reddish purple – a bit like dark blood, Alfie. (Knowing what would appeal to him.) It's a nice new word for you all. Anyone who likes it can write it in their word books. Let's all say it together, looking at the board. Ma–gen–ta. Mag–en–ta. Right. Now get on quickly with your diaries.

Evening. Time to do the marking.

Mrs Wilton smiled and gold-starred Leila and the story-bag and the one magenta sock. And smiled even more when she came to Alfie's grazed knee and the 'magenta bludd' that 'spirtid out', and Rose's sister's new magenta nail varnish that got tipped all over the carpet, and Ethan's visit to his nan – who just happened to be wearing her best magenta dress.

'Seeds,' murmured Delia Wilton. (Comfort for a hard day.)

Edward bided his time – then took to wearing odd socks – even when they'd been carefully paired by a mother who'd have preferred to be doing something more interesting.

KANT'S DAY OFF

When Kant saw the time, he knew he must be dreaming.

'Good lord! I must be dreaming!' he said aloud – in his dream, of course. 'I never wake up at that time.' He made a small movement of his head towards the time-piece. Not that anyone was there to see. He was alone. Alone in his dream.

'This is the strangest dream I've ever had,' continued the philosopher, 'a dream of reality – in as far as we can know it.'

He went first to the window, as was his habit in waking life, opened it to breathe in the fresh air that stimulates the brain. Königsberg looked just a little strange, as if lit from a different angle.

'Of course, at this hour, the city is, indeed, lit from a different angle because the sun is higher in the sky. It's later.' He was about to close the window again but paused. 'On second thoughts, it's probably because I'm dreaming that it has an eerie brilliance. Dream-light.' He checked the time once more. 'At this hour I am normally at my desk. At my desk in my room in my house in the city of Königsberg on the River Pregel (frozen November to March), a city which grew up around the castle built in 1255 by the Teutonic Order ... ' He heard his young school-boy voice running on in his head. An odd sound. Like the odd light. He hadn't heard it – even in his head – for a long time.

It was just over a week since his fiftieth birthday. Yesterday had been the last day of April. So today was ... Well, it would depend. If this dream was happening before midnight, it was still the thirtieth of April, if after midnight, then the first of May. And the dream city was bright and blooming. Inviting. The iron grip of a ponderous Prussian winter had been loosened and this lovely morning had placed in the opening

Kant's day off

fist a sweet posy of spring flowers. Who could refuse the invitation of such a city?

Since he was dreaming, there was no need to bother with ablutions and breakfast and all the fussiness of dressing.

He passed a man on the stairs, vaguely resembling someone he knew from his waking life. But the face was changed by dreaming – the eyebrows oddly raised in two startled arches, the eyes beneath staring and terrified.

'Poor chap,' murmured Kant to himself. 'Clearly having a nightmare. At least *my* dream's a pleasant one.' He tapped the man on the nose with the tip of his forefinger saying, 'Cheer up. It's only a dream.'

The man opened his mouth. 'What are you doing, *Herr Professor?*'

Kant, now thoroughly warmed to the freedom his dream bestowed upon him, replied, 'I am tapping you on the nose, then I am going out for a walk in my nightshirt.'

And he did.

The fresh spring air was lovely around his naked ankles. It took delicious liberties with his legs and played with the hem of his white linen shift.

'Hope it's not going to be one of those common old dreams where the night-shirt gets shorter and shorter,' chuckled Kant, blowing a kiss to the staring housemaid who was supposed to be sweeping a front step. He checked the length of the nightshirt. No problems – so far.

Finding himself in a wide thoroughfare, Kant stopped, a little smile pulling at the corners of his mouth. 'There's something I've always wanted to do and, since I'm dreaming, nothing can harm me if I do it.' And he made straight for the middle of the wide, cobbled street, paused to savour the moment, then, with a light step – almost a skip – he proceeded down the centre of the busy road.

He chuckled at the astonished expressions on the faces of

horse-riders as they veered away from him at the last moment, and at the way the terrified horses rolled back their enormous brown eyes (they were very close) with the sudden, dramatic change in direction. And he laughed out loud at the green-liveried driver of a coach and six whose face turned to a mask of terror as he struggled to manoeuvre the morning-fresh team of horses and the heavy vehicle out of the path of the cheerful apparition dancing towards him.

Suddenly, Kant felt a hand grasp his elbow and he was propelled firmly to a less exciting location on the left side of the thoroughfare.

It was a few seconds before he recognised the dream-changed face of his handsome friend, Friedrich. Taking the beloved face in both hands, he did what he'd wanted to do for years and met the full, delicious lips with his own. Handsome Friedrich, mouth now gaping, could only stare as Kant skipped backwards away from him, calling, 'My best wishes to your good wife!'

Turning a corner, Kant found himself in a street that formed part of the route for his normal afternoon walk. He plucked a sprig of some unnaturally bright purple flowers from a window-box, twirling the stem between his thumb and forefinger as he made his way jauntily down the familiar street. There was a peculiar, other-worldly stillness about it. He was aware of people at their windows and in doorways, but a general hush held the air. He was used to feeling the eyes of Königsberg's inhabitants upon him: the rumour had come back to him that they set their clocks by his presence in the streets – so regular was his walking-out time. But in his dream it was different: he had not set out at four o'clock in the afternoon. (Would they dream their clocks were wrong?) People were looking at him in a different way, as if he were ... a bride! White dress. Flowers. Walking down a hushed aisle with all eyes upon him.

But there was no altar at the end of the street. Usually he turned right. So, for his dream, he'd turn left ... and left again

Kant's day off

... and arrived in the busy, colourful market. The smell of fruit roused a dreamy hunger. Apples. That's what he wanted.

The purple flowers in his hand were beginning to annoy him, so he stuck them into the cleavage of a buxom girl whose dress was simply crying out for such attention. She laughed good-naturedly – even when he added a friendly pinch to her retreating behind. Then he spotted just the apples he fancied – apples well-stored since the previous autumn. Still crisp-looking. He picked up two and walked off – who needs money in a dream? – and, after only a moment's hesitation, began to juggle with them ... the way he'd done as a lad.

The stall-holder called after him in what must have been a special dream-language (he had certainly not heard the words before) – in response to which Kant caught both apples in one hand and, with the other, raised the back of his night-shirt.

'And not many people have seen *that*,' he called over his shoulder. 'Call it payment in kind.'

A worm-eaten turnip narrowly missed Kant's left ear, but caught an old lady square in the face, precipitating a most vivid nosebleed. However, Kant's attention was now on the group of children collecting around him and chanting, 'Do it again! Do it again! Show your bum! Show your bum!'

'Huh!' mused Kant. 'Youngsters – they never change.' Then, facing them with a conspiratorial smile, announced, 'I'll let you in on something much more interesting than a bare backside,' and snatched a little wooden flute from one child and a jester-like hat from another. 'Follow me!' And he put the hat on his head and the flute to his lips and made a noise with it – not an actual tune, because he didn't know how, even in his dream. The children jostled and ran behind him, laughing and calling out words Kant had never heard before: that dream-language again! Feeling the energy of the children blowing him along from behind – like a wind pushing into the future – he began to realise how exhausting it surely was to be a teacher of young children. So much energy! Still playing a weird melody on the little flute and half dancing over the cobbles, he glanced over his shoulder at the rowdy band whose numbers were increasing by the minute. *If I can only get them sitting down quietly to listen to me, what things I could tell them ... show them! But they'll never sit still and listen at this time in the morning. We'd better take some exercise first – tire them out a little, make them happy to sit down for a bit. Then they might pay attention.*

So he snaked up and down the side-streets, taking the longest possible route to the quiet square he had in mind, and thinking to himself this was the best dream he'd ever had ... and in fact what a wonderful thing dreaming was, allowing an unmarried professor of logic and metaphysics to lead away a whole troupe of children in broad daylight ...

And being busy with his thoughts, it was some time before he noticed that the rabble of youngsters was no longer pressing at his heels. A noticeable gap had opened between them. And they'd quietened down considerably. Their energetic noise had sunk to a resentful grumbling. Some were dragging their feet. Some leant (rather melodramatically, Kant couldn't help thinking) on their friends for support.

'How much further?'

'Nearly there! Best foot forward. You can do it!'

One more street and there, indeed, they were – the quiet square. The large monument on the far side had a flight of wide stone steps leading up to it. Ideal for his young audience! Gratefully, the children staggered and stumbled towards the steps and flopped down with a general moaning and groaning.

'Cheer up!' grinned Kant, still sprightly and on his feet in front of them. Removing the jester hat and placing it, together with the flute, on the ground beside him, he hummed under his breath something that sounded a bit like, '*Row, row, row your boat gently down the stream ...* '

A curious little brown and white mongrel approached the hat

Kant's day off

and began sniffing at it, keeping a wary eye on the unfamiliar figure watching him. When Kant – suspecting the dog was about to piss on the lovely bright hat – tried to shoo the dog away, it began to bark at him.

'Aggression, as usual, brought on by fear,' mused Kant, pulling up his nightshirt slightly so he could squat down and try to make friends with the little dog. And after a few minutes he was, in fact, able to stroke it. It even began to wag its tense little stump of a tail and ... yes! ... he got it to lick his hand!

'There!' he said, standing up again and looking at the children.

But they were all fast asleep on the steps – curled up against one another like a large basketful of puppies. Kant sighed. 'Oh, dear. What a shame. There was so much I wanted to tell them. I felt I was about to give the lecture of my life. And I seem to have worn them out just getting them this far and ready to begin. What a shame. What a shame.'

He tried shaking one or two of them gently. A single, sleepy eye-lid lifted a moment, but unable to make the immense effort any longer ... closed. He stepped back and looked at them, paused, then raised his hand in a sort of secular benediction. 'Sweet dreams, my dears, sweet dreams.'

He picked up the hat and the flute and placed them by their sleeping owners, then walked slowly from the square, murmuring, 'I hope some of them at least saw me make friends with the dog before they nodded off.'

He hadn't gone far when a distinct rumble came from his stomach.

'It seems I'm hungry,' he said aloud, waving and blowing kisses to a group of middle-aged ladies staring at him from the doorway of a cloth-seller's shop. 'I wonder what sort of meal my dream is going to come up with. I'll call on Heinrich. He always keeps an excellent table.'

Heinrich's housemaid looked rather strange with that expression on her face. It made her seem older, somehow. But she was niftier than ever on her feet. He'd never seen her flit up the stairs at such a speed – not in his waking life. It was wonderful how time and space – the constants of 'reality' – could bend and melt in dreams. And here was Heinrich himself – *wheeee!* – down the stairs in the wink of an eye.

'Sorry to arrive out of the blue like this, Heinrich, only I've been out there dreaming for some time and was feeling a bit peckish and I thought to myself ... '

'My dear man, are you all right?'

'Never felt better. Just a bit peckish, and I knew you wouldn't refuse an old friend a spot of supper. And I've got something terribly important to tell you.'

'Hannah!' called Heinrich.

The little housemaid with the dream-changed face and oddly speeded-up movements reappeared.

'Hannah, tell cook to send up ... er ... a cold-meat supper for two right away ... in my study, not the dining-room.'

'Supper, sir? At this hour?'

'Dreamers' privilege,' pronounced Kant, before Heinrich had time to reply. 'Freedom to do what you like when you like – *how* you like. Just try it!'

Heinrich nodded in a slow, deliberate, rather odd manner and the maid moved off at her accelerated dream-speed towards the kitchen.

Heinrich led Kant upstairs to his study and pulled a couple of chairs up to a small table near the window which looked out from the back of the elegant house.

'Now, *Herr Professor*,' Heinrich began, gazing with quite unnecessary seriousness, Kant thought, into his face, 'tell me what all this is about.'

'If only any of us really knew,' smiled Kant. 'But I do believe I'm a step closer, at least when it comes to the matter of the planets.' He had lowered his voice to one fit for school-boy secrets. 'And as a thank-you for the supper I've invited myself to, I'm going to let you into the most tremendous secret.'

'My dear friend, you have clearly been working too hard. Your mind is everywhere at once – metaphysics, history, epistemology, morality, religion, and now the further reaches of science. It's too much ... too much ... '

'*Balderdash!*' exploded from Kant. 'The more a man thinks, the more he *can* think. Besides, thinking is the greatest pleasure in the world. Now listen – but keep it secret for the moment. I'm still working on the fine details but it's so tremendously exciting I simply *must* share it with you.' A prolonged rumble came from Kant's stomach. He leaned forward. 'Gas!' he whispered. 'The planets are condensed from a mass of gas!'

'My dear friend, you really must take some time off. Why don't you ... '

But at that moment the maid appeared at the open door and sped to the table with a tray of cold meats, bread, cheeses and wine.

'Will there be anything else, sir?' She was already backing towards the door.

'Just inform my wife I'll be going out shortly and will be needing the carriage.'

'Heinrich, why ever didn't you say you were going out. I do hope I haven't delayed you. I say, this is excellent wine! A veritable *dream* of a wine!'

'I am going out because I am taking you home.'

'No need for that, dear fellow. I'll be quite capable of walking through the streets of Königsberg unaided once I've a spot of supper inside me. Besides, I want to make the most of this night.'

'So I see!' Heinrich looked startled by the rapidity with which the capacious glass emptied. And even more so when it was held out for refilling immediately.

Talking it over with Genghis Khan

The effect of four consecutive glasses of rather good, strong wine began to turn the room around Kant into even more of an unfamiliar, wavering dreamscape, and he was vaguely aware that his sentences were twisting and turning upon themselves as he tried to explain so many things ... so many things ... until he began to sound, even to himself (though he couldn't do anything about it, it seemed) quite sentimental about reconciling British empiricism and German rationalism. 'If only ... if only ... ' Yes, sentimental and, soon, almost lachrymose ... and it was so tiring, so tiring to explain about all that and the planets and why people should ...

The ride home in Heinrich's carriage was a vague affair ... although the rattle of cobbles beneath the wheels seemed to hurt his head, for some illogical reason, so that he wanted the comfort of resting it on his friend's obliging shoulder.

And when he became aware of his own bed beneath him once more, he knew the dream was over.

Kant woke at his usual hour. Remembering the dream, he smiled to himself, then swung out of bed, went to the window, threw it open and breathed in the good fresh air. Once dressed and breakfasted, he sent for his secretary. The man (whose nose he'd tapped in his dream) stood hesitantly at the door.

'Come in, then, come in.' Kant was already at his desk. 'Now, I have no engagements today, as I recall, so we'll ... '

'Excuse me, *Herr Professor*, but you are delivering a lecture at the university at eleven o'clock this morning.'

'I think you'll find that's tomorrow, Wilhelm. I distinctly remember it was to be the second of May.'

'It *is* the second of May, *Herr Professor*.'

Kant was very still for a number of seconds. His secretary did not interrupt this brief time of reflection.

'Are you sure?'

'Yes, *Herr Professor*.'
Another pause.
'Absolutely sure?'
'Yes ... *Herr Professor*.'
'Then yesterday ... ?'
' ... was the first of May, *Herr Professor*.'

An odd kind of smile made Wilhelm's face look unfamiliar – though not unkind.

'Oh ... dear ... ' said Kant, slowly. He covered his face with his hands. 'O ... dear ... '

BIG

He certainly had a big one – the biggest I'd ever seen. And the hairiest. How old was I when he started coming to our house? The age when people *are* their faces – when you draw them with enormous heads and startling mouths on stiff, twiggy little bodies.

He was just one of an endless carnival of weird ones my mother would invite into her single life. He stayed longer than most. It was always talk, talk, talk, talk, talk ...

'Why does he come here?' I asked, fearing she might be planning for him to become my father.

'Just to talk,' she said. 'We like talking about books and ideas.'

'Would he still come even if you didn't make his favourite dumplings every time?'

She laughed. 'There's a lot of him to feed. Dumplings are nice and filling.'

A giant. He'd sit there looking at me from his big, hairy face, me all silent eyes above the table-cloth, expecting him to fee-fie-fo-fum me any minute – though it was the dumplings he was there for: I knew that really. But a little shiver down the spine – not entirely unpleasant – could be achieved by staring at his enormous face, the black beardiness adding a good few inches all around it and not quite hiding the red lips and the moist hole of his mouth and the pink flap-flapping of his talking tongue.

Others who came to the house would bring me sweets. Not him. Not a single jelly baby. Just once an old bit of rock. A stone. Shiny-ish turquoise-blue. A 'peacock stone', he called it, shimmering it in the light for me. We sat it on the window-sill for a bit, but I tried not to look at it so as not to remember

Big

the vast gorilla hand holding the little stone in a sunbeam and trying to make it shine for me. There followed a number of years for it in a drawer with old bits of string, an unfranked stamp on the torn-off corner of a brown envelope, a chop-stick with a tiny red dragon on it, two shrivelled conkers, a bent drawing pin, and other such seeming necessaries of existence.

Some calendars into the future – how old was I? ... the age of moody stares, walking alone, age of love, hate, hormones – I was, indeed, walking alone, staring moodily, full of hate and wanting someone to love, full of hormones trying to make me woman, when ... there he was like a big old Gulliver stretched out in the long grass by the disused railway cutting I'd made my dangerous brooding ground. Yes. There he was, vast-bellied, spread-legged, gorilla hands under his not-quite-as-big-as-I-remembered-it head, eyes out of action, an open book making a little roof on the rise and fall of his enormous chest.

Curiosity (never the better part of valour, having killed so very many cats) put a brake on my tip-toeing past him. I paused by the top of his head. What was he reading? *The Travels of Ma* ... AAAAHH!

Gorilla gripping my ankle ... going ... going ...

Who was more winded, him or me? Me landing on top of him, feet in his face. Iron clamp around my ankle. Too surprised to scream. Finally, a small voice (mine) saying, 'Don't hurt me. Remember the dumplings? ... and the peacock stone?'

A moment silent. Then such a volcano of laughter that I did a 'hear-no-evil' and screwed up my eyes, too, against it. But still the ankle was manacled, though the giant roar calmed into words.

'Well, if it isn't little Lune-eyes grown up!'

'Lune-eyes??!!'

'Lune as in the moon. What I used to call you in my head. You sitting there with your great big moon eyes just above the horizon of the table, looking as if you thought I'd eat you up.'

(How did he guess?!)

I stopped struggling, but his grip gripped on.

'Does the great dumpling-maker know you're here? Not the sort of deserted, out-of-the-way place a girl should be seen dead in, if you don't mind me saying.'

That well and truly touched the panic-button of my heart which obligingly made ready for fight or flight, banging away in there, ninety to the dozen ... Deserted place – girl – dead ...

A voice that seemed to come from the clouds said, 'Please don't kill me. My mother would be so sad.'

Red mouth open – but no laughter. No words, even, at first. Then, so gentle – oh, so so so so gentle. 'Oh, little Lune-eyes, you didn't think ... not me ... not *me*, surely ... '

'Then please let my ankle go. You're hurting me.' Voice a little nearer now, though not yet properly in my mouth.

Startled to see his own hand there, reddening my leg, he looked at my face, back to my ankle, then my face again.

'Answer the questions right,' (grasp already loosening), 'and I'll let you go. But no running away, and you must tell me how your mother is. It's been a long time ... Deal?' The other great gorilla hand was held towards me to shake. Declining, I nodded. (Humour him.)

'Right. Which would you rather be, a savant or an ignoramus?'

'Not ignoramus. The other one.'

'A sage or a clod?'

'Sage.'

'An imbecile or a bibliophile?'

'The second one.'

'Scholar or noodle?'

'Not a noodle!'

'That's better. You look nice when you smile a bit. You're mother's clearly doing a good job on your education. I think

Big

we'll let you live! Besides, the giant has already dined.'

Funny, but the minute my ankle was freed, I was wishing his hand there again – though maybe not quite so tightly.

I kept my promise and didn't run away. Just sat there, staring out over the long grass, him sitting next to me – Titan, Thor, Jove ...

'How is your mother?'

Having never given the subject a moment of my moody time – 'mother' just 'was'; there was no 'how' involved – I hesitated before saying, 'All right ... I think.' I risked a sideways glance at him. Had they been lovers? 'No!' my soul cried out. 'Not that giant on my little mother!' ... though I could see he might be nice to snuggle up to, just for a cuddle: nothing more.

'Does she still make beef stew with those wonderful dumplings?'

I shook my head. 'Gone veggie. Cheaper, she says.'

'Tell her the "philosopher" sends his very best wishes.'

'I will.'

'And make me a promise.' He was suddenly very, very serious.

'What?'

'No coming here on your own ever again, or I'll have to come all the time just to make sure you're safe. An out-of-the-way place like this is all right for giants like me, but ... '

I was fed up with the place anyway. I'd find somewhere new for blue-mooding about in.

'I promise. I really do.' Then, 'Remember the peacock stone? We've still got it.'

'I gave it to *you*, did I. I've sometimes wondered where ... '

'You can have it back.'

'Wouldn't dream of it. Just hold it up to the light for me from time to time.'

After supper, I went to the bits-and-pieces drawer and scrabbled about for the peacock stone. I tried holding it up to the sixty-watt bulb over the table. It shone a little bit, but not very much. It needed daylight really.

Before I went to bed, I looked along the shelf where the philosophy books were. He'd called himself 'the philosopher'. The thinnest one had the word 'Protagoras' on the cover: it said it was one of the dialogues of Plato (I'd heard of him). I slipped it from the shelf when my mother was out of the room. Somehow I was sure that reading it would make me feel close to ... And if I met him again, I wanted to be sure to have something 'philosophical' to talk about.

I got into bed, stowed the peacock stone under my pillow, and opened the book ...

Where have you come from, Socrates? No doubt from the pursuit of the captivating Alcibiades. Certainly when I saw him only a day or two ago, he still seemed to be a handsome man; but between ourselves, Socrates, 'man' is the word. He's actually growing a beard ...

There was a strange, tingling sort of excitement in my body. I knew about older men in Ancient Greece treating young boys as if they were girls. Was Socrates big and powerful like the "philosopher", giver of the peacock stone?

In the loneliness of my adolescent's bed, I suddenly felt how nice it would be to cuddle into the body of a man huge enough and wise enough to protect you from all the fearfulness of being alive.

I fell asleep as his enormous, hairy arms closed around me.

I dreamed I was Alcibiades.

'SAY "HELLO" TO THE FAIRIES, KARL'

[Translated from the German]

London, 22nd June, 1873

Liebe Hannah,

Thank you once again for the lovely time you gave me in Trier. It was nice to talk over 'the old days' and to see once more the places that had meant so much to us when we were girls together. If I hadn't have married Arthur, perhaps I would still be living just around the corner from you. Since his death, I *have* thought of coming back, and my visit certainly stirred up those feelings once again. But I've been in 'exile' for so long now and have made many dear friends here in London and, at my age, I don't think I could take another major upheaval – especially without Arthur. And, quite frankly, I find society a little more free and open here than in Prussia. That's no doubt why London attracts a certain number of 'intellectual refugees' – probably not as many as Paris, but certainly its fair share, including, of course, that tragic Marx family I was telling you about, Jenny and Karl, the ones from Trier. His father was a lawyer and hers some high-up government official, but you'd never think it as they haven't got two ha'pennies for a penny and have been living in the most unhealthy conditions which must, surely, have contributed to the deaths of their children. To lose one child is bad enough, as I know, but to lose *three*, even if one has six! No wonder Karl's like he is. Sometimes I wonder how his wife puts up with him. But I'm very fond of Jenny and she tells me she understands about Karl's 'work'. He writes a lot and is quite into political things. 'Trying to make the world a better place,' is how Jenny sees it, she says. Trying to make it more equal and to get people to understand why it isn't, at the moment. Bit of an uphill task I'd say, and you can't help admiring people who have a go, especially when they've got so many worries of their own, like the Marxes have. But I do feel so sorry for those children.

The Marxes are at the front of my mind today because Karl popped round yesterday: they never forget my birthday – well, I don't suppose *he'd* remember (men don't, do they), and I know it was Jenny who sent him round with the usual little bunch of flowers. I used to help them out quite a bit in their early days here, when we were neighbours – especially when I found out where they were from. Arthur actually remembered Karl's father (converted Jew, apparently) and it was nice to have neighbours I didn't have to struggle to speak English with.

I don't know what the weather was like in Trier on 21st June, but it was the most glorious Midsummer's Day here and in came Karl, all gloom and doom and in a hurry, not even realising what day it was (apart from my birthday). Anyway, I made some silly joke about God giving me a beautiful day as a birthday present. You never know quite what to say to Karl! I just said it without thinking and, of course, he starts mumbling something intense through his big bushy beard, something about religion being like opium. And it was only then that I remembered how very much against anything like that he really was. Calls himself a 'materialist', I think it is. Now I'm not really religious, as you know, Hannah, but I do believe in keeping an open mind. There's such a lot we can't understand, can't know for certain, us with our little human brains. Why be so *categorical*? Why not leave a little space for the imponderables, the impossibles, and the perhapses of life? It would be a dull old life if everything was just as it looked, if everything was completely logical, if there was no room for imagination, things we can't quite explain, invention, even silliness! Take all

'Say "Hello" to the fairies, Karl'

that away and people start doing some *very* nasty things to each other.

Well, I could see Karl getting himself into a state about the time and wanting to be off. The call of 'History', I wouldn't be surprised. Between you and me, Hannah, he thinks quite a lot of himself. That's all very well, but I didn't think it'd hurt him to give me a few minutes of his time on my birthday. After all, I used to give them plenty of *my* time when they needed it. Not that I expect any special thanks for it. I was just being a good neighbour. But I thought it would do Karl good to step off the ladder of 'History', just for a few minutes. I'm sure it's not good for anyone to be so intense and one-track.

I'm not stupid. I know that to him I'm just a silly old woman, a bit of a bore, especially as I can't really talk about politics. But I've lived in the world a good deal longer than he has, and I've lived the complex life of a woman in a man's world – which is more than he has – and I decided, rightly or wrongly, to … well, not to beat about the bush any longer, I made him walk down the garden with me. It's getting a bit overgrown as I can't afford a regular gardener and my rheumatism stops me from doing too much myself. But it's lovely. The trees are quite big now and I get a lot of birds. You'd never think you were in London. There are quite a lot of wild flowers, especially at the bottom of the garden – some lovely delicate pink ones, the colour we used to call 'damask' when I was a child, after those wonderful roses. Sort of *greyish* pink, if you know what I mean. I don't know what the flowers are called. Emily says they're weeds and I should pull them up. Her little Gemima (she's the youngest of my grandchildren, only five, bless her) says they look like fairies with their little petal skirts. 'Please don't get rid of the fairies, Grandma,' she says. Speaks perfect English, of course. You'd never dream she's more German than not. And once she'd said that – about them being like fairies – I just didn't have the heart to pull them up, weeds or no weeds. They may not do any good for the garden, but they're lovely to look at – such a delicate colour. And when I sit by the open French windows and look down there and see them, they make me feel happy. Probably because they make me think of little Gemima. What a comfort grandchildren are, aren't they, Hannah? – the feeling that a little bit of us will go on in this world after we've left it.

But I've gone completely off the point. Sure sign I'm getting old! Well, I took Karl by the hand and led him out into the garden, saying there was something I wanted him to do for me. He went a kind of apoplectic purple and said, 'I'm not dressed for gardening, Elsi.' I didn't take any notice. One of the few nice things about getting old is that you can pretend all sorts of things and get away with it. Anyway, I kept my hand firmly on his wrist and led him outside. 'Look up at that tree, Karl,' I said. 'Elsi, I'm not a tree-lopper. Get your daughter to organise someone to come and do it for you.' 'No, no. I don't want it lopped. I just wanted you to look at how beautiful it is. It's full of birds you know. You can hear their wings rustling sometimes. Makes you realise where people got the idea of angels from. But it's lovely, isn't it?' After a few seconds, he did seem to see some of the beauty of it – at least, I like to think he did. Then I took his wrist again and led him down to the bottom of the garden and showed him 'Gemima's flowers', as I call them, and I said to him, 'They're weeds, but they're beautiful, aren't they? Gemima calls them "fairies". That colour used to be called "damask", you know.' I'm not sure whether I was meant to see the way he rolled his eyes, but I did. Though I pretended not to. I just tightened my grip on his wrist and stood my ground.

'What is it you want me to do out here, Elsi?' he said, looking fidgetty again. 'I just wanted to show you.' 'Show me what?' 'The fairies. I wanted you to be able to say a nice cheerful hello to the fairies, Karl, that's all.'

Quite honestly, Hannah, he was so anxious to get going by that time he would've stood on his head and recited the Lord's

'Say "Hello" to the fairies, Karl'

Prayer if he thought it'd make me let go of him. It was a good job none of his political acquaintances saw him at the bottom of my garden talking to fairies! I don't know what made me do it, really, but it's a sight I'll remember to my dying day. It brings a smile to my face even though my hip's really playing up today.

This little story's just between you and me, Hannah. I wouldn't want it spread about. I expect Karl's got a certain reputation to keep up.

Anyway, I've rambled on long enough. There's not really much else to tell you since it was only a couple of weeks ago that we were together. I do hope you'll come and stay with me before too long so I can try to repay all your kindness during my visit to you. I'm looking forward to taking you to the theatre. I remember how much you used to like Shakespeare, even in translation. Perhaps 'A Midsummer Night's Dream' will be on somewhere and we can say hello to some more fairies!!

Thank you again for the lovely time we had together, and I do hope little Friedrich gets completely well again soon.

With fondest love,
Elsi

NIETZSCHE, MY DARLING

You want me to come right out with it and confess?

Okay then. Yes, it probably happened because I fell in love with Nietzsche. That's right, the German philosopher, Friedrich Nietzsche. Don't look so surprised. I know he's not the average woman's idea of a pin-up, but then I'm not an average woman, am I. Perhaps I should've been someone truly terrible ... like Hitler. But so far I've only killed one person.

Nietzsche. I put his picture in an oval frame and beside it a little china vase of flowers. Always fresh ones. Just lawn-daisies, once, when that was all I could lay my hands on. No-one turned a hair, assuming it was a great-grandfather, I suppose. Didn't even recognise Nietzsche. That's what they're like around here.

It helped me to cope, that picture. When people came round – after David ... went – and started on about all the traffic coming through the village or the food at the Hotel de Caca or wherever they'd just got back from, I'd simply glance at those burning eyes in that oval frame and the tune of '*Once I had a secret love*' would fill my head and drive out their *silliness*.

There was a day when Anita Dunlevy ('Neighbourhood Watch') paused in front of the frame. My heart leapt with hope. Had she recognised him?

'Must've made kissing very difficult, those big, bushy moustaches back then.' That's all she said.

It was probably disappointment that dictated my reply. 'Perhaps they didn't waste much time kissing back then. Maybe it was ... you know ... straight in.' (Explicit gesture.) 'No beating about the bush, so to speak.'

She just put the 'Watch' leaflets through the door after that. Fine by me.

Nietzsche, my darling

Nietzschean Rule Number One: be yourself, utterly.
Nietzschean Rule Number Two: maintain only discriminating contacts with other human beings.

As you yourself said, my darling, 'Have about you people who are like a garden, or like music on the waters in the evening.' Anita Dunlevy? I don't think so.

I crossed her off the Christmas card list, along with old Mrs Purkiss who'd died soon after David. (Roads to freedom.)

And anyway, my darling, I love the feel of your huge moustache against my hairless woman's lips when you press your face into my imagination – when we lay together at night and you enter me with all your possibilities.

Disguise. I want nothing more to do with it.
 I used to dress myself up, over and over, as one of the botched and bungled of this world. The door-mat type. Not any more. Not now I have Nietzsche – my hero, my comfort, my philosopher of the dangerous perhaps.
 Yes, I know *someone* has to clear out the world's cupboards. But not me – not any more. The expense of spirit in a waste of being-what-other-people-think-you-should-be. Their regurgitated ideas. 'Cathy Sick-Pot, This Is Your Life.'
 Not any more, it's not.

Once, my darling, there was a planet dancing in my mind.
 I had the pick of the star-bright masks made for youth. I wore one for a while, smothered in the golden stars of future. It was called 'university'. It's where I first set eyes on you, my darling – though only in the distance, then. A nod and a smile. Friends in common. I never suspected how much you'd come to mean to me.

For three years the planet danced seductively, outrageously with and in my mind, teaching me to tease the seven veils from the world. I got about as far as number six.

'Quite a catch.' My family's verdict on David. I was "the first girl in the family to marry a doctor" – they didn't say "the first girl in the family to go to university"..

A village practice to start with. Just a stepping-stone.

Stepping-stone? Mill-stone.

I taught for a while at the local school. Then I was pregnant.

Next it was all that earth-mother stuff – healthy country living, fresh air for the children, property cheaper than in London and having got the house just as we wanted it. All so terribly *reasonable*. Irresistible.

Earth-mother.

Twins then Tom. All boys.

Boisterous.

I remember learning, at primary school, how they used to collect rubber from trees by cutting into them and attaching little cups for the rubber stuff to run into. The trees bled whitish latex. I remembering wondering if it hurt – whether the trees got used to it.

He died trying to overtake a tractor. Head on into a meat lorry.

He always was impatient.

One of our little jokes. A doctor who was im-'patient'.

Everyone very ... supportive. Hoped I'd stay on in the village. Knew I would. Knew I'd put the children first – wouldn't 'uproot' them at such a time.

Leave their roots securely in the earth. With their father.

I was, apparently, much admired for how well I was coping. Subtext: 'Why aren't you *broken* by this tragedy? Why not throwing yourself on the funeral pyre?' (*Übermensch*, dears, *Übermensch*. Even then.)

Nietzschean Rule Number Three: affirm existence

Though I never intended it to end in a killing. But sometimes people leave you no option.

Long evenings without David's 'paperwork' to keep me busy. No need to earn a living. Life Insurance is a many splendoured thing. Didn't even have to get rid of Mrs Everett who'd always 'done the basics' for us. I could read in the evenings, once the boys were in bed. The planet began to dance again. To jig about a bit, anyway.

Until his mother decided we needed her to live with us – to 'help me with the boys'. No. I'm not that stupid. To make sure I had no chance of falling in love. Clearly, it was a matter of inheritance. A matter of *control*.

How could she do it to you, Nietzsche, my darling? – that sister of yours, warping your life's work. With her 'Come and look at what I've got for you, Herr Histler. Just what you need. Cred-ib-il-it-y. Intellectual re-spect-a-bil-it-y. Behold the works of my brother's hand. Read in a certain way – and with minor changes and omissions – they could be useful to you ... couldn't they? Please by nice to me, Herr Guns-and-Ovens. Look what I can do for you!'

The picture is vivid. Nietzsche's decrepit sister licking Hitler's dick.

No wonder you sometimes seem a bit funny about women, my darling – what with your sister and the syphilis.
  But I'm not like that.

I would be your slow spider that crawls in the moonlight ... and the moonlight itself – returning, returning. I would stand in the gateway with you, watching the return of the moon and knowing the stars were not above but all around us.

Soon after she moved in, the planet stopped dancing again. It simply lay down, exhausted, and went to sleep.

I joined things to get away from her. The usual village stuff – church choir, W.I., sewing circle, charity groups.

The choir didn't last long. Asked me to tone down my powerful contralto. I claimed I couldn't. (Or was it already more a case of 'Why should I?') There was nothing for it: I had to throw myself into the ICSS – the 'Ittelbury Church Sewing Symposium'. *SYMPOSIUM??!!* Yes, well, I suppose they did gossip ... those 'Idlers and Cobweb-Spinners of the Spirit', as I re-baptised them. (Verbal subversion. Sad weapon of those who own no other – which I didn't then.) They'd just started a mammoth project: replacing all the church kneelers. There was an awful lot of stitching ahead. Kneelers. One up from doormats, anyway. And the theme was 'love'.

Love defined all love expelling – love fastened down with a million threads.

But we're Gullivers, us Übermenschen, aren't we, my darling? The little people may run all over us for a bit, tie us down with a million petty fetters, but in the end we'll be up, up and away ...

Or maybe she simply wanted to be looked after, David's mother. Her life-time of looking after others: now it was her turn. So it goes on. And on. She didn't have a daughter and David's married brother had gone to America just in time.

I couldn't do anything right.

Each time I went out, it was the full, inquisitorial spotlight

Nietzsche, my darling

in the eyes afterwards. She was afraid I was meeting a man. Sometimes I put on perfume for the sewing circle – give her something to think about. Just to say, 'I would if I wanted to and you can't stop me. Ya-boo-sucks to you, "Grandma".'

Nietzschean Rule Number Four: Do not let others unself you.

Mrs Everett handed in her notice over Grandma. Very direct accusations regarding dust, apparently – on the tops of the wardrobes. While I was out. But for Mrs E. it was 'last straw stuff', really. I told Mrs Everett I wished I could hand in my notice and escape the old girl, too. We had a little cry together.

But I don't cry any more, my darling. I'm utterly Übermensch now.

Grandma's line was I had plenty of time to do my own housework. Subtext: I was wasting money that could go to the boys later – plus she didn't want me to have any energy left for 'other things': drudges don't. 'Her boys,' she started calling them. They took after David – all three of them. I scarcely got a genetic look-in.

Simmering rage of the slave.

The tiger turning and turning in its cage, yearning to bite the hand that feeds it the wrong-tasting food that's already dead.

I started pretending I suffered from constipation so I could get away from her and read for a bit in the toilet. And that the long, hot baths were what David used to recommend for my back problem.

'Back problem? First I've heard of you having a *back* problem.'

'It started after the twins. I didn't tell anyone – except David. I believe in putting up with things – in case you haven't noticed.'

Yes, I actually said that. To her face. ('Hello. Hello. This is Doormat to *Übermensch*. Doormat to *Übermensch*. Message. I am making progress. I am making progress. Over and out.')

Grandma grunting. 'Seems to me you spend too much time in that bathroom – what with one thing and another.'

A life of strength and good will, warmth and beauty – that's what I wanted. Want.

Though I never thought I'd kill for it.

I was getting a bit behind with my kneeler. I'd done all the boring plain stuff round the edges, but some of the others were already on their 'texts' – the usual stuff from St Paul, mostly: love not being puffed up, et cetera, et cetera. The less verbal went for variations on a theme of doves.

Then it came to me. Just like that.

I marked the first part of the text on the canvas. I wasn't one of those who could do it by counting. I didn't have the patience.

'**THAT WHICH IS DONE OUT OF LOVE ...** '

Jane Fothergill looked over my shoulder: 'What would we do without St Paul,' she said.

What, indeed. (A secret laugh. A secret love.)

I absented myself from the 'Symposium' the following week so I could get on a bit faster. 'Grandma' was impressed by my assiduous application. 'There's a deadline,' I said, putting the finishing touches to '**ALWAYS**'.

The next evening I completed '**TAKES**' and '**PLACE**' and did quite a bit of the filling in between the letters – that boring blue colour. 'Church blue', I call it.

I sat up late on the Saturday night. Last bit – '**BEYOND GOOD AND EVIL**' – all finished by 2 a.m. ...

Next morning I popped it in a John Lewis ('Never knowingly undersold') bag and left it at the Vicarage when I knew they'd

Nietzsche, my darling

all be at Morning Service.

Having lit the blue paper, I retired immediately to wait for the explosion.

... which never came. No-one twigged. They're like that here.
It was meant to be a decisive gesture. Point of no return.
Not one of them knew it was Nietzsche rather than St Paul.
Or maybe they didn't even bother to read it.

I like to imagine your words, my darling, glowing through the dusk, somewhere among those musty pews. I like to think of some knowledgeable visitor noticing my kneeler and wondering about the woman who'd sewn it.

If it weren't for the vertigo, I might have tried for the top of the crucifix – stuck Übermensch *over the* INRI. *Maybe they'd have noticed that. Just how far does one have to go?*

You should know, my darling, you should know.

How long will they go on simpering about imaginary angels? How long ignore this dancing planet? Or their own possible humanity?

Never used to suffer much from PMT. If there was something especially distressing on the news around that time, I might find myself blinking away tears. That was all. Just a few hormones. I could cope.

But after 'Grandma' had been living with us for a while, I started getting these raging despairs. A bleakness almost beyond bearing.

'Oh, pull yourself together. It's only the menopause coming,' she 'comforted' me. 'You'll not be fertile much longer.'

Other progeny. That's all she was worried about. Didn't want David's boys – *her* boys – having to *share* anything. *Inheritance.*

Rage. Despair. Bleakness. For two or three days a month, the curtain drawn back. That craftily sequined, embroidered

cloth – that seventh veil – removed ...
And there it was. Existence revealed. Life's fanny.

The problem is, even on the majority of days, when the seventh veil's rewound around it all, the knowledge of what's beneath does not go away. The rage fades, but the cool, intellectual knowing of it stays and stays and stays.
Is that just *hormones*?

Was your philosophy just the power fantasies of an invalid, my sweetheart?

No. I would not be ... *reduced*.
She started saying I didn't clean the bath out properly. She said it didn't *shine* the way a bath should. I said nor did I, but she chose not to hear. Anyway, she wouldn't have recognised a metaphor if it'd jumped up and locked its jaws onto her sagging backside.

The twins did come back from university for the funeral. (With their dirty washing.) Tom ('her baby') was on some course in France. I didn't see the point of dragging him home. Of course, the three of them'll be fine now – financially. Which means I don't have to worry. (Roads to freedom.)
I was credited with having 'yet another tragedy to cope with'. 'No,' I said. 'Her death wasn't a tragedy. It was a silly and totally avoidable accident. She wouldn't use a slip-mat in the bath. She didn't like the feel of the rubber on her arse.'

Nietzschean Rule Number Five: truths are illusions of which one has forgotten that they are illusions.

Okay. So I made it up. We never did have a slip-mat.
Now, if I'd said 'bottom', things would have just gone on

as before. But using the word 'arse' in referring to the recently deceased placed me beyond the pale. Perhaps it even made them suspect my role in Grandma's exit. But I braved it out.

Nietzschean Rule Number Six: do not fear your neighbours and there will be no necessity to tyrannise over them.

A simple refusal of tyranny. Both the giving and the taking of it. It can be done. I have said, 'It shall be thus'. And thus it is.

If she hadn't gone on about the bath not being shiny enough, I wouldn't have polished it. Furniture polish. Half a can.

When she slipped, she knocked herself out. And drowned.

At least it was nice and shiny for the ambulance men. It wasn't an *embarrassing* bath to be found dead in. Though I'm not sure she'd have been pleased to have been so very naked in front of them.

Headphones. Wonderful things. You can have the music up as loud as you like and it doesn't disturb anyone – even with the windows open.

And you can't hear the phone. One or two people have put a note through the door to say they've been trying to get in touch. But the church roof can cave in tomorrow as far as I'm concerned. *I'm* not going to make fucking jam for it.

You berated your sister for trying to reconcile opposites. You were all for the glorious uncertainties of the world. You'd approve the opposites in my life, my darling. Isolating myself from society, I have power over it. I appear to be alone, yet my life swarms with the great. I stride about with them. Bach, Beethoven, Brahms, Rachmaninov ...

Myra tells me off about it, walking on the hills on my own. 'Not as if you even have a dog,' she says. 'Asking for trouble.' But then she doesn't know what it's like, being an *Übermensch* – doesn't know how strong and free you are. (She thought it was Thomas Hardy in the frame.) I tried telling her I now live by my ...

Nietzschean Rule Number Seven: re-evaluate your values in the light of what you honestly do believe and feel.

'Once I had a secret love ... '

Spring's best up there on the hills. Daffodils. Golden trumpets blasting out their music, affirming existence, its beautiful possibilities.

'Now I shout it from the highest hill -
Even tell the golden daffodil ... '

Though it's autumn now, of course. Strong wind blowing everything fast forward towards winter. Vigorous clouds. Sunday morning. I'll be up there once all the good-'n-evil brigade are round their sacrificial roasts. I'm beyond all that primitive stuff – way, way beyond ...

Headphones. Last movement of Beethoven's Fifth blasting through my bare white flesh ... my bare, white murdering flesh ... and I'm shouting – shouting myself to the world, shouting for the love of it, shouting and shouting for you – for *you, you,* Nietzsche, my darling ...

FEATHERS

After a lonely Sunday lunch and a little rest, Annie Hodge picked up the large-print books from her bedside table (a white pillow-feather had settled on the top one: she blew it off) and checked inside. *Horribly* overdue. She hadn't even finished them. She'd resorted to 'Large Print' under pressure from a well-meaning librarian, but the choice was limited and mainly not what one wanted to read while one still had all one's marbles.

She manoeuvred the books into a bright orange Sainsbury's bag, put on as many clothes as she could and went out into the snowless, grey cold of a January afternoon.

There was Sunday opening now, until four. But the bus was late and, by the time she reached the library, it was twenty past. Perhaps there'd be someone inside tidying up – someone obliging …

It looked hopeful: lights were on. But the door was locked. Putting her face to the glass, she peered in. It was teeming with people! Some kind of party? Fancy dress? A party to launch the Book Festival? … But that was in March. A wedding, maybe? People got married in funny places these days. A librarian getting married? Hazel Hawkins? Surely not!

Then her eye caught something going on behind the 'Issues' desk. An old man had cornered a girl – no more than twelve or thirteen – and had his hand between her legs. Annie pounded on the glass door … but her gloved hand made little sound against the noise of the party. Desperate to save the young girl, she found her front door key and tapped sharply on the glass until the sound penetrated and everyone stopped what they were doing and stared towards her. Annie pointed anxiously to the old man and the girl. Those nearby took a look … and shrugged as if to say, 'What's the problem?' The girl herself made a rude sign at the old lady.

Annie drew back and walked off, heart pounding, into the gathering dark.

* * *

'Who vas zat?'

'How the hell should *I* know,' sighed Lolita. 'Now let's get this straight. It's not the same with girls, Mr Ashenbach. You have to touch us differently ... like this.' She took his hand, closing her eyes to avoid having to look into the face of the bizarrely made up old German.

He was just beginning to make progress when a fat kid in National Health specs appeared. 'Five minutes,' the boy wheezed.

'Five minutes *vhat*?' The old man was annoyed at yet another interruption.

'To decide.'

'I have made my decision.' Aschenbach scanned the boy's clumsy flesh: it stirred no lust in him.

'What about her?' The fat boy nodded towards the girl.

'Fine by me. Anything's a welcome change from Mr Humbert.'

And now an asthmatic little Frenchman was helped up onto a table and addressed the company.

'*Mes amis*, I 'ope you 'ave all found your desire. You 'ave until dawn to enjoy your – 'ow shall I say eet? – "little 'oliday". I will appoint a scribe to record your experiences 'ere in zis book.' He held up a hard-covered, unlined notebook resembling a normal hardback but empty of print. (Suddenly all eyes were averted: nobody wanted to 'scribe'.) 'And finally, a big "*merci*" to Mademoiselle 'Azel 'Awkins, zat oh so rare person, an UNTIDY LIBRARIAN ... ' ('Ooohs' and cat-calls.) ' ... who omitted to re-shelve zat copy of '*Owards End* before returning 'ome. To Mademoiselle 'Awkins!' He raised an imaginary glass.

'Hazel Hawkins ... ' 'To Hazel ... ' hung in the air. Then the noise level rose as all prepared to plunge into their adventures.

But some of them stopped in their tracks, looking up. Thinking it was Icarus falling again, they wanted to enjoy the fleeting mythic moment before rushing off to new lives. Someone said, 'It can't be Icarus. It's *two* figures falling.'

'Must be Gibreel and Saladin,' said someone else. 'But there *should* be the sound of them singing: *"To be born again, first you have to die ... To land upon the bosomy earth, first one has to fly"*.'

Two tangled figures splattered to earth. Collecting themselves together and standing up, they were recognizable as those two old friends, George and Lennie.

'Hey, George, this don't look like no farm. Ain't gonna live off no fatta the land here.'

'Too right, Lennie. But don't you recall how we left all that behind us. And you mustn't call me George no more. I'm Saladin Chamcha. Can't ya get that inta ya head, Lennie?'

'And who am I, George?'

'You're Gibreel Farishta. How many more times I gotta tell ya?'

'And what we gonna do, George?'

'We're gonna be *diff'rent*, that's what we gonna do. No more farms and no more of your damned *rabbits*.'

'No more *rabbits*, George!? ... '

'NO MORE DREAMS ABOUT STOOPID FUCKIN' RABBITS. No more sloggin' our guts out for hardly no wages. No more social fuckin' realism. It's gonna be *MAGIC* from now on. But if you and me's gonna inherit the earth, first we gotta *fly* ... '

... which is just what Emma Bovary felt she was doing as she charmed her way around the highest social circles of *In Search of Lost Time*. Having swapped places with the Duchesse de Guermantes, money was no longer a problem for her – nor boredom. As the focus of flattery among a glittering cast of Proustian Parisians, she laughed, was affectionate, witty, *reasonable*. Shimmering in damask-pink silk, her changeable eyes unclouded by worries about debt, she'd found the match she'd dreamed of in the Duc. Boring old Charles Bovary and his disgusting operations seemed little more than a nightmare – and arsenic was the last thing on her mind as she circulated among her guests.

But just as she paused to reflect that this was truly the happiest day of her existence, the doors burst open and a balding man in less than tip-top physical condition thundered into the *salon*.

Flaubert cast angry eyes around the sumptuous Parisian room then bellowed, 'Emma Bovary, get back to Rouen IMMEDIATELY. What *do* you think you're playing at?'

'I'm *playing* at being the Duchesse de Guermantes and having a *wonderful* time – not that dreadful provincial life you *thrust* upon me, you miserable, syphilitic old codger.'

'How DARE you! Get back to your book, you slut!'

Emma raised her chin and stared back at his challenge. 'I'm no longer under your control, Monsieur *Flow-Bare*.'

The author turned purple so suddenly that Doctor Zhivago (who'd wandered in by mistake) was concerned. But, at that moment, Marcel Proust, their *animateur*, crawled out from beneath the table.

'Gustave, *mon ami*,' began Marcel, still on his hands and knees with the white table-cloth draped over his rear, '*calmez-vous*. It is not such a big *problème*.'

'Not for you, *Monsieur*, but the Duchesse de Guermantes is causing HAVOC in my novel. She's sorted out Emma's finances through her connections with eminent Parisian bankers and now there's absolutely no reason for Emma Bovary to commit suicide. My novel's heading for a happy ending. It's a *disastre*!'

Everyone just laughed at his apoplectic rage. Dr Zhivago persuaded him to sit down until his breathing regularized.

Marcel held out to him a glass of Côtes de Rhône. 'Here, *mon ami*. Let us drink to happy endings, eh?' They raised their glasses. '*Au bonheur*! To happiness!'

Helen Schlegel had been quite happy in *Howards End*, but, having helped liberate others from their given lives, she felt obliged to participate. Fancying herself as a character in a Virginia Woolf novel, she flicked through a couple, saw that *Jacob's Room*, like her own story, started with a letter, and jumped in.

It wasn't quite what she'd expected, however, and she found herself writing to her sister in the old way.

Dearest Meg,

Jacob Flanders has turned out to be a most complicated young man and I'm finding the whole escapade exhausting. Picture me – never having climbed a mountain in my life, and PREGNANT – taking a stuffy Greek train to Olympia and, yes, CLIMBING THE MOUNTAIN. When I finally get to the top, all I can do is lie down on my back and stare at the sky. Nothing but infinite blue! Then a bird plummets from that azure dome (a bird of prey falling upon a rabbit, I suspect) and I'm remembering Icarus and thinking how such myths start from everyday occurences.

I shouldn't complain since it was my fault that the whole thing started – mine and Hazel Hawkins'. If she hadn't been preoccupied with romantic thoughts about a certain second-hand book dealer (the one who picks through the library sell-offs), she would no doubt have noticed Howards End *on the floor at closing time, would've re-shelved it, and that would have been that.*

As you know only too well, dearest Meg, 'making trouble' is a habit of mine ... though for the best of motives. And I hope some good will come of it in the end.

What made me do it? The wonderful sense of freedom, there on the open floor instead of squeezed onto the shelf in the usual boring neighbourhood. (That TEDIOUS Captain Hornblower!) The bliss of the 'unexpected' made me feel more ALIVE. And I wanted others to be more alive, too. You know what it's like when someone's taken our book out and you find yourself staring up from the page into their lives and thinking, 'How dreadful ... how absolutely and utterly DREADFUL' (quite as if one were Samuel Beckett). Sometimes one wants to scream up from the page at them, 'NO! This reading business isn't a nice little "heritage" activity for when there's nothing else to do! Literature is SUBVERSION – it's REVOLUTION. It's teaching you to think, to question. Don't read me because it's a "nice" thing to do. Read me to CHANGE THE WORLD!' Oh, Meg, it's so hard sometimes. Do you think me quite, quite mad?

When I pushed open the cover and stood up off that page, I'd never felt so strong and happy and sure of what I had to do. And once I started pulling all the fiction off the shelves and setting everyone free and seeing the joy and possibilities of it all, I KNEW I'd done the right thing – especially when Monsieur Proust came up with the idea of having us write our new adventures in that book. Just imagine, Meg, if such a book were to be published! Think of the EXAMPLE it would set to the people who read it – how it would show them they don't have to be trapped in the grey story life's given them.

But I must go. It seems I'm now off to fight in the Great War.

By the way, do you know what happened to that boy who helped organize everything at the start? The fat one with glasses? I meant to thank him.

Your affectionate,
Helen

Feathers

The fat boy Helen Schlegel was referring to was sitting alone, on a park bench, sick to death of being teased and of other people's stupidity, squinting (through glasses with one cracked lens) into the darts of sunlight falling through a sycamore tree, trying to imagine a better life for himself.

'What's up, Sonny Jim?'

The boy nearly jumped out of his pale skin. An extraordinary creature was beside him. A woman, but so *large* – wearing a helmet crested with purple and vermillion feathers and a matching cape which enveloped her from neck to feet … an outfit totally at odds with the cockney voice that had addressed him as 'Sonny Jim'.

'Fevvers,' she said, by way of introduction.

'Piggy,' said the boy.

'Well, if Fevvers is good enough for me, I reckon Piggy's good enough for you. What you doing 'ere all on yer tod? Not joining in the fun and games?'

'I wanted to be Harry Potter, but all them books is out. What about you?'

'Not a lot on offer for the likes of me. I tried to find *Flaubert's Parrot*, but … '

'You'd need *wings* for that.'

'Exactly, young man.' Fevvers gave a sly smile. 'In Paris they didn't call me *l'Ange Anglaise* for nothing. Wings, Piggy, wings. We all of us needs 'em but only some of us 'as got 'em.'

'That's silly. There's no people in the world what's got wings.'

'Seeing is believing, Sonny Jim.' At which she carried out an ungainly clambering manouvre to stand on the bench, fiddled with the neck-fastening of the feathered cape so it fell in a soft, vivid, vermillion landscape around her ankles. Piggy gazed up at the enormous woman in a pink body-stocking, a spangle of sequins covering the bits of a lady you weren't supposed to see and, open-mouthed with wonder, saw the great, gaudy wings unfurl and stretch out, with a shuddering rustle, above him.

Talking it over with Genghis Khan

Fevvers looked down with a wide, lipsticked smile. 'Is she fact or is she fiction?' She moved the huge wings back and forth until there was enough breeze to bear her weight up off the bench ...

Piggy swivelled his head to follow the great human bird as it circled twice before landing – somewhat heavily, legs apart – in front of him.

'Seeing is believing!' smirked Fevvers.

'You could do Peter Pan,' suggested Piggy.

'Nah.' Fevvers crossed her enormous arms. 'Don't do kids' stuff. I'm strictly for the grown-ups. But you want an adventure, right? How's about a visit to "foreign climes"?'

'I don't want to go to no tropical islands ... '

I was thinking more of a trip to the "continong". Gay *Paris*. I revisit the scene of past glories and you get to ride on me back.'

'My auntie always says naughty things go on in Paris. My auntie ... '

'Oh, *sucks* to your auntie! It's only people what's afraid of life thinks that way. Paris is where you get to *live* ... And I've just remembered this French novel what could be the answer for me. A kind of Icarus story, only it's by this funny French guy ... Raymond Something-Beginning-With-Q ... Won't be a copy in *our* library. Bit too out-of-the-ordinary. Bit too *European*. It's called *Le Vol d'Icare* – "The Flight of Icarus". There's a bloomin' great library in Paris. Bound to be in there. Climb aboard, Sonny Jim ... '

It took Fevvers a longer run and a lot more muscular activity than usual to get airborn with the fat boy wedged between her wings and clutching the neck of her leotard for dear life. But once they were up and away, it was mainly a case of gliding with the occasional few flaps to maintain height. There was a tail-wind and, in no time at all, England fell away into the sea at Dover, and France was already in sight. Such a little bit of water keeping them apart ... the tiny waves down there making a pattern like the skin of some blue-green amphibian. Then the wide fields and villages of northern France ... churches ... a sprinkling of war cemeteries like patches of spilled talcum powder ... And just as Fevvers was beginning to feel the ache in her shoulder-blades, there it was: the perfect perch, sticking up from the prone body of that most beautiful city ...

'I'm going to have to grab onto that,' Fevvers shouted over her shoulder, pointing to the rapidly approaching top of the Eiffel Tower. 'Hold tight!'

She circled, judging her distance and speed, then made straight for it.

'Phew! Made it!'

'I ... I can't look down. It makes me feel ... '

'DON'T BE SICK – not on me fevvers, for Gawd's sake. I'll never get rid of the pong.'

'Can't we ... go down ... please.'

'Just getting me bearings ... ' At which point a fortunate current of air brought a magnificent hot-air balloon within hailing distance. 'BON-JEWER! NOUS CHERCHONS LA BIBLIOTHÈQUE NATIONALE ... THE NEW ONE.'

'Follow the river ... past the *Jardin des Plantes* ... Four tall towers like half-open books, one at each corner of a big square with a bit of forest dropped in a hole in the middle. Are you looking for something particular there?'

'A BOOK,' Fevvers called back.

'Then you're going to the right place. About ten million to choose from ... ' At which a strong breeze carried the balloon suddenly away and caused Fevvers such an alarming wobble that she was forced to stretch her wings for balance. Piggy groaned.

'Hold tight, Sonny Jim!' And she launched herself onto the breeze and swooped sickeningly down towards the rooftops of Paris.

Next time Piggy opened his eyes they were circling right above the four towers of the library, and he could see the tops of trees in the deep well between them. People walking around and between the towers stopped, looked up, shouted, pointed at the great bird ...

'Here we go!' Fevvers hurtled down, straight for the green heart of the *Bibliothèque*.

Crash ... Crack ... Rustle ... They plunged through the branches, grabbing hold where they could, in a flurry of bright feathers and expletives.

With no room to stretch her wings, Fevvers was obliged to clamber down through the trees, swearing each time she felt bits of plummage pulled out or snagging painfully on spiky twigs. But she'd faired better than Piggy who was laid out, concussed, on the ground below.

With a heavy jump from the lowest branch, she was back on *terra firma*. But with the sides of the little square forest enclosed by glass, it was like being in a bizarre kind of aquarium. A bedraggled Fevvers shoved her way through the trees to the nearest glass wall on the other side of which hundreds of people were seated at tables, poring over books, too absorbed to notice the six-foot bird-woman flapping bright but tattered wings at them.

She thumped on the glass.

No response.

She'd never been so totally ignored before. It was an odd experience, and she began to feel smaller because of it ... Yes, she definitely had a shrinking feeling ...

If any of the readers *had* looked up at that moment, all they'd have seen was a medium-sized green parrot lurching and squawking among the trees. And had the sound-proofing not been so effective, they might have heard the parrot saying, 'Talk, talk, talk – that's all you can do ... ' for, having fallen like Icarus at the end of *Le Vol d'Icare*, Fevvers had inadvertently thought herself into another novel by the same writer. But at least, as Laverdure, the long-suffering parrot of *Zazie dans le métro*, she was able to fly up through the branches again ...

The journey back was so exhausting that, arriving 'home', the confused parrot just had time to squawk 'Pieces of eight' before plummeting to the library floor, apparently stone dead. But in the confusion of trying to get back to their original texts, no-one noticed. The late dawn of a January morning was breaking and the Librarians would soon arrive. Though most 'made it back', a few ended up between the wrong covers, dreaming themselves differently and later taken out by puzzled readers. (Wasn't Emma Bovary supposed to take arsenic?)

Hazel Hawkins was distraught! There seemed to have been an intruder ... or an earthquake: half the fiction section was scattered on the floor. But it didn't take long to return the books to *where they were supposed to be*. (Helen Schlegel groaned to find herself once more enduring Captain Hornblower's seaman's yarns. Fevvers, her bruises still painful, let out a few choice words on being squeezed into a gap a millimetre too small for *Nights at the Circus*.)

While tidying up, Hazel came across a book *with no classification number*, its cover entirely plain. No time to peruse it (a brief glance suggested it was one of those weird, 'experimental' novels: it even appeared to be hurriedly written by hand), she slipped it into her bag to look at over her solitary supper.

Tuesday. The library staff had never seen Hazel Hawkins in sequins and would never have guessed she owned a pink feather boa. The manager was all for phoning the doctor, but her Deputy said, 'Let's see what happens. At least she's smiling for a change ... '

Hazel was on 'Returns' when Annie Hodge finally brought back her Large Prints that bright Tuesday morning. The moment she saw Hazel in sequins and feathers, Sunday's 'event' fell into place: the launch of some new library 'initiative' to jolly things up a bit.

'Not really to my taste, what's in Large Print, Hazel,' murmured Annie.

'I've just the book for you, Miss Hodge.' Hazel beamed a crookedly lipsticked smile, producing the strange, handwritten, untitled book from her bag. 'It could change your life!'

'Any book worth reading should do that. But I don't suppose it's in Large Print.'

'No problem. We'll scan it into the computer, turn it into large print format and run it off. The fines due on these, I'm afraid, will more than pay for the printing.'

'Miss Hawkins, you're a genius!'

'I know.' Hazel winked.

Later, as Annie passed the library window, she saw Hazel, cross-legged on a cushion, surrounded by small children. Some were stroking the feather boa, some touched her sequins, but all were listening with rapt attention as she read.

Annie smiled. A change certainly *had* come over Hazel. She'd never liked small children in the library: noisy, sticky little things that left the place in a mess, she used to say. But now ... Was she in love? ... Or was it the effect of the book?

Long may it last, anyway!

Annie knew she would treasure, to her dying day, the image of a once frumpy librarian now kitted out in sparkles and feathers, happily introducing the next generation of readers to the liberating wings of 'Once upon a time ... '

PICTURES FOR AN EXHIBITION

1

But why start with the shoes?!

A little pair of shiny (till the paint dries), and for a moment empty, black shoes.

Then the legs, wet and sticky, feeling the brush hover a little to create the curve of a calf. A hesitancy. A little too pink, possibly?

The clothes? Probably quite plain as I'm just a detail and so quite small. Arms now, stretched forward, extended in giving. Offering something. To whom? To what?

Lots of hair tumbling softly, comfortingly, over the shoulders. Colour?

A pause. The difficult part. A change of brush, perhaps. One of those with just six hairs.

The nose tickles, but the cheeks are caressed into place. And then, at last, almost painful with the precision of it, first one ... then the other ...

Eyes. And I'm looking straight into the pebbly gaze of an enormous swan. I wasn't expecting that! Its neck is stretched towards me, taking the bread that has been painted onto my outstretched hands. (Is it a bad joke, or has he forgotten I'm terrified of swans? – since the park that time ... I'm beginning to wish I'd never asked him to put me in one of his pictures.)

And now that I have eyes I can see he has dressed me in an ordinary blue dress and given me dull brown hair. I look a bit like Alice in Wonderland – only more boring. (Maybe that's how he sees me ...) But he's painted me into a perfect English summer's day – the picture he was copying from a card

Talking it over with Genghis Khan

someone sent him. The lake in front of me is very still. There are probably lots of trees – Grandfather has always been good at trees: trees and skies. But I've no idea what's behind me.

A long sighing. It's finished. Some fidgetty noises as of things being arranged, cleaned, packed away. Then, passing momentarily across my field of vision, from left to right, his huge figure – somewhat stooped, grey clothes hanging loosely from his light frame – shuffles off into the blankness that is the place I am aware of to my far right but which I cannot see. I can only look straight ahead.

He's forgotten to give me a mouth.

I want to call after him, 'Come back! It isn't finished! You've forgotten ... '

But, of course, I haven't got a mouth so I can't call after him.

I begin to wish it were the eyes he'd forgotten. Will a part of me have to look forever into the relentless gaze of a pebble-eyed swan reaching its beak towards me to take and take?

But one must be grateful for small mercies, I suppose: a perfect summer day, a beautiful garden ... If only I knew what were behind me.

The light has begun to fade in the little room where he paints, so he definitely won't be coming back, not today. I'm left voiceless.

Here, in the picture, the summer day still glows – golden, late afternoon – despite the twilight in the wider world.

And, quite suddenly, the created stillness is broken by a small but distinct 'plop'. Rings on the water. A fish has jumped or a frog leapt in. The swan extends his neck to the full, rouses his stiffened muscles from their pose, stretches his enormous wings and moves them a couple of times back and forth as if in a half-hearted practice for flying, then sinks into a swimming position and paddles faultlessly away.

I can turn my head!

There are trees to one side, their tops glowing in the late

afternoon light. I flex my arms and hands, stiff from reaching out to the swan. A dragon-fly skims the water just in front of me with a flash of electric blue.

If it's a garden, there must be a house somewhere ...

Yes, there. About fifty yards up a gentle slope is a wall, and just beyond it the side elevation of a lovely old house. I hope I can go in.

Should I first walk a little around the lake? – before the light goes completely? Maybe not. The trees are looking shadowy and beginning to come alive in the evening breeze. Darkness rustles in them, even though the light hasn't completely gone, and I'd have no way of shouting for help if ...

The swan is in the centre of the lake, heading for a small bushy island, dignified and luminously pure against the darkening water.

It's only when I turn and begin to walk towards the house that I realise grandfather is definitely much better at trees and skies than he is at people. My body doesn't move easily. My legs feel lumpy and wrong, my torso too long from the waist to the hips, and too short above that. My arms are long and angular, not quite matching the over-sturdy legs. But he has given me sharp eyesight and enough brown hair to hide the unnatural conflation of my upper organs (I can almost touch the breast with the chin!) if I arrange it carefully, as I do now, before approaching the house.

I walk alongside a weathered, uneven wall until I come upon a rough wooden door partly open. It leads me into a walled garden that has the beauty of slight neglect. Natural shapes have begun to re-establish themselves over pruning and training. From the pear-tree, spread and pinned against the wall, small arms reach out over the lavender bushes. Nasturtiums trail idly, unchecked, across the path which is softened in places by moss. Impudent tufts of grass and wind-sown seedlings sprout from earthy cracks in the paving, untrampled by frequent walkers.

Talking it over with Genghis Khan

A creaking – perhaps a movement – to my right. I sense someone has slipped in through the side door to the house which opens onto the walled garden – the sense of something said in a low voice. Nothing ... definite: just a feeling.

A bat swoops very close. I shiver. There's a chill in the dusk and I only have my blue summer dress. Perhaps they'll let me in – let me spend the night there. I'd promise to get up early to be down by the lake to feed the swan before Grandfather comes. I'm hoping he'll notice my missing mouth: it wouldn't take a moment to add it.

I knock at the side door and wait. Though how will I explain myself, without a mouth? There's no answer, anyway, and for a ridiculous moment I imagine grandfather has painted the people inside the house without ears.

In the end I lift the latch and let myself in.

A dimly-lit, stone-flagged room used for laundry. There are old-fashioned wooden clothes-horses everywhere, draped with pieces of white linen. Some are clearly sheets and pillow-cases; others are smaller – triangles and strips of all lengths and widths. Strong smell of soap. At the far side is a step up to a slightly open door – which I pass through ... into a spacious hallway with a chessboard floor of black and white tiles. I walk across the dim foyer to a flight of wide stairs, carpeted in faded green, and stand in the shaft of bright light coming from the landing above. I begin to climb, expecting a voice to challenge me from behind or a looming figure to appear on the landing and bar my way.

It doesn't happen.

The landing leads to a wide corridor with doors on either side. Small noises come from behind them. Murmuring. Running water. Something dropped. Two quiet laughters. I listen at each door in turn, until I find one that suggests a silent, unoccupied room where I hope I can sleep for the night.

Thinking I've found one, I twist the brass knob, open the door and slip in. Closing the door quietly behind me, I turn ...

2

I'm not sure who's more startled, them or me! Two young men, both in summer dressing-gowns over striped pyjamas. One looks somehow familiar ... But the other – dark and aristocratic-looking – doesn't. Before my interruption, they'd been occupied with a half-finished painting on an easel. A table is strewn with the debris of art – squeezed out tubes of paint discarded without lids; chipped saucers used as palettes; old bits of rag smelling of turpentine; cleaned brushes drying in an old vase.

'Yes?' says the aristocratic one, peremptorily. 'If you've come for the tray, we haven't finished yet.'

The other speaks more gently, haltingly, with a stammer and odd movements of his face. 'S-s-s-sorry, b-but if you c-could possibly c-c-come back later ... '

I should turn and leave straightaway, of course, but I can't resist running over to the window to see if it looks out over the lake.

'Hey! What do you think you're doing?!' The aristocratic one strides after me and grabs me by the arm. 'You don't belong here. You're not in a nurse's uniform. Explain yourself. Speak!'

I shake my head and try to pull away from the angular, dark features and alarming white bandages thrust near my face.

'Are you d-d-dumb?' asks the other.

I nod.

'G-g-g-give her a p-piece of p-paper and a p-pencil.'

Instructed to write down my answers to their questions, I struggle horribly. Grandfather really has made a bad job of putting my arms and hands together. Only after a great deal of effort do I manage to write the word 'SLEEP'.

'You want to sleep here?!' I nod. 'Why?'

Rather than grapple with the pencil again, I rub my upper arms and make shivering movements, then point to the window.

'C-c-c-c-cold? ... outside?'

I nod and try to smile with my eyes.

'I've got an idea, Edward,' says the dark one. The two whisper together for a while. Edward doesn't seem very enthusiastic about the 'idea', but eventually shrugs as if to say, 'Okay, if you like.'

They turn to me. 'We'll do a deal with you. If you'll model for us – not naked, don't worry – we'll let you sleep here for the night, on the sofa. We'll even give you a blanket. But you must go early in the morning, before the nurses are around. Understood?' I nod. He takes me by the hand and leads me to the unfinished picture on the easel. 'Edward's having trouble with one of the figures.' He points to a little card propped up beside the easel. It's a crudely tinted photograph of a painting, the caption beneath declaring it to be 'Coast Scene with Rape of Europa – by Claude Gellée (le Lorrain)'.

I try not to be alarmed by the word 'rape'.

In the foreground, a woman in lilac drapery sits side-saddle on a white bull. There are three women with her and, to the far left, four more seated on the ground around a large tree. To the right, other cattle graze. The sea is only a foot or two behind them and is quickly – and improbably – deep enough for several large sailing ships to ride at anchor not far out. Two men in a rowing boat are making for the shore. In the far distance, purplish-grey hills swell, and behind them, faintly, mountains ... or maybe clouds.

When I look again at the canvas, the problem is obvious at once. Most of the picture has been skilfully copied – apart from the figure seated on the bull. On the card, the clumsy tinting of the figure has blurred the outline, and the woman is in an odd enough position anyway.

It's a very strange picture. Each individual detail is realistic – each cow, each tree, the waves, the complicated ships – but, put together, there seems no sense in it at all. The dark one notices

Pictures for an exhibition

my puzzlement and laughs.

'Do you know Ovid? Probably not. This woman,' he points to the one sitting on the bull, 'is Europa. Jupiter fell in love with her, disguised himself as a white bull and carried her off to have his wicked way with her.' He puts on the expression of a villain from a Victorian melodrama and twirls an imaginary moustache. But he doesn't finish the story.

'D-don't frighten her, L-Lewis,' says the other.

'She's not frightened, are you? She's a sensible girl and is going to do as she's told because she wants to spend the night in here where it's warm, not out in the chilly night air with the bats and the owls and dark, rustly trees – isn't that right? Now, look at the position of the woman sitting on the bull and remember it. Come over here ... ' He piles a couple of big cushions onto a high stool. 'And up you come ... ' He picks me up and sits me on the top. He reaches for a walking stick from the umbrella stand in the corner and places the curved top in my hand. 'This is the bull's horn. Now, remember the position of the woman?' I try to get myself into the shape of her. 'No ... swivel your hips a bit more ... and elbow up – bend it! ... and reach towards your neck with your finger-tips.' He stands back to assess the pose and to compare it with the little reproduction. 'That awful dress is no good for the drapes, of course, Edward, but get the figure right underneath and the drapes will take care of themselves. Does she look about right to you?'

'F-f-f-fine.' Edward smiles at me, but I feel myself begin to turn very pink under the intense scrutiny as he starts to paint and I feel the strange sensation of being emptied of myself, and to know he will soon discover my less than perfect proportions. A cry is gathering inside me – a cry that will yell how it isn't my fault, that my body was made this way by my grandfather who ...

Edward!

I turn to look straight into those eyes I know so well ...

'Keep still, can't you girl!' roars Lewis, and strides towards me, dark face lowering with anger.

This is madness!

I slide down from the back of the bull and, dodging the hands of the women who try to reach for me and hold me back, begin to run along the water's edge, past startled cattle, too frightened to look round in case he's on my heels. I stumble slightly, but right myself, and notice, just a few yards ahead, a detail I'd not seen on my first glance at the picture – a wooden rowing boat pulled up onto the shore. I glance behind me. There's just a chance ...

Though already breathless, I manage to heave the boat out into the water, clamber awkwardly over the side – almost capsizing it – and, heart pounding and ears singing with fear, struggle the oars out from under the seating planks, get them into the rowlocks and, with a few clumsy but effective strokes, pull the boat well clear of the shore ... just as he reaches the water's edge and bellows at me to come back.

I know that once I'm on the sea, he can't get at me, and the two other rowers in the bay cheer me on. Though so badly out of breath from my run, I can't relax my efforts as there's a light but steady on-shore breeze and I'd drift rapidly back to land if I didn't pull against it. So on I go, on and on ...

3

... until at last I'm able to pull around a low promontory. I slow down a little and keep parallel to the coast for an hour or so, watching the landscape change to a less mythological one of neat fields and modest but solid houses.

And it isn't long before I reach an inlet and the possibility of landing presents itself. And that's what I do – though my utter fatigue makes it a labour of Hercules to drag the small boat up the gentle slope of the shore. I look around for assistance – but the place is utterly deserted ... though, in the distance, I see the reddish-brown tones of houses and hope for a civilised reception there.

Dishevelled, damp skirts clinging to my thighs and calves, I leave my little barque with the water still lapping about its bows – unable to pull it any further – and hope the tide is already at the full and will not rise further to take the empty vessel away, in case I need it for future flight.

I clamber up the bank, grasping clumps of tough marram grass, and find myself on a sandy track or road, very long and straight, leading off into the distance directly towards the settlement I'd noticed from the water. The road is bounded by well-tended fields and a number of very tall, spindly trees, curiously bare until their upper reaches, as if all lower branches had been stripped for some purpose of husbandry.

As I pass the fields, one or two of those tending the crops call out a friendly greeting to me. Is it Dutch they're speaking? (So I must be in Holland or some part of Belgium ...) I cannot, of course, return their greetings vocally, but give a friendly wave in acknowledgement of their pleasantries.

Then I notice, coming towards me – though still some way off – a young man whose clothes are of the same warm tones and comfortable cut as the buildings scattered here and there. With him he has a dog, of medium size, that keeps obediently to heel. I sense his gaze upon me as we draw nearer each other. I must have presented a peculiar sight in that civil landscape – my hair Cassandra-wild from flight, my clothing damp, limp and generally neglected. But so courteous does the young man prove to be that, as he draws level with me, he removes his curious round hat and bows.

Fearing he will, after this show of what was probably accustomed courtesy in these parts, simply pass on, I try to indicate, by dumb show, my need for assistance. He notices, at once, the reason for my non-vocal method of communication. As luck would have it, he's an artist and has with him a bundle of his trade's necessities slung from his shoulder – from which he now withdraws an implement and proceeds to endow me with a mouth. Not a proper painted mouth, of course – just a somewhat faint, 'drawn' mouth which might fade in time or with over-use. And though the voice itself is also lacking strength and resonance, it is at least a voice and will serve me for the time being.

The first thing I do with my voice is to thank him, and then to enquire about the locality. He informs me we are in Middelharnis and that the road or track upon which we are standing is known simply as 'The Avenue'. I ask if I am likely to be kindly received in the town ahead. He pauses before replying: 'Yes ... most probably. But there are ... dangers here about. Watch out for soldiers.' He notices that his dog has run ahead, and calls him back. 'Here, Hobbie! Heel, boy, heel ... ' But the dog stands defiantly, nose twitching, smelling the adventure of the road. 'We have only just set off,' the young man explains. 'You are welcome to accompany us, but it will be a long road and the outcome of the journey uncertain.'

I thank him and explain that I am so fatigued from my earlier journey that I will simply proceed to the nearby town and seek rest and shelter there. Wishing him luck with his journey, I thank him again for my mouth. He bows again and turns to go ... then looks back at me and says, 'But do be careful. This pleasant country is experiencing some ... difficulties.'

'Is that why you're leaving?' I ask. But the dog is barking, urging his master on, and he seems not to hear my question. I watch him go. He doesn't look back and his pace would be too quick for me to keep up. I turn towards the approaching town.

4

Tired and wet, I can scarcely put one foot in front of the other. And it's getting colder. A bank of dark cloud is drawing itself across the sky and I sense the damp, raw edge of approaching snow. I try to hurry so that I reach the town of Middleharnis before the snow starts to fall. But my legs are so awkward and I stumble on stones and ruts and before long the first flakes begin to drift down.

I come to a fork in the road: it's impossible to decide which one will be the shortest way to the town. I take the left fork ... but soon it seems to be veering away from the friendly-looking group of houses ... though a large stone at the side of the road bears an arrow, a distance, and the name of another town not too far away. I can't actually see it because the snow is coming so thick and fast now, stinging my face and deeply chilling my whole body in its silly little blue frock. Larger and softer the flakes come, making a quick accumulation on the ground.

Figures hunched, huddled. Odd ghosts burdened with firewood. Despite the cold and the snow, life goes on. Sharp, white geometry of roofs. Brown bronchia of trees will soon be hung with lace. People watch from doorways. All look friendly. A small, cheerful town. The best of ordinary life. I would like to stay here for a while. To rest.

But how can I find words to properly tell what happened next? The margins of history are scribbled with such crimes. I hear a great rattling sound of armoured soldiers on horseback. The people, who had been about their daily business, despite the hardship of the snow, begin to run for their houses. One calls me in, screams at me to get away from the soldiers. I watch the whole thing from an upstairs window in one of those modest, civilised houses.

Tied to the trees, the helpless horses bow their heads, turning from the dreadfulness of humans.
Fresh blood on the trampled snow.
A man is trying to comfort a woman.
The mothers pleading.
The children clinging.
The helpless horses.
Break down the door. Red hose and a halberd.
Crow in the tree-tops.
Dead children in the snow.
The dogs smell blood.

The Massacre of the Innocents. When I saw it in the book grandfather was using for his copies at that time, I knew he would choose it. He loved to paint snow. But I was afraid he would choose this one to put me in. I didn't want to find myself sitting in the snow and wailing with a dead baby in my lap.

'Why do you always copy someone else's pictures? Why don't you paint something from inside your own head.' He went on cleaning his brushes. 'I'll buy you a big new canvas for your birthday, but it's to be for your *picture – no-one else's.'*

I didn't recognise myself in the foreground. I must have run out of the house to try to help when I realised what was happening. I'm holding a small boy by the arm. His mother has given up and is sobbing hysterically into a large white handkerchief. One of the murderers has the child's other arm but is looking away from him, speaking to an armed soldier on horseback. The sword is drawn. The child, gazing up at me in hope, is a moment from death. My hand is extended, trying to push the soldier away – or make him look into my eyes and see if, so doing, he can still hack a small child to death. All around me are terrible shrieks and sobbing and the pathetic whimpering of the doomed and terrified children.

Pictures for an exhibition

O, brave soldiers!

The child's small arm is warm in my hand. (I shall never, ever forget the feel of his little arm which my hand could encircle completely.) In five seconds dogs will smell his blood.

... and I am running, running, running
sometimes slipping in the old snow
running and shaking my head as if the picture could somehow be made to drop out of my mind
leaving the screaming town behind and running, stumbling, struggling, and running again until my lungs are bursting, though the picture still throbs in my head, on and on and on and on ...

5

A huge field of untrodden snow, extending in all directions as far as the eye can see.

Silence at last.

The new white canvas.

I sit at the edge and wait. I know where I am. My gift to him. I'm waiting to see what he will paint.

But while I am waiting a message reaches me. Grandfather is dead.

Remembering the many pictures he has painted, I plan a modest exhibition. He was undoubtedly talented. If he had lived at a different time in history, who knows what he might have become.

I'm left looking out across the untouched snow of the still blank canvas I'd given him for his very own picture. The funeral will take place on the other side of it. I must set out straight away if I'm to be on time.

Stiffly, I get to my feet and stretch. The sun comes out as I begin to walk across the canvas, thinking of Grandfather.

The snow begins to melt. Odd, dark shapes are sticking up through the melting whiteness. But huge and twisted roots make no sense in a treeless landscape. I have seen hands of hawthorn root clawing at the soil, but never so human a looking one stretching up, as out of a quicksand, yearning for help. A curiosity to put with the driftwood I have collected and placed for decoration in the hearth. I pull at the root to see if it will come loose easily.

I am holding two human fingers which have snapped off. My stomach heaves. I am shaking. I drop the fingers. The vomit is vivid on the snow – which melts more quickly with the warmth of it, just there, and something else begins to emerge from the slowly sinking whiteness. I can scarcely look, knowing what it is. It's always been there, just below the surface. Skull beneath the skin. Rotting head beneath the snow. 'Somebody's son.' The jaw is stretched wide in a death-shout.

But what was I really expecting to find in Grandfather's head?

And, hideously, Time is a film run backwards. Flesh, grey and pitted at first, begins to grow over the screaming skull. It becomes less grey. The gums are covered now, pink, the eye-sockets filling with their living jelly. One unshaven cheek is complete. The other will not be: it has been ripped away and bleeds modestly onto the dingy snow which still, mercifully, covers the lower part of the dying man whose yell is now but one among a swelling chorus of moans and screams and dying curses. I look up, out across the scene. Only occasional flecks of white are left now on the canvas which seethes with the wounded and dying, the terrified horses desperate to be free of the unimaginable mud.

To my right, two men are sunk on their knees, cradling an agonised third whose stomach is ripped. They are both sobbing. One of them is bleeding from the head, but doesn't seem to

Pictures for an exhibition

notice. His blood drips and mingles with the ooze of the dying man. He dies. The injured man closes the childishly startled eyes. The other man stares about him and begins to shake and utter gibberish sounds. He is very young. But with a pain in my reluctantly believing heart, I recognise Grandfather – and the dark-featured man with him was Lewis, whom I'd last seen bandaged in the big house where ...

Oh God, take me back to the summer garden. Let me stare into the eyes of the swan for eternity. Anything, anything rather than this ...

I rifled through the stacked paintings in the little room he called his studio. They were all there – except the one I longed for most. The summer garden with the big house that had been turned into a kind of hospital. Had I missed it in my anxious haste? I looked again, flipping the canvases heavily against each other. Looking and looking, and every time pausing at the blank white canvas, knowing, finally, why he could never fill it with a picture from his head.

I pull my feet from the sucking mud and all I can hear in my head is the stuttering, shell-shocked gibberish, and Lewis wounded and half-fainting, leaning on my so-young grandfather who clutches his friend to him. And the voice telling me I must get to the other side for the funeral. The sucking mud. The rolling eyes of the terrified horses. Hands clutching at my legs as I try to struggle through the hellish mess of men crawling, dragging themselves what they think is forward. I can feel something rising in my throat. I have felt it before. At the Massacre of the Innocents.

There's no colour. The mud sponges up the blood, is largely made from blood and the other leakages from dying men and animals. My legs are caked with it. I struggle on, trying not to look, hands clamped to ears, trying not to hear. Disfigured monstrosities pull at me. Stumbling, I get covered in filthy ooze. Dead eyes look into mine. My throat is bursting. The journey is endless – and how, if I get there, can I possibly go into the chapel – the suffering so utterly beyond the imagination, so utterly beyond the ability of words or music or painting to tell, that I don't know how one can possibly ... how one begins ... how we ... how ...

6

Then I see there's a bridge and two people, dressed as if for a funeral, walking side by side on it. As I reach the bridge, a terrible sunset – or is it sunrise? – spreads luridly across the sky, bathing everything in a bloody light. And I'm on the bridge and running, running past the two people dressed as for a funeral, the shrieks and moans and gibbering of massacres still in my ears, hands clasped tighter and tighter over them, trying so hard not to hear, not to run mad with the sound, my throat bursting, my mouth opening though with nothing but silence silence silence

7

or is it that I can't hear the soul-splitting cry that's inside me?

I take my hands from my ears

and immediately my arms are filled with a child, a dead child, who might be mine, though it doesn't matter whose, and still no scream, only a mouth stretching as if to

the child's head hanging back at a broken-necked angle, the tiny nostrils where no life is and the roaring hurtling us into a future which is also past and another land and this land and the town is so full of explosions that all the screams and running feet are silent, even the screech of the dying horse and nothing is recognisable in the grotesque distortions which have become reality, the dead child still warm in my arms as I try to run out of the picture and into another canvas – no matter what, it can't be worse than this shrieking despair and terror – but I can move only to the edge of the picture and no further, trapped here, useless breasts bared, with the dead child for ever and ever and made to look up to the empty – no not empty but filled with metal and fire – heavens, and I feel the tongue growing in me, pointing straight up, tongue of fire growing from the throat, a pointed flame and finally I hear the voice, my own voice, leaping out from me – a great and unbelievably echoing scream

[The well-known paintings referred to in the story are, in order: 'Coast Scene with Rape of Europa' by Claude Gellée (called le Lorraine): 'The Avenue, Middelharnis' by Meindert Hobbema: 'Winter' by Lucas van Valckenborch: 'The Massacre of the Innocents' by Pieter Brueghel the Elder: 'The Scream' by Edvard Munch: 'Guernica' by Pablo Picasso. I have been unable to trace the initiating picture of the garden and house: it used to hang in my grandparents' sitting-room when I was very young. As far as I know, my grandfather never painted an 'original' picture, though there is a very small chance the summer garden painting might have been an early attempt to do so. My grandfather fought at Yprès.]

LOOKING FOR
LITTLE MISS UNIVERSE

Joy. Absurd joy from an old cheese packet tossed to the side of the road from a summer picnic. A circle of cardboard. Faded, soggy, but the grinning and ear-ringed cow still faintly there. *La Vache qui rit*. Those little French 'Laughing Cow' cheeses the children always liked. I picked it out of the grass and half-melted snow, held it out in front of me like a mirror and began to laugh. Loud, uproarious laughter such as I'd never laughed before. The only sound for miles, bouncing away across the snow-speckled, bird-deserted fields – until a bright yellow car came round the corner, quite slowly. The grey-haired driver tooted in a friendly way at my laughter, took one hand off the steering-wheel to give a thumbs up, his face creasing into a grin.

Old man in your little yellow car, I loved you. Loved you with all my laughter.

Then the noise – my laughter or the car, or both – disturbed a hare: it went streaking across the field where dark clods were breaking through the whiteness that pained the memory. Those vast wastes of ice ...

'Walk,' my husband had said. 'Walk. That's what I did when ... It can help – a bit.'

So I went off on my own and walked. The usual route we took together, the long one – footpath skirting the two fields, then right, along the lane, over the style, through the copse then right again by the lane that veered drunkenly as it followed some ancient stream, as far as the fork in the road where we would normally bear right again along the road that led back to the farm, where we'd have parked the car.

But my mind still seethed with her last days – it was the first time I had watched someone die – so I took the left fork and hoped something less familiar would take my attention and help me.

Little difference. Nothing to engage and distract the mind: the remaining snow even obliterated all variance of colour and tone so that the images remained, hovering in front of me, overlaying the scenery. The sepia photograph of her as a child, there, in its tarnished frame propped at an angle on the dark-wood dressing table. (And there the woman, old, so old, propped at an angle on the sad hill of white pillows, eyes closed mostly.) The child's eyes direct into the camera and a sepia smile. (A faded nightdress straightened by the visiting nurse.) And the little girl in a sepia dress thrown over with a net of stars and a crescent moon, a halo of points and a wonderful wand with its almost symmetrical star. Skin still lovely, even now, though the jaw and eyes are sunk. *'Little Miss Universe'*: the caption written on the photo in a flowing, old-fashioned hand.

Not so very long since she last spoke – something about seeing children playing in the sunshine, and then goodnight. Her last words. Before that it had always been what time was it, what day, as if hovering on the edge of timelessness but glancing back, always, sadly, to that place where such things mattered. Where was she?

Breathing. Moving a little from time to time. Eyes opening occasionally, but not seeing what we saw. She would never come back but had not yet gone. Had her life seemed very long to her? From smiling child, there, in the photo, to these sad pillows? Or did this seem the longest part, this wandering wherever she was wandering now? Did she want it to be over, be free to go, finally, into oblivion? Or was even this better than that?

The lane went on, rising slightly now, open fields on each side extending to a near horizon, as they often did around there, dipping gently again and revealing more of the same. Nothing startling. No sudden plunge to the sea.

Towards the top of the incline the brown of the thawed road gave way to a light brushing of white, as if walkers and drivers came this far and no further. There was just enough room, using the verges, to turn a small vehicle.

Over the brow of the hill. Not quite what I expected, but almost. Further fields. Wider. Bleaker. Little in the way of trees or hedges, so that a thin wind moved easily across the land, blowing up a light smoke of powdery snow from the surface, less thawed here. It blew across the lane. My shallow footprints filled in a moment. Snow blew past my ankles as I walked and my left cheek began to sting with the wind which was much colder now. But it was pleasant to feel the numbness settling in, helping to grow a film of ice over the pictures in my head. Perhaps this was what he meant, the way it could help. So, though good sense told me to turn back, I didn't.

A slight dip, then a further gradual climb. Snow in the air, blown against my left side, forcing me to turn my head to the right rather than concentrate on the road ahead that was climbing now. Breathing more heavily with the cold and gradient. (Her breath coming hard, from time to time, before slipping into minutes of quietness.) Was the sky darkening? Reaching the crest. Trying to look. Snow in my eyes. Going down. The wind easing. The snow, too. Then looking – and the heart turning ...

A vast valley. Arid. The snow petered out half-way down the hillside, but after that there was only rock and scree, and even the broad valley bottom was utterly bare of vegetation. No water ran there. (We'd tried to squeeze a little water into her mouth from a sponge, she was so parched; but each time she choked.)

Looking for Little Miss Universe

Deeply fissured slopes rose on the other side, as if water had once run there abundantly and carved out great walnut forms from the bare rock. There was a fascination in the hideousness of it. (My little girl poking, with a bit of old stick, the dead and eyeless fish on the shore of the lake ...). Total stillness.

... until I saw the speck of brown moving irregularly along the valley floor. You would have said it was a child hopping and skipping as it went, if a child could have been in such a place. The most melancholy sight I'd ever seen, and I wanted only to be down there with that other living creature so that we could at least keep each other company in this sudden sterile waste.

I began to move down the hillside which, though steep, wasn't precipitous. But several times my feet sent stones bouncing before me down towards the valley floor. The echo of them, in all that silence, soon caught the attention of that small figure moving below. Once or twice the figure stopped and I wondered if it were looking towards my progress down the hill and hoping I'd be there soon.

But as I came within a reasonable distance, the figure stopped for some moments, clearly looking towards me as if trying to decide what to do, then, having decided, began to run – not towards me, but away across the valley to the bald, fissured hills on the other side.

'Wait!' My call echoed across the valley. 'Let me come with you!'

But the small legs beneath what I could now see to be a bluish tunic moved even faster, stopping only once to brandish some kind of stick at me.

Once on the flat of the valley floor, I too began to run, careless of how my feet slipped on the loose stones, falling two or three times but scrambling upright again and making the hills sound out with my 'Come back! Come back!'

The greyness of the sky dissolved as sudden sunshine switched the valley into vivid patterns of utter brightness and utter black where the twists and turns of the bleak, gouged hills shadowed themselves. Into one of these blackened fissures I pursued the fleeing figure.

My eyes rejected the sudden plunge into the dark, giving the figure time to gain ground. But I could hear the light steps and panting breath and plunged on, even when I found myself in the mouth of a cave from which not a single bat flew out and through which no water dripped. And when I saw that the figure carried something emitting a small, glimmering light, I knew that if I kept it in view I wouldn't plunge down a sudden crevasse nor hurtle into icy waters a thousand feet deep where blind, transparent fish would nibble my swollen carcass.

Never had I know such dryness of the earth's surface. And the air, too, rasped the lungs with its total lack of moisture. It was air that made you greedy for more air, only it hurt so much when it came that you tried not to want it, but still ... still ...

Sometimes the light disappeared for a moment in the convolutions of the cave, but it always came into view again. I wondered if it really were trying to escape me or were deliberately leading me on. But quite suddenly there was another light, brighter, towards which the glimmer moved. A spot of daylight. It grew until the small light carried by the fleeing figure was swallowed by it. I tried calling again, but my throat was so raspingly dry no sound would come at all.

A small silhouette paused against the daylight of the cave mouth – then it was gone. And because I was trying to see whether it veered right or left, I didn't notice the sudden unevenness of the cave floor and fell, hitting my hip so painfully that I felt faint and had to sit on the ground for a minute or two with my head between my knees.

As soon as the pain and faintness passed, I stood up – a little gingerly – but found I could walk and was soon standing in the very mouth of the cave, shielding my eyes against the excessive brightness of an immense plain stretching unguessable distances. Its furthest reaches merged with the sky.

It was only a brief and gentle slope from the cave to the start of the plain – a slope sparsely dotted with the dried remnants of stunted trees and scrubby bushes. From one of these, towards the bottom of the slope, something hung, stirring and turning in the light breath of wind. In the absence of any other goal or meaning (the figure having apparently vanished) I went to investigate the only thing that moved in the bewildering immensity stretching into nothingness.

A torn, limp piece of darkish blue gauzy material stitched with metallic stars. That was when I began to cry – though through the blur of tears I delicately extricated the fragile rag from the thorny twig that had ripped it from the costume.

Holding it lightly, reverently, almost, I made the last few steps down to the flat ground and walked some paces out onto the start of the plain, wiped my eyes as best I could with my hands, looking this way and that for the slightest sign of a moving figure.

Nothing.

I gazed back towards the hills through which I'd passed by means of the cave. They were not fissured on this side but swept upwards, grandly, though no birds soared around their craggy tops. Nothing. Not a sound. I walked further out onto the plain, hoping to get a better view of the hillsides in case a small figure were moving there.

Any creature would be so piteously tiny under the unspeakable immensity of that sky. Nothingness beating down. Not a dark sky, nor a particularly bright one. Just a whitish-grey luminosity arching so absolutely over everything ... that was also nothing.

The plain was dust. I stooped and picked up a handful of it – let it run through my fingers.

Then the corner of my eye was caught by movement back among the rocks and broken, desiccated trees on the slope beneath the soaring cliffs. The little figure was clambering with the intensity of a crab-searching child on a beach, glancing back every few seconds as if expecting a parent's voice to warn about going too far, getting lost, slipping – though I knew it was me she was keeping an eye on, to check I wasn't pursuing her. Perhaps, if I didn't follow her so obviously, I'd seem less threatening and she'd let me come within hailing distance.

Sauntering back towards the slope at the cliff-base, diagonally, so I was making in her general direction without appearing to be in pursuit, I watched the frail little figure in her ragged costume. When she looked round the next time, I held up the torn remnant of her star-scattered dress as if to return it. She seemed to scowl a moment, sensing a trick, as children do, then carried on clambering and scuttling away, trying to hide as she went, like some nimble kind of crustacean herself. I was sure that, hurrying from rock to rock along the base of the rising ground, just where it met the plain, I would be able to advance on her.

But at that very moment I felt the first drops of moisture on my face and hands. It was raining – lightly and steadily at first, little dark spots on the dust – then suddenly heavier. I tucked the blue remnant up my sleeve so the stars wouldn't get wet. Where was she? The rain was becoming torrential, and I could hear thunder ...

A sudden flash of lightning revealed her standing on a large rock higher up the slope, thrusting her little wand towards the skies like a diminutive Prospero whom the elements were refusing to obey. The remains of her little dress whipped backwards in the wind and she tried to wipe the wet strands of hair from her face with so child-like a gesture – despite all the dramatic business with the wand – that I wanted to weep. But how could I know I was weeping, with the rain already streaming down my face?

Looking for Little Miss Universe

As the storm built up to a terrifying display, electrical charges ripped and lit up the skies above the infinite plain. Humbly I crouched behind the rock, thinking of that little creature so exposed, standing up there so bravely against the terror of the storm.

I crouched behind the rock until the storm was over – by which time it was night. It was impossible to see her by starlight alone: I walked out a little way onto the plain. So dry was the ground there that already it had absorbed all the rain. I thought that maybe I would find some comfort by laying on my back beneath the stars and tracing their familiar configurations, those giant dot-to-dot puzzles invented by the Ancients. Yes (I settled my hands behind my head and looked up), there was the Plough in Ursa Major, there Orion – and good old Betelgeuse and Rigel – and Canis Minor. How strange to see a little dog in the sky – even to think of it! How strange to see a sky writhing with scorpions, serpents, flying horses, crabs, lions, rams, bears, fish, charioteers and hunting dogs. I tried to trace the shapes – but I couldn't make myself see them any more. The best I could do was a backwards question-mark where Leo should have been, and a few figures from a geometry text-book. The sky I looked at had nothing to do with anything human. Immeasurable darkness with a random scattering of whitely glowing stones. I pulled the creased and tattered gauze from my sleeve and held it spread against the sky, for comfort. ' ... How I wonder what you are.' One finger on the piano. The fragment of her costume was no more than that, and I was holding it up against Mahler's Eighth ...

I would cling to the nursery rhyme. Everything else was too much. The sky beyond writhed with nothingness and points of light that knew nothing of their own existence. The patterns – that drew things together and kept things apart – had gone for me. And those patterns were not inevitable, anyway. It would be easy to superimpose others. It was only our hopefulness that discerned any pattern at all. I held the scrap of material to my cheek and felt the stars cold there.

I must have slept briefly, for the next thing I remember was the horizon brightening in the east. I thought of shooting stars and wondered if any had fallen while I slept.

I sat up stiffly after those hours on the hard ground, and looked around. No sign of her. Then I noticed something white on the ground in the direction of the hills and, with no other immediate call on my attention, went to see what it was.

A feather. A pure white feather, large enough to be a swan's, soft enough for a dove's. Turning it over in my hand, I remembered what she used to say if we were out for a walk with her and found feathers on the ground – that they'd dropped from the wings of passing angels. The whiter the feather, the more beautiful and important the angel.

And some yards ahead was another ... and beyond that another still. Like a fairy-tale trail in a forest, the angel feathers led me on. I picked them up as I went, eyes always just a few yards ahead of me and so not noticing that I had skirted one of the hills and was entering a different landscape.

Sand ... and, a short way ahead, some kind of stone objects strewn about the desert. There were no more feathers (but I had a handful already), just broken monuments – stone angels. Here a wing, there a cherub head and a slowly eroding shoulder. Half a leg with the toes still perfect. Another head – the nose shorn off. More and more bits and pieces of wings, arms, chubby fingers. With the feathers held tight in my left hand, I crouched and touched the stone wings with my right.

Then she was there, standing beside me, scowling down.

But I had to look away. The fiery light from her wand was bright as a comet. As if out of consideration for my mortal eyes, she dimmed it to little more than a sparkler. I dared not speak, but offered her the feathers. She managed to take them without touching my hand. She turned them back and forth several times contemptuously, then, still scowling, handed them back. This time her hand just brushed mine. The cool delicacy of that touch spoke more of angels than all the purest feathers and wishful monuments in the world. The desert became grass. The stone angels were still there, still broken, but she had gone ... and left me in a huge, overgrown garden.

Looking around, I was just in time to glimpse a small figure flitting away through the broken statuary into the further reaches of the garden. The wand was now a dandelion clock, the white seeds of time-telling streaming off behind her as she ran in the strange sunlight of that unworldly place.

Foolishly, I'd thought she wouldn't want to leave me after that nearness, that touch between us. And I still hadn't given her back the shred of dress. I stood up to follow her and was astounded to see the nearness of a great stone edifice, a sublime, overawing building towards whose vast, arched entrance she ran. Pursuing her as quickly as I could through the long, hummocky grass, I came close enough to see her tiny bare feet on the big stone steps. Then she was in through the door and gone. I followed.

A museum of natural history, it seemed. An old-fashioned one, abandoned in the middle of nowhere. Turning right, I was with the primates, stuffed and dusty. There was an unconvincing model of 'the missing link'. Bare feet could not be heard on the stone floors, but the tiniest rustle, heard clearly in the utter silence, told me she was there, somewhere.

Through lofty chambers and endless corridors, all lined with bears and dogs and extraordinary cats, reptiles, fish, spiders of every hideousness, beetles of every mandible size and wing-colour and configuration the imagination of a bizarre god could conjure. Star-fish and dragon-flies, horrid, fleshy plants dredged up from under ghastly seas. Sharks with devil faces and astounding ribs from whales. On and on in a maze of bone and hair and scales and veins and flesh preserved or imitated, teeth and claws, maggots and eye-balls, locusts and termites, dinosaur spines and beaks of freakish birds ...

I longed for a broken-nosed Socrates, a tapestry of grape-treading peasants and lords with elaborately-hooded falcons on their wrists ... for just one illuminated page of the Book of Kells, a ridiculous French costume from the eighteenth century, or even the exquisite idiocy of the Crown Jewels ... Anything rather than this infinite fleshly slowness of Evolution run backwards, a world unmade, starting with the apes and laying out every contingent little mutation, the laborious processes of billions upon billions of matings and birthings and dyings of all the creatures, all the forms of life that lay behind the making of a speaking animal. There was no speaking here, no language. Even the labels were mostly faded or missing. But always just the rustle of *her* a little ahead of me, in the next corridor, round the next corner, in the next chamber. I tried to use my voice to call out to her to stop, but it was swallowed by the vastness of it all. I was afraid of language falling away from me altogether.

What I wanted most was to hear a joke. A pun. Something silly. To play with language, toss it up in the air, catch it any old how and hug it to me. All those wonderful words. All those complicated, intricate, wonderful little wittering noises streaming out from the Earth into the utterness of the slow and silent universe. I wanted to scuttle away from the absolute.

How could she be there? Where was there?

My arms ached to take her to me, cuddle her, comfort her – as she had, once, me. I wanted to speak words to her.

The exit door was wide open. The sunshine was brilliant outside – made to look even more astonishingly bright by the gloom inside the museum. The slightest of rustles. Quickly I held out the starry net. She paused, fractionally, in the doorway and glanced back at me just for a moment. But the brightness was so great that it streamed around her tiny silhouette,

Looking for Little Miss Universe

dazzling the neck and waist and little legs almost to nothing. I tried one last step forward with the starry rag. But in that instant, she was gone.

I didn't follow for a while. I just stood, looking towards the doorway until the brightness began to fade a little and I knew the day was edging away from its zenith.

Just outside the door was a bush, its buds still tight but there ready for spring. I checked for thorns. It was just spiky enough to hold the starred rag without tearing it. I hung it there and gave one of the stars a last touch.

From the door, a path led through the garden, past a thick screen of trees and out into a lane I recognised.

The sun was low in the sky now and there was the familiar cold of snow-dampness in the air. Remnants of snow still whitened bits of the verges and dappled the fields ahead. A crow laughed slowly, and was silent. Some sparrows squabbled in the hedge for a moment. I wanted to shout something silly. I tried a few nursery rhymes – just the first lines – in my head, to practise my human voice again: 'Little Miss Muffet sat on her tuffet ... ', 'Solomon Grundy, born on a Monday ... ', 'Hey diddle diddle, the cat and the fiddle ... ', 'Twinkle, twinkle little star ... '

But the words got no further than my throat. And it was as I blinked away the tears that I saw the old cardboard cheese packet. But it was supposed to be a dog laughing at a cow for jumping over the moon, and here, instead, was the cow laughing at itself, perhaps. Had it caught sight of itself in a mirror? Those ear-rings! Ridiculous! Amazing! Wonderful!

Hurray for the ridiculous!

Long live the silly.

Praise to all the daft little things of human life.

Long live laughter ... Our only ammunition.

MR DAVIDSBÜNDLER COMES TO CALL

or

'IF ON AN AUTUMN MORN A TRAVELLER...'

The children are at school. Tuesday morning, so the washing's done. You stayed up late to finish the ironing to have today free. You've made a good cup of coffee, sat down at your desk, filled your old black fountain pen (you still prefer to write first drafts by hand), opened a new pad and have written a sentence that's been forming for some days – the start of a story about a woman who buys a book incorrectly bound, consisting of the same eight pages over and over again. Not a metaphor for your life, really ...

You like the feel of the pen and the easy slipping of the page beneath the old gold nib. It reminds you of your school days when the future was ...

It's such a dank and misty morning out there, and you are here in the circle of warm light, taking experience and shaping it in (what you think is) your own way. You've just begun to write the second sentence when ...

... the door-bell rings. You ignore it. You don't want any Avon cosmetics nor to go to underwear parties. All you want is a little peace and quiet.

It rings again. Mormons or Jehovah's Witnesses?

... and again.

You throw down the pen and stomp to the door. Forming on your tongue is the politely dismissive venom you keep ready for all proselytisers. Forgetting the caution of the safety chain, you throw open the front door, your prepared rebuttals about to leap from your mouth.

Mr Davidsbündler comes to call

But you find before you a poor specimen of humanity, undernourished with burning eyes in a pale face, strangely attired in a trilby hat, long black coat (shoulders flecked with dandruff), and gripping a bright, multi-coloured carpet-bag in a leather-gloved hand. The word 'murderer' forms somewhere in the cortex of the brain. But before it can trigger a slammed door, the man produces a little card with the name 'Davidsbündler' in the centre and, beneath it, in smaller script, 'Book Promoter'. Something strange has happened to Time. You're a little girl again; your mother is telling you there are lots of encyclopædias in the house because Great Uncle George used to go from door to door, selling them. You asked if he had a little electric car like the milkman who also went from door to door. No, she'd said, he just carried some samples about in a big bag.

'I don't need any encyclopædias,' you say.

'That's just as well, because I haven't got any,' replies the man, replacing the card in his pocket then raising his hat to you with a gesture you haven't seen for a very long time. Despite his name, he does not appear to be German (no trace of an accent) – though he does look a little foreign.

'Then what books are you promoting? I've got a house full already; I could probably sell *you* some!' You try to joke away the odd situation.

'But I'm not *selling* books.' He feels in his pocket and withdraws the card again. He puts down the carpet bag and points patiently to the words. 'Book *promoter*.'

'But surely you can't *promote* books and not *sell* them.'

'Yes you can!' He beams like a little boy and you notice how blue his eyes are. 'I try to persuade people to *read* books. I don't have any for sale.'

'Then what have you got in your bag?' Words like 'stranger', 'madman', 'never accept sweets from' et cetera start to bubble somewhere in the brain.

'Books,' he says. '*My* books.' He lifts the carpet bag onto the doorstep and unfastens it. It's full of books, most of them far from new. 'I lend them to people to read.'

'Jehovah's Witness' leaps from the cortex; that's what they do – lend you their books. Then you see one or two titles. *Crime and Punishment* is on top. 'Mad axe man' rises from the literary cortex.

'How much do you charge?' you ask, coming to the conclusion that this is a new form of begging among former intellectuals in recessionary times and hoping to be rid of him by a simple cash payment and get back to your desk.

'Oh, I don't charge!' he responds, as if offended.

'Don't be silly!' you laugh. 'How can you earn a living?'

'That, dear madam, is my own affair.'

'But don't you mind lending your own books to strangers? Don't you find that people ruin them with coffee stains and dog-earing the pages? And some never come back at all!'

'Perhaps the borrowers love them so much they can't bear to part with them so "forget" to give them back.'

You laugh. 'I think you're very naïve.'

'And *I* think *you're* cynical and selfish.'

You're about to slam the door in his face, but the carpet bag's blocking it.

'I'm sorry,' he says, charming and salesmanlike again. 'I didn't mean to offend.'

'But,' you protest, 'people just don't go around the streets lending out their books in the cause of literature.'

'But wouldn't it be nice if they did?!' His eyes are bright.

You try to find a reply, grateful when he speaks again.

'You think I'm a con man, don't you.' He narrows his eyes. 'You even thought I might be a murderer, didn't you, especially when you saw *Crime and Punishment*. Mad axe man, that's what you thought. Well, at least it shows you've already read it – though you might want to read it again!' His face regains its innocent gaiety as he reaches into the bright bag then begins to thumb through the old paperback. 'Let me remind you. The most famous murder in literature!' He clears his throat and begins to read.

'*He could hold out no longer, put his hand out slowly to the bell and rang. Half a minute later he rang again, more loudly.*'

You begin to shrink and panic somewhere deep inside, but cannot act. It would be unreasonable. The parallel is coincidental. There's not really a hatchet in the bag nor concealed under his coat. This is the doorstep of a suburban house. This is now. This is England.

' ... *He took out the hatchet, raised it with both hands ...* '

'Morning!' A cheery voice breaks the hideous vision. Mrs Benn on her way to the corner shop.

'Hello!' You half smile and half wave. She's craning her neck to see what the travelling salesman is selling you.

'Damn!' he mutters. 'Always interruptions!'

'Just what I thought when you rang my bell,' you say, determined to live. You are not going to be the victim of a mad axe man and will close the door then call the police.

But he looks so hurt and disappointed. 'I'll have to start that bit again,' he sighs. And does. And you do nothing.

When he's finished, he stands there, head lowered. You break the silence with, 'I'd forgotten just how very ... '

'It's years since you've read it. Why not read it again?' He snaps the book shut and offers it to you.

'Oh, that's all right. I've got a copy ... at least, if it ... '

'Borrow this one just in case.' You find yourself taking the book from him. 'I'll call back in a couple of weeks.' He closes the bag, picks it up, raises his black trilby hat with that old-fashioned gesture, turns, and walks down the path into the mist, whistling a tune you recognise but can't quite place.

You look down at the doorstep where the carpet-bag had stood, as if expecting some magic symbol to be left behind. Not so much as a dent in the doormat. Slowly you close the door then make your way to the bookshelf housing 'Literature: Foreign': French ... Italian ... Russian. Chekhov ... Ah! D for Dostoyevsky. There's a gap between *The Brothers Karamazov* and *The Idiot*. How annoying! Who borrowed it? But you need a cup of coffee and a few moments to calm down before going back to your writing. The cup rattles a little against the saucer as you carry it to your desk and prepare to open the book to see if Mr Davidsbündler has written his name in it; much can be learnt from a signature.

You open it ... and tumble into an abyss. Your name, in your own distinctive hand, looks back at you.

The next two weeks are scratched by wakeful nights and periods of silent introspection which makes you less than relaxing to live with. You're asked, more than once, if you're 'all right'. If only you could tell someone about Mr Davidsbündler. But it would sound too ridiculous. And the proof – the book he left with you – is inscribed with your own name. It's your own book, so who would believe you? But you have, of course, been re-reading it.

The night before the two weeks will be up is utterly without sleep. And you haven't quite finished the book, reading it more slowly than when you were seventeen and gobbling your way through Russian literature. You wallow in it. You skimp the housework, hurry the ironing, buy convenience meals to win time for Dostoyevsky.

It's nearly morning as you reach the very end, your heart in your mouth as you read, '*The book belonged to her ...* ' The children are stirring. ' *... acquaintance with a new and hitherto unknown reality.*' Small feet padding to the bathroom. ' *... subject of a new story.*' Sleepy voice – 'Mummy.' '*Our present story has ended.*' The door opens. 'Oh, you're in *here*!'

Once they've been taken to school, you make a cup of coffee as usual, sit at your desk and pretend you really are going to do a bit more to that story about the woman who buys a book

Mr Davidsbündler comes to call

consisting of the same eight pages over and over. But glancing at the clock you can't tell if the throbbing is time ticking away or a fearful pounding of your pulse. You write a few words, then cross them through bad-temperedly. Pull yourself together. It was obviously a daydream. This morning is one of clear sunlight; no carpet-bag-carrying commercial traveller in culture is going to step out of the mists of your imagination this morning. Now, just take up thy pen and *write*.

You pick up the pen.

The door-bell rings.

You think you may pass out or be sick.

It rings again.

Picking up *Crime and Punishment*, you hurry (as well as you can on wobbly legs) to the front door. You want to be rid of the book – even if it has your name in it. Thrust it at him, close the door, and let him be gone.

But it isn't so easy when you open the door to his smiling face and the polite raising of the old-fashioned hat, the expectancy and pleasure of his glance at the volume in your hand.

'Good, isn't it!' he begins, as if continuing a conversation not interrupted by the passing of two weeks.

You open the book at the title page. 'Can I ask how you ... came by this particular copy? You see, it happens to be ... mine!' You point to the distinctive signature.

Mr Davidsbündler blanches to an even paler shade of pale and seems genuinely lost for words.

'I ... let me think ... ' He takes the book, turns it over this way and that, as if trying to unlock some buried memory. 'Ah ... that's right ... I *had* a copy – my own – but it wasn't returned. When I called back, the borrower had moved away or died or something. I replaced it with this one from a second-hand shop in ... '

'But I'd never have given my copy of this book to a second-hand ...

'No madam, of course not. I expect you lent it to a friend. The embarrassment of keeping it so long being too much to bear, they got rid of the guilt by getting rid of the book ... without actually throwing it away.'

'But the chances of it coming back to me ... '

'I agree; it's the most bizarre coincidence I've ever come across. Made me feel quite ... strange when you told me. The odds must have been billions to one.' He hands the book back to you insistently. 'No! I wouldn't feel happy keeping it, madam. Each time I saw it, it'd remind me of the bizarre coincidence of its path back to you. Too disturbing to carry around. But what can I offer you this time?' He unfastens the bag with a flourish and you are still a little surprised that it's not full of dusters and cleaning fluids – or religious pamphlets. 'Goethe? Flaubert? Kafka?'

'Something a little less violent this time, I think,' you find yourself saying, though you'd had no intention *whatsoever* of borrowing another book.

'Yes.' He looks around. 'On a crisp, golden morning like this, one doesn't want to grope around in the mists of poverty and guilt. On a morning like this, one wants ... ' He delves into the bag. And instantly you know what he'll bring out.

'Proust!' you both say together, neither of you amazed.

He turns to the title page hesitantly. 'Just making sure!' he grins, and shows you, with a relieved flourish, the signature of F. Davidsbündler ... though it's the same edition as yours, the one you read in Paris when ...

'But I only have the first volume at the moment,' he apologises. 'A gentleman not far from here has had volume two for some time now. I call occasionally. It's been with him to several European countries, apparently, and he still can't seem to ... But one mustn't prate about clients: most unprofessional!'

Your interest is aroused by the idea of the 'gentleman not far from here' reading Proust: you didn't think there was another literary soul for miles. Wild schemes begin to form of Mr Davidsbündler helping to set up networks, an underground movement against ...

' ... And I guarantee,' Mr Davidsbündler is saying, 'that this volume will fall open at the key passage about the madeleine.'

He's right. It does. Even in your own hands – which is where you now find the book.

'Can I ask you a great favour, madam?' he raises his hat. 'Would you be so kind as to read *me* that little passage? I think you have just the right voice for it.'

And though it seems even more bizarre than the circumstances by which the Dostoyevsky found its way back, you find yourself on your own doorstep about to read Proust to a madman in the clear light of a suburban autumn morning. Even more unsettling is the realisation that you'd rather be doing this than anything else in the world – and you begin the famous passage.

'*Many years had elapsed ...* ' And you continue down to '*Whence could it have come to me, this all powerful joy?*' You cannot go on. You are smiling. The feel of the familiar book in your hand and the words themselves have unlocked for you certain feelings which ...

Mr Davidsbündler, too, is smiling. 'Thank you, thank you,' he all but whispers, 'though I have a confession to make. The unlocking of memory by the taste of the madeleine dipped in lime-flower tea is surpassed, I believe, by this ... if you will allow me.' He takes the volume from you with his gloved hands, turns the page, and begins to read.

'*And just as the Japanese amuse themselves by filling a porcelain bowl with water and steeping in it little crumbs of paper which ... the moment they become wet, stretch themselves and ... become flowers or houses or people ... so in that moment ... the whole of Combray ... sprang into being ... from my cup of tea.*'

A respectful moment's silence. He looks up. You are both smiling the same smile as the echo of the last words hangs between you. 'Cup of tea.'

And it seems perfectly natural for him to be sitting at the kitchen table while you pour two cups of 'English Breakfast' tea from a very ordinary tea-pot, apologising for the lack of madeleines but offering him a digestive biscuit instead. Simultaneously you both dip the biscuit in the tea and wait for the memories ... but laughter blows them away.

'It really does have to be madeleines, I'm afraid,' he says.

You are beginning to like him extraordinarily. He has reminded you of the greatness of Great Literature. He has reminded you – a little painfully, perhaps – of your youthful ambition to be a Great Writer. And it's demoralising, always comparing yourself to the giants.

His bright carpet bag is there on your dull kitchen floor. Is it only 'classics' he carries?

'Do you carry anything really up-to-date?' you ask.

'Indeed I do, madam.'

He sets down his cup and bends over the bag. For a split second you think again about the axe ... He retrieves a slim volume.

'I think you might like this one.' He begins to read.

'*The children are at school. Tuesday morning, so the washing's done. You stayed up late to ...* '

Vertigo.

Ears pound, head spins, legs dissolve ...

But somehow you must have found the strength to eject him, for the next thing you know you're sitting at your desk, trembling, as you read, over and over, your own words: '*The children are at school. Tuesday morning ... the washing has been done ... The Children ... the washing ... the children ... the washing ... the children ...* '

PINK

The abduction took place by starlight.

She was asleep, though not in bed. She'd nodded off, fully clothed (except for shoes) stretched out on the *chaise longue*, and Camilla hadn't liked to wake her. Retreating on respectful tip-toe, she'd turned off the main lights, leaving the little bedside lamp glowing its usual subdued pink. Even the curtains were left unclosed in case the light rasping sound should disturb the gently snoring sleeper. The long window was left slightly open, too, for the pleasant breath of the summer-night breeze.

Camilla herself was fast asleep by the time the four figures slipped through the open window into the pinkly flounced bedroom, threw a dark blanket over the sleeper, and whisked her away.

At first she was under the impression that this was another of those suffocating dreams that had been plaguing her lately – but she soon began to suspect that this was different. In her dreams, the source of suffocation – pillow, duvet, a large bottom – was always pink. *This* was black. *This* was leering reality pushing its dirty face right up against hers, forcing its way into her precious dream-time.

Aware of being moved from one place to another, she didn't struggle or call out silly, obvious questions like, 'Where are you taking me?' or 'Why are you doing this?'. She'd no doubt find out soon enough. It would probably involve a demand for money – the usual, boring kind of kidnapping.

Eventually, the movement stopped. There were four voices, all female – though one was rather ... *lusty*. The discussion seemed to be about whether to unwrap her yet.

Yes.

Gingerly, they sat the bundled figure on a chair, aware of her frailty, and carefully removed the dark blanket in which they'd transported her.

And there she was – a slightly crumpled, wingless fairy-doll, shimmering with a crystalline pinkness and silveriness in the dim light. Yet not quite a fairy doll: the face was very, very old. It was also heavily made up – which seemed, oddly, to make it look even older. And two shrivelled little feet hung down beneath the hem of her rumpled skirt, not quite reaching the floor.

But the ancient fairy put on a brave smile, momentarily disarming her abductors.

'Is it possible to have a little more light, do you think? I don't see quite as well as I used to and it seems somewhat dark in here.'

'You'll get used to it, lady.' (Young voice. American.) 'Maybe removing those false eye-lashes would help let the light in. They must intrude awfully on your field of vision.' The girl stepped towards the crumpled pinkness as if to rip the eye-lashes from the mask-like face. But one of the other women grabbed her and pulled her back.

'No, Dolores. That will do no good – neither to her nor to our cause. The idea of bringing Dame Barbara here is not to punish her but simply to make her listen and reconsider.'

'And who do I have the honour of listening to? – who, exactly, is helping me to reconsider whatever it is you wish me to reconsider?' She peered through the gloom. In fact, her eyes *were* beginning to grow accustomed to it and she could now make out the general outline and colouring of the four females standing before her.

The broad creature with the lusty voice (slightly West Country?) announced herself as Alison. The very civil young woman who had prevented 'Dolores' from ripping off the eye-lashes introduced herself as Dorothea. Surly Dolores now

Pink

insisted on calling herself something else – it began with 'L' but the old lady didn't quite catch it. And the woman in some kind of nun's outfit, only bright red, said she could call her Offred.

'Well, my dears, and what can I do for you?' enquired Dame Barbara, pleasantly.

'Cut the fairy-godmother crap,' snarled Dolores. 'It's *us* that's going to be doing things for *you*, lady.'

'That's extremely generous of you, my dears, but I'm not sure I actually *need* anything done for me. I have always been a very active, daring and independent woman and, what's more, I now have Camilla and quite a few other people making sure that everything runs smoothly so I can just get on with my literary life, you know.' (Scoffing grunt from Dolores; belly laugh from Alison; wry smile from Offred; a searching, compassionate look from Dorothea.) 'Oh, I see. You're one of those political groups that doesn't believe in servants and such like. That would account for the amount of red some of you are wearing, I suppose. Well, let me tell you, my dears, a literary life would be impossible without servants of one kind or another. But then,' (she sighed) 'so few people really understand what a literary life is like. And why should *you*, my dears, be any different?'

'You have absolutely no idea who we are, have you?' Offred was gazing at her with a kind of mesmerised disbelief.

'*Should* I know you? ... Oh, you're not from one of those peculiar writers' groups I've spoken to on some occasion or other, are you? You'll have to understand I've spoken to so many people in the course of my long career that it would be impossible to remember them all.'

'Lady, don't you ever *read* anything? (The surly tone had changed to one of puzzled amazement.)

'Read??!! Heavens, no! I don't have time to *read*. I'm a writer, not a *reader*.'

'But ... '

'Oh, you really *don't* know anything about what us writers are like, do you.'

'But ... '

'In fact, you don't know much about anything, I'd say. Now, if you'll allow me to give you a few tips. Take Alison here. So, you can't help being past your prime, Alison, but you could still attract a mate, you know. It's never too late, only *do* see an orthodontist and get that gap between your front teeth closed up. It doesn't help, deary. And I know it might be your age, but you look permanently flushed. Make-up, dear, make-up. Covers a *multitude* of sins ... so to speak. And do try to avoid red. Who wears red stockings *these* days? And that ridiculous hat! You look like one of those women who dresses from jumble sales! A few inches off those hips, too – and try to avoid that sarcastic laughter: men don't go for that, dear.'

'Look here, you silly old crumpet ... ' (Alison – aka 'the Wife of Bath' – planted her hands on her ample, red-skirted hips), 'I've been married five times and have had more lovers than you've written books.'

'Oh, I doubt it. More than seven hundred?'

'Holy Saint Fanny!'

'*Touché*, darling.'

'But I can't believe you really don't know who we are.'

'Any chance of a clue, sweetheart?'

'Ever heard of Geoffrey Chaucer?'

The ancient fairy shook her head. 'Sounds like one of those modern designer labels. I did know of a Geoffrey Johnson-Smith once ... but that was a long time ago.'

'Never heard of *The Canterbury Tales* ... by Geoffrey Chaucer ... the father of English poetry?'

'Oh, *poetry* – who reads that *these* days?!'

The Wife of Bath's face was turning redder and redder, and she looked in severe danger of succumbing to some nasty medical emergency. Offred took her aside and tried to calm her down.

Dorothea had faith that her own steady persistence would pay off in the end.

'I agree, Dame Barbara, that the fourteenth century was quite a long time ago and that maybe not every writer knows their Chaucer as well as perhaps they should, but I'm sure, as a woman writer yourself, you will know the novels of George Eliot ... you know, Mary Ann Evans? The one who used a man's name so she'd be taken seriously? One of *the* great writers of the nineteenth century?'

'Oh, the nineteenth century! Who bothers about that *these* days?'

'But you must've heard of *Middlemarch*. I'm the heroine, Dorothea Brooke.' She reached into the deep pocket of her full-skirted grey dress and pulled out the Penguin edition. 'I'm not being immodest but, really, it's a wonderful book. If you haven't read it, you should.' She handed it to the old lady.

'But, my dear, it's simply enormous! Why, I can scarcely even hold it! This ... ' (she peered at the name on the cover) '... George chap clearly needed a good editor – get rid of all the unnecessary stuff, all the padding. You say you're the heroine. So, what happens to you?'

'I marry an older man to help him with his career. He's well off and highly respected – but he turns out not to be a very loving husband ... not in the way I want. Then I fall in love with a much younger man, and when my husband dies ... '

'... you marry the young man ... who doesn't have much money or a position in life but you're going to be blissfully happy and ... '

'So you *do* know the book!'

'My dear, I know my *own* books. But I can't imagine why your George took so very many pages to tell a story like that. I could've done it in ... '

'Lady, I really think you're missing the point.' (Dolores.)

'And I suppose *you're* the heroine of a book, too – though I can't imagine what kind of story would use a girl like *you* as the main character.'

Dolores reached up her sleeve and pulled out an average-sized paperback. 'A world best-seller, lady. Ever heard of *Lolita* by Vladimir Nabokov – one of the greatest writers of the twentieth century?'

'I bet he hasn't sold as many books as *I* have.'

'But, lady, that's not the point.'

'So what *is* the point? People write to get published and sold and read. The more books they sell, the better.'

'Yes, but what *kind* of books, lady, what *kind* of books ... '

'Ah, so you're not the "Red Brigade" after all – you're the *élite* brigade!'

Having succeeded in calming down the Wife of Bath, Offred came over. With her reticent, ironic manner and rather slow, Transatlantic voice, she took quiet but firm control.

'You won't know me, but I narrate *The Handmaid's Tale* – a futuristic, science-fiction-type novel by a wonderful Canadian writer that you won't have heard of called Margaret Atwood. You won't like it. It isn't a happy story. It's largely about the subjugation of women.'

'My dear, how dreadful for you! Some writers have absolutely no conscience about what they do to their characters. Do you not even have a happy ending?'

'That's somewhat beside the point. As time is getting on and rosy-fingered dawn will soon be waking up the larks, and ghosts will be fading on the crowing of the cock, we'd better get down to business. The reason for bringing you here tonight – let's make no bones about it – is to try to reform you. We want to make you understand that, well, quite frankly, your books do nothing whatsoever to help the position of women.'

'So, you're not the "reds" *or* the "élitists". You're those dreadful femi-what's-its. I should've known. Now, if I could give women like you one magic gift, do you know what it

Pink

would be? ... A sense of pink.'

'A sense of ...*pink*?!'

'Yes, my dear. Pink – and all it means.'

'A gift I would decline.'

'Suit yourself, if you want to wallow in your own misery. But my heroines are a lot happier than you are, in the end. They find fulfilment of their feminine nature in beauty and romance.'

'Excuse my directness, Dame Barbara, but your "books" are dangerous rubbish. They are read mainly by women who haven't a hope in hell of living a life of beauty and romance. They're ground down by endless housework, child-bearing and child-caring, not to mention badly paid, exploitative, low-skilled work. They're distracted and dehumanised by continually trying to make ends meet, by being second-class citizens in what's *still* a man's world. It's a life in which they can never be the winners.'

'That's probably a *little* exaggerated, my dear. I doubt such women have any time at all for reading. But let's say you're right about my readers. Wouldn't you agree that each of my books gives them – how shall I put it? – a little "time off" from their difficult lives?'

'But that doesn't *solve* anything. It just keeps them in chains – feeding them some sugary kind of dream life that'll never happen to them.'

'Offred, darling, you are a great deal younger than I and naturally impatient. It takes a long time to change things in this world. It won't happen in the life-time of the women who read my books. And, while they're waiting for you femi-what's-its to put it all right, I just try to make it bearable. You told me your own story was not a happy one. Did your author not allow you any little escapes from your dreadful situation?'

'I do manage to scrounge brief periods for travelling back in time in my imagination, to my husband, my daughter, my mother ... '

'There you are then! You understand exactly what I'm getting at. An escape into imagination.'

'No. No. You're making it harder for us to change things. You're ...'

'My dear, I feel very sorry for you and the hard life your author has burdened you with. I hold no grudges against you for bringing me here but, as you know, I have a tight schedule. If I don't start dictating my next book first thing tomorrow morning, I won't meet my deadline. The literary life is a demanding one, you know. And it looks as if it's growing light already.' Whitish grey light was, indeed, filtering in. The puckered, made-up, but not unkind face turned in a slow reconnoiter of the surroundings. 'Where exactly are we, by the way? I don't recognise it.'

'The new British Library,' said Dorothea, helpfully. 'We thought it would be ... appropriate.'

'Mmm. Not as nice as the round Reading Room in the old British Library ... the one in the museum. That had *much* more atmosphere.'

'You knew it, Dame Barbara?' Dorothea was wide-eyed with surprise.

The pink fairy gave a knowing smile. They each began to wonder if she'd been teasing them all along.

'My dears, I wish you well. I wish you success and happiness. And I wish you pink. Now, are you going to take me back home, or do I have to use my imagination to get there?'

SPEAK, GARGOYLE

Gar-goyle. Garg-oyle. My name echoes with twisty bits of other words – 'ghastly', 'gargle', 'goitre', 'oil' and, just for good measure, 'boils'. The bits have stuck themselves together, my staring stone ugliness right there in my name. Gargoyle. Mouth leering in a gargle with oil. And I am old ... old ...

The wind whistles round us up here. Slowly lichen spreads its gritty sunshine, and years and years of its yellow creep are whited over in a single crap from your ubiquitous pigeon.

Here we go ... Flutter ... Claws ... Wait for it!

Over seven hundred dizzying years leaning out from this ledge, staring up at the endless carnival of clouds and down at the tiny little people way, way below. A few developments in that time, of course: the bicycle; steam-engines; motor-car; the aeroplane (big surprise, that one!); rockets to the moon ... *great* increase in noise of all kinds. Though some things never change. War. Pigeons.

Pigeon-shit. The only thing we have in common with cathedral saints – them with their smug other-worldliness, eyes rolled up to invisible crowns of glory floating across their mythical heavens. What bugs me is that people know who *they* are, those holier-than-thou simpletons. I s'pose it's their clothes, and all that paraphernalia they have with them: rather a lot if you ask me, considering they're supposed to have given everything to the poor.

But who can name a single gargoyle, eh? We're just a bunch of uglies to you, aren't we. Mind you, I'd rather be gargoyle than any of *them* with their horrible deaths and imaginary crowns and having all those tedious bits and pieces to hold onto all the time – great bunches of keys, dolls-house churches, those arrows, that *awful* spiky wheel ...

I'm quite at home up here, glaring out from the heights of gothicness, my neighbourhood laced with flying buttresses, my companions an interesting and varied bunch – old doggy-faced Glomagog there, farting away as usual by the next buttress along. Bog-eyed Chobkin a bit further on. The other way there's Cubalub (dab hand at aiming rain-water onto the pates of passing clergy) ... and then Obsity. Oh, we've had some good times ...

Ouch! Get yer claws trimmed!

... mostly. But the trouble is ... well ... after seven hundred years it seems I ... don't have much time left. At least, I *may* not have. Rumour has it that recent inspection discovered certain bits and pieces of this great Gothic 'project' to be unsound, unsafe, likely to tumble upon the heads of the little gawpers down there. It seems possible that I shall be replaced ... replaced by a sort of 'clean copy' of how they think I would have looked fresh from the imaginative chisel of the stone-mason Jankin, who could not construe his letters but who was able to persuade wonders from resistant stone. It will be a false memory of me.

Something nasty in the rain has eaten into me, apparently – though, personally, I think certain of the feathered kind cannot entirely escape blame for the situation. And I suppose my edges have also been nudged and rubbed by the centuries, seeing as I'm so old, so old, with day night day night day night a strobe-light passing over me ...

Already the ghostly self that will take my place seems to hang in the air, just out of eye-shot. I feel its cream-coloured inanity hovering there. It's me – but not me. I've earned this darkening of my stone, these imperfections of my surface. Smoothness of

Speak, Gargoyle

skin indicates the ignorance of youth, doesn't it? – though I've heard what stratagems are pursued, in some quarters, against the wrinkles – the very *signs of life*, of having lived, of ... Ha! No offence, but if you'd seen what I've seen so often and so long, you too might baulk at the prodigious coxcombing of you 'youthful' creatures that belch out your gases and squirt out your wastes like the rest of us ... only less publicly, perhaps.

Apologies. This sourness arises, no doubt, from my fear, my regret, my wish to remain, just here. You see, I always felt my position was *preparing* me for something. Storing up sights and sounds and thoughts, catching sound-waves from far and near, feeling them vibrate against my stone, enter me, inform me. It was all preparing me for – what? Suddenly it may all be over. What will I have done with all that 'preparation'?

So I thought if I could get someone to listen, to hear me before ... before a witless simulacrum – some whited, mere *memory* of me – usurps this place from which I've looked out, bog-eyed with wonder and terror, so long – so *very* long – it'd be some comfort in the uncertain days ahead. There are things I want you to know from old Gargoyle here before I get stuffed away in the most boring corner of some museum, the part that's first to be closed when the 'flu hits and there aren't enough guards to go round – or put to doze away the rest of Time in a dust-choked corner of some 'builders and renovators' yard – or sold to a private collector and stuck on a plinth as a conversation piece.

Lot of activity down there – lorries. Huge amounts of scaffolding being delivered. An area at the side of the cathedral screened off as a builders' yard. 'Cobbett and Cobbett. Restorers. Hard hat area.' Oh well, I suppose it's inevitable, but before I ... 'go', I'd like to talk about the 'status' of us gargoyles.

Oy! Bog off, you pea-brained dumper ... you ... you ...
pebble-eyed flea-hotel!

Talking it over with Genghis Khan

OUCH!!
Some of us are trying to have a conversation, if you don't mind, but I don't suppose you'd know what that means, would you.

Our status? Believe it or not, we used to have some. Now we're just the novelty item. You point. Laugh. Move on to the seriousness of saints. Though I suppose I have to admit to our origins in the humble functions of plumbing. But, my friend, the ability to void waste water through a centrally-placed pipe is not the sum of *your* being, is it? – though clearly this is one of your attributes, along with philosophising, politicking, inventing machines, and falling in love. Like your proverbial prophets, we gargoyles have not been properly recognised – for, despite, appearances to the contrary, we are the face of *reason* ... in the sense that our faces are a sane and reasonable response to the *unreason* of the world as is, as was, and as likely to be.

Longevity puts me in a position to give history lessons – history I remember so can vouch for. Mediaeval Europe, for example. I remember a field of caterpillars excommunicated for eating the new crops. Yes, a bishop – educated man, supposedly – went out into the fields, spread his arms and pronounced the words of expulsion from the Community of God's Church. I imagined the caterpillars laughing as the gobbledegook of the bishop floated above them on the spring breeze – laughing as they carried on chumping away at the tender shoots, a few of them choking, perhaps (for it's never a good idea to laugh and eat at the same time) – which would have been a shame as a choked, dead caterpillar can't turn into a butterfly. A plague of caterpillars. But just think what the butterflies were like that summer!

Now the year is 1474. A chicken – yes, a chicken – is put on trial for laying a basilisk egg. The verdict was guilty, of course (the bird having come up with no viable defence) and the chicken executed. Not so very unusual at the time. Plenty of

Speak, Gargoyle

God's dumb creatures were tortured by good Christian citizens to extract 'confessions' in those days. But what would any god worth his salt think of followers who did that to another living creature, eh? – Or of grown men who slaughter each other and believe they have God on their side? Dare I mention the delicate subject of the Somme? ... or Auschwitz? Dresden? Hiroshima? Vietnam? Iraq? Well, excuse me, but it's about as reasonable as putting a chicken on trial. And how many chickens these days get a fair hearing before the chop? Look to your plates, carnivores!

Oh, yes–yes–yes ... sorry–sorry–sorry. I know. We gargoyles always give offence. But only because we speak uncomfortable reasonableness, as I was saying. Sometimes the world's enough to make a gargoyle sick – hence the expression of so many of us. Our makers knew what it would be like, looking out from up here, seeing everything and never a chance to close a blind eye. Some of us simply laugh. It's the only wise thing to do. The only alternative –

OUCH! I told you to piss off!

– though one can't *always* manage laughter, of course.

And it's particularly hard at the moment. For yours truly, anyway. It's the prospect of being removed from my companions. For we gargoyles are *very* sociable ...

Ouch! OUCH! Cut it out. Go on – scram.
We can do without the choric comments from you,
you gibbering moron. Thank you.

Yes, we really do like each other, us gargoyles. We positively *revel* in the differences between us – unlike some of you, if you'll excuse me mentioning it. By your standards I suppose we're all cranks, eccentrics, odd-bodies, outsiders, marginals, conundrums of strangeness. All different. Well, what's the use of friends that just mirror yourself? You've *got* yourself already! Why should I fret that Ramekin along there has pointed goblin ears and pulls a silly face? Why object to Glomalog's dog-faced, human-rumped individuality? What's wrong with Blumbaloo's hairy-headed fish body? Clubalub's goatiness? Fulvashim's beard and breasts? And why blame Chobkin for being so bog-eyed, frog-mouthed, serpent-tailed, and angel-winged? I love the quirks and phizogs of my friends. We laugh at each other, true, but it's not 'put-down' laughter: it's just for the fun of it all. And among my friends, androgyny reigns – or, rather, a complete disregard for the category of gender. We are what we are: Grobolinch, Quibanish, Obsity, Hodip, Loochigant, Suliphit, Yodicus ... Oh, my stone is ripe for weeping at the thought of how I'll miss them when ... No: not when. If ... IF ... IF ... *IF* ... for nothing's absolutely certain yet.

Ouch! OUCH! ... Yuk! Not again!
Have you got an incontinence problem or something?

Hate it when it runs down behind the ears like that.

Oy. Stop pecking. That hurts, you know.

Spirit of mindless violence, that's what they are.

Two men down there, looking up. Hard hats. Expecting my fall to be imminent, perhaps? Bright yellow plastic, the hats are. Easy to see – but not much protection against me, I can tell you, should I come down upon their heads. But they'll not do much more today. The light's going. Already the tourists have taken their pointing fingers home in coaches to dream of cathedral gift-shops.

The limpid eye of evening closes. Cloudless.

Nothing between the top of my head and the moon. The

moon. Last night a tarnished gold plate on an ebony table. Tonight, a fine silver crescent balanced above the mosque of the world. Magical eyebrow of the sleeping sky. Dimmer and deeper into dreaming the world below me goes, and I am left here, fronting the dark.

And for one who must watch through every night, what comfort? The staring is hard. It's goodnight without lullaby. Vast unimaginability. Stupendous immensity. Ineffable marvel of the universe made manifest.

Have you ever spilled a tube of glitter across a glove of black velvet? That few inches of stardust to the rest of the planet Earth is as our galaxy to the Universe. Or maybe even less. That's how big it is out there. Yes, we're that tiny. Yet people still go in for their own 'God's Big Plan For Me' theory. 'Your Fate in the Stars.' 'Your Week in the Stars.' Huh! Your *dandruff* in the stars!

No, we are not dangling on cottons from the stars. With all the looking I've done through all the nights of seven centuries, I can tell you I have never once seen a single thread from the stars. We're on our own. No hot-lines to God. No big plans. No puppet-strings from the heavens to us. We're on our own. We must learn to live with this, our own loneliness, or run mad. It is *we* who make the world, little by little by loving it.

Even its pigeons? Yes, I grudgingly admit it. Even those grey and brainless scourges – from which night at least provides a temporary respite.

The first bird. Even before the light. He's noticed a slight fading of the stars, no doubt. (Not a pigeon, of course: they're too insensitive.) The greenish hand of dawn reaches for the comforting blue blanket of the day, draws it slowly across the sky that the world might live with a little less terror – if a little more error.

Early start. The scaffolding's going up.

Talking it over with Genghis Khan

> *Ouch! here it comes. First crap of the morning.*
> *I hope you've got alternative arrangements.*
> *I might not always be here, you know.*

Actually, they're not particular where they do it. They choose us out of spite because we're all different and they're all the same.

> *At least I'm not going to end up squashed in the road.*
> *Oh, no. Not two of you. I know what that means.*
> *Oy. Why don't you go and copulate down there*
> *on St Paul's head for a change, eh?*

(Always at it. No wonder there's so many of 'em.)

The workmen seem a cheery lot. Singing away. Insulting each other. Quite inventive. Bawdier than old Unctoff, one of them is – and that's saying something! I feel like calling out to them. Bit of 'camaraderie'. But they wouldn't be expecting it. Wouldn't like to cause an accident.

I don't want to speak too soon, but the scaffolding does seem to be working a treat regarding the, er, 'feathered kind'. The brief evening of life relatively peaceful. Small mercies must be counted.

Wonder what it's like in the museum. Stuffy, I should think. Constant temperature. No change of seasons – no feeling them on my face. Perhaps some neglected corner of a builder's yard *would* be my preferred 'after-life'. Dusty, yes, but I'd still get to feel the first spring sun, as up here – the tickle of rain, abrasive hail, the searing blaze of an unprotected summer, passing caress of whirled autumn leaves, frost nipping your crevices. Then, most lovely of all – snow. Snow falling on gargoyles.

Why the most lovely of all? It gives us new contours. And all so white! Makes us smile at each other's newness. Glomalog's lion claws thickened to elephant feet. Ramekin's goblin-ears

Speak, Gargoyle

losing their points to human curves. Chobkin's frog mouth stuffed with crystals, while the breasts of Fulvashim are decently covered for once. The eagle-wings of Unctoff turn angelic (about which much teasing!), while goaty old Cubalub is smoothed to your perfect sheep.

Snow on gargoyles. It makes us see each other differently. No longer the familiar, haggard stones with irregular dressings of pigeon-shit. The beauty of it! A transformation.

The workmen are so close now. I can hear exactly what they're saying. And it's not nice.

Oy. Yes, you. You won't look so good yourself, mate, when you're seven hundred years old.

Seven hundred years. Not so very long after all, now it's over. Or possibly over. Vivid recollections of the day I was put up here – hoists and pulleys and winches and ropes and wheels and the turning of some kind of spiked machine. And the ground falling away, away, away so dizzyingly.

Looking at that lot down there, one wonders if cathedrals would ever have got finished had their builders taken as many 'breaks' as your modern workman.

Going to a lot of trouble to protect the glass – original stuff, apparently. But why so much fuss about preserving *that* when they don't care two hoots about replacing *us* with mere lookalikes. A conspiracy against laughter, against obvious old age, that's what it is. But who wants eternal youth? – youth, with its pains and its pimples, its excoriating embarrassments, its intolerable intensities. Give me old age and laughter in the face of it all. Laughter, that returns all things to their place in nature. Neither more nor less.

Lot of walking around on the roof suddenly. Talking, too. I have so much to say and no time left to say it, by the looks of things. Seems to be raining slightly. Smell of damp pigeon feathers? No. I'm imagining it. Nostalgia. They're staying away. Too much human activity.

Well, it looks as though today's the day.

Tears? – No, no. It's only a little rain.

Is that some kind of machine? I am to be 'cut off'.

The workmen suddenly attentive.

And I feel hands on me ... Hands ...

THE 'BIG D' GANG

or

"THE CASE OF THE DOUBLE QUINCUNX"

1

'We are not dealing,' said the Chief Constable, an ominous seriousness in his voice, 'with your average London bus-stop graffiti artist. These fellas are clever.' He cast a quick but meaningful glance around the room. 'They get the C and the K the right way round.'

There was a general shifting and murmuring among the special group of officers hand-picked to try and unravel the capital's latest mystery.

'The responsibility to solve these crimes rests with each and every one of us. They are no ordinary crimes. If allowed to continue, it wouldn't just be London at risk: they could become a threat to the State itself.' He spoke these last words in a low voice which nevertheless managed to emphasise the tremendous importance of the task that lay before them. They had never known the Chief C. to be quite so serious.

Suddenly the door was flung open by a uniformed officer, very pink in the face and rather dishevelled in general.

"Scuse me, sir, but there's been more incidents. The phones are going mad.'

The Chief C's brow furrowed slightly in puzzlement, then he realised the officer was possibly speaking metaphorically and that the 'incidents' he mentioned didn't actually refer to the capital's telephones 'going mad' (which would have been a 'new development') but to the police station phones ringing more frequently than was their custom.

'Well?' He waited for the officer to clarify the situation.

'It's the libraries, sir.'

'The libraries?'

'Yes, sir.'

'Arson?'

'Oh, no, sir – nothing like that.'

'What, then?'

'Things ... written on them, sir.'

'Things?'

'Yes, sir. Words, sir.'

'What kind of words?'

'All sorts of words, sir.'

'Can you give me an example, officer?'

'There is one that springs to mind ... ' All eyes turned to him, expectantly. He looked a little uncomfortable and fidgeted his fingers. 'It's, er, "crap", sir.'

The murmur of disappointment from the assembled company, however, encouraged the harassed officer to expand. 'It's not just that, sir. It's in funny places ... and sometimes it says "not crap", sir.'

'Correct spelling?'

The officer turned an even deeper shade of pink. 'Didn't think to ask, sir.'

The Chief C. sighed irritably. 'These details are important, officer, in this particular case.'

'Sorry, sir. I'll go back and check.'

But before he could close the door, there came the sound of raised voices and the unmistakable wailing of a young Italian woman in a state of extreme distress.

2

Piers Porter, private detective, was just pouring his wife a glass of sherry when the telephone rang. They had planned a pleasant, relaxing evening listening to their new double CD of *I Pagliacci*, so it wasn't surprising that Piers cursed mildly under his breath when he heard the tedious voice of the Chief C. on the other end of the phone. They only ever called Porter as a last resort. He was expensive. He specialised in unusual cases, his well-groomed exterior belying the quirky mind it housed – a mind capable of following the most bizarre manoeuvrings of the criminal psyche.

As the Chief C. talked on, Piers sipped his sherry and occasionally moved the receiver a little way from his ear. He was eventually obliged to respond.

'My dear chap, I do think this can wait till the morning. Graffiti, no matter how widespread and incomprehensible, plus one hysterical Italian waitress, will scarcely dismantle the State as we know it over night.'

He paused while the Chief C. spoke some more.

'Of course ... Yes, yes ... I suppose it could lead to someone getting hurt, though I rather doubt if things have got that far yet ... Yes, yes ... first thing in the morning. It does, indeed, sound like a most interesting case. I'd be quite pleased to be involved.' He replaced the receiver and stood thoughtfully sipping his sherry for a moment or two.

'Who was it?' called his wife, Laetitia, from the kitchen.

'Oh, just the Chief C. with an interesting little case for me. Here.' As she came through to join him, he passed her a glass of the expensive amber liquid. 'I told him it would have to wait until tomorrow. I've been looking forward to this evening.' He smiled his school-boyish smile and they clinked glasses. 'To *Pagliacci*.'

3

Next morning, Shepherds Bush Road was unhelpfully veiled in mist as the Chief C. and Piers Porter made for Hammersmith Library. But the neat, variously coloured graffiti were nevertheless visible on various parts of the building's outer structure. Piers Porter scanned the building carefully, occasionally nodding, going closer, standing back, looking up, or approaching a window and peering through, as if trying to determine which books were housed directly behind the graffitied areas – all without saying a word. The Chief C. followed him – physically if not mentally, for he had no idea how the Private D.'s mind worked.

Suddenly Piers made for the entrance, and the Chief C. followed him into the library.

Despite the early hour, there were a good number of people at the desk – and there seemed to be a great deal more noise coming from them than was usually encouraged in a library. In fact, one might say they were positively *clamouring* while, on the 'Returns' desk, growing piles of books, opened at various pages, were clearly turning the usually phlegmatic librarian into a besieged bundle of nerves.

As the two men approached the crowd, the people parted in response to their air of automatic authority. But, just the same, the Chief C. flipped a small card from his pocket and flashed it at the flushed librarian.

It took Piers Porter a mere second to ascertain the reason for the clamour of the pensioners and middle-aged ladies who, inevitably on a weekday morning, made up most of the noisy group. On each of the exposed pages there were neat, handwritten messages in various brightly-coloured inks.

'Shall I get the finger-print boys in?' asked the Chief C., ominously.

'I don't think so,' smiled Piers. 'It would lead to the arrest of half the local population.'

The 'Big D' Gang

The Chief C. looked puzzled. Piers sighed. 'A great many people have handled these books,' he explained with slow emphasis, as if speaking to the deaf.

It took a moment more for 'the penny to drop'. And when it finally did, the Chief C. – not a man easily embarrassed at the best (or worst) of times – flushed slightly.

'Let's just take a look,' suggested Piers, somewhat regretting his sarcasm. And the two men began to look at the 'messages' with which the books had been inscribed. Whereas Piers merely glanced at them and made a rapid assessment, the Chief C. took out his notebook and began copying them meticulously into it, noting the title, author, and category, in case it should be significant.

'*Sentenced to Love*,' he wrote, 'by Serena Smiley. Large print – Romance – page 17. "Dear Reader, just because you're getting on a bit and your eyes aren't as good as they used to be, you shouldn't have to be reading this rubbish. As you move towards old age, seek wisdom, not silliness. Boycott this garbage. Demand good stuff in large print. Or buy a magnifying glass. Yours, A friend."'

'*Rat-Pack Nightmare*, by Sid Quinn page 23. "Some books are to be tasted, others to be swallowed, and some few to be chewed and digested. Quote, Francis Bacon. Spit this one out, Dear Reader, before it poisons you."'

He was about to start copying out a third one when the Private D. turned from the pile of books with, 'I've seen as much as I need to.'

'But what shall I do about them all,' wailed the librarian. 'I can't Tippex them all out. It'll take forever! And if I withdraw them from circulation, there'll be an outcry. These happen to be some of the most popular books!'

'Put them back on the shelves,' said Piers, with such steady assurance that everyone seemed, quite suddenly, to calm down. 'Just put them back and let's watch and wait.'

'What about the, er, graffiti outside?' the Chief C. asked, hesitantly, in case there was an obvious solution he hadn't quite arrived at.

Piers shrugged. 'Do as you like – leave it or remove it. What's going on inside is more significant.' His gaze followed a group of library users who had already wandered off to select new books, and most of whom were examining their choices carefully – even thoughtfully ... some even looking at many pages, no doubt searching for further messages.

Meanwhile, Piers Porter and the Chief C. made their exit and headed for the patrol car. Scarcely had they opened its doors, however, when the Station contacted them on the radio and they were obliged to proceed immediately to the Argosy Gift Centre whose windows had been daubed with strange foreign words that no-one could understand but that were felt by the owner, Mr Gombrich, to be vaguely threatening. In one sense, he was right.

4

Piers Porter stood before the garish window of the tacky gift shop and laughed. Neither Mr Gombrich nor the Chief C. could see the joke and were accordingly annoyed and humiliated by the ignorance that kept the joke from them.

'Well, what's it all about?' demanded Mr Gombrich, when he could take it no longer. 'Just tell us what it says.'

'It says *Lasciate ogni speranza voi ch-entrate*,' replied Piers, in perfect Italian.

'But what does it *mean*?' huffed Mr Gombrich, impatiently.

'"Abandon all hope you who enter here,"' proclaimed Piers, still scarcely able to stifle a smile. 'It come from the Big D. himself – Dante, the Italian poet,' he added, by way of explanation, for obvious reasons. 'The inscription over the entrance to Hell.'

The 'Big D' Gang

Mr Gombrich stared at his glittering palace of gifts with a hurt expression. Perhaps he knew that the large, shiny, china horses were not quite perfectly moulded, with those ridges along their spines where no craftsman had filed down the joints. Perhaps he knew that the cheap, veneered little grandfather clocks did not have the same resonance of the originals, and that the little glass chandeliers would never produce the startling sparkle of real crystal. But, if he could have put his half-formed instincts into words, he might have said he dealt in dreams. And Piers Porter did not need to be told what lay behind the Argosy Gift Centre: a childhood in a bare room, an instinctive love of beautiful things that could never be afforded, an instinct which had never been placed in fertile soil. Little education to speak of, but an ability to add up numbers and, after years of hard work, his own little shop where he could sit all day crammed in among cheap, token versions of the things he would have liked to own but never would. He dusted the little alabaster Venus every day, always keeping the price a little too high for his usual customers – customers who thought the possession of a chandelier, and as many other fancy things as their homes could hold, would somehow open doors for them into that leisured realm of power and sophistication of which Piers Porter himself was, in part, a product.

So, despite the laughter, Piers understood it all. He even felt sad, and couldn't help thinking that a few decent books would have done more to 'open doors' for Mr Gombrich and his customers than any number of formica-finish grandfather clocks – even those that had *tempus fugit* inside the circle of gilt Roman numerals. Feeling suddenly sorry for the fat, wheezy little man, he made up a story to account for his laughter.

'You see, when I was at school, we played a prank one April Fool's Day – put a banner up over the Head's study with that very same quotation on it. It brought back so many memories.' He shook his head convincingly, as if trying to disperse them.

Mr Gombrich was somewhat placated, recovering his self-possession sufficiently to call the window cleaner in to get rid of the Dante that was obscuring the special bargain prices he was offering in the run up to Christmas.

On their way back to the car, Piers noticed a small group of people around the window of 'Medusa's Uni-sex Hairdresser'. A large reproduction of the head of Botticelli's 'Venus' had replaced the usual portrait of a pouting punk in the centre of the window. But he did not draw the Chief C.'s attention to it. Others would no doubt do so in the course of the day. He didn't wish to be delayed any longer, having a luncheon appointment at the Ritz.

'I can't make it out,' murmured the Chief C., shaking his head. 'I can't make it out at all.'

Piers Porter smiled to himself, but did not reply.

5

On arrival at the Ritz, Piers Porter edged his way past the overalled workmen who were trying to remove the words 'ONLY CONNECT' which had been painted in large, yellow letters on the outside of the illustrious hotel. Having deposited his coat, he made his elegant way to the usual table where an affable, slightly greying gentleman of portly stature was already waiting.

'Max, old boy!' cried Piers. 'How terribly good to see you again!' They shook hands energetically.

Although they'd spoken on the phone quite often in recent months, it was some time since they'd met face to face. Max's jacket was a little shabbier, his hair a little greyer, and his face a little more lined than the last time Piers had seen his old friend, but otherwise he had remained, in the tradition of old friends, unchanged.

The 'Big D' Gang

'So,' began Piers, as they seated themselves, 'how are things in the world of publishing?'

Maximilian Feinster, one of the few remaining 'gentleman publishers', shrugged. 'One lives,' he said, 'though only just. It's difficult to compete with the big conglomerates. It all comes down to distribution and advertising. Precious little we can do about it, really.'

Piers noticed, with a pang of regret, how the edges of his friend's shirt-collar were frayed, even though as immaculately pressed as ever.

'Oh, come on, Max. There's always something you can do. *Semper undefeated* and all that.'

But Max shook his head. 'Truth is, I'm getting weary of the battle. Just want to withdraw into my own little world up at "Dolcets" and forget what's going on out there.' He nodded in the direction of the entrance and all that lay beyond. 'Huh! Graffiti on the Ritz!'

Piers suppressed a smile. Maybe his friend had not noticed the nature of the graffiti.

'Anyway, what about you?' Max, as always, displayed the good taste of not 'going on about' his own troubles. 'Any interesting cases lately?'

'As a matter of fact, yes. I think you'll find it somewhat amusing.'

At that point they were asked if they wished to order, and since they both took the same dishes each time they lunched there, the ordering took only a moment and Piers was soon launched into the details of the new case, which would be as safe with Max as with a priest in the confessional.

By the time the *consommé* arrived, Piers was relating how the Italian waitress had become hysterical. When she went to clear one of the tables, she found an extraordinarily generous tip. She was about to pick it up – 'no doubt relishing the thought of some harmless little luxury it would buy her,' Piers embellished – when she noticed some Italian written on a napkin left carefully folded beside the tip. 'Can you guess what it was?'

Max shook his head. He had never quite had the wit to keep up with Piers.

'*Lasciato ogni speranza ...* '

There was no need to finish the quote. Max had caught on at once and burst into Max-like laughter. (People at the next table turned around.)

'She thought ... ' Piers could scarcely contain his own mirth, '... she thought Lucifer himself had been in the restaurant and was putting temptation in her way.'

'Jolly decent of him to leave a warning!' Max was enjoying the joke the tremendously.

'Apparently it's spreading like wild-fire.'

'Good old Dante – the Big D. himself!' Max gazed into the distance as if remembering a long-dead friend and the things they used to get up to together.

By the time they'd finished lunch, Max Feinster was in a considerably more optimistic mood than when Piers had arrived. 'Pop back to the office with me, will you; I've got something I rather think Laetitia will enjoy,' said Max, as they were helped on with their coats.

'Fine, but I mustn't stay long. I'm seeing someone at four.' Piers glanced at his watch.

As they entered Burlington Arcade they were greeted with the unmistakable decibels of Scriabin's *Poème de l'extase*.

'I say, this is a new thing.' Max was obliged to shout very close to Piers' left ear. The climax of the piece was drowning the shopping talk of high-class customers and tourist-class window-gazers alike. Some looked baffled and confused, others angry. If it'd been a little closer to Christmas, they mightn't have minded a few choruses of 'Ding-dong Merrily on High', but the all-pervading presence of the *Poème* was putting them quite off their shopping. The little bits of crystal and the lure of cashmere could not cast their usual spell while the music insisted upon attention. A couple of unusually elegant shop assistants stepped out into the Arcade as if trying to ascertain who was responsible for the extraordinary intrusion. But by this time, Piers and Max were through the Arcade and heading for Cork Street.

6

Four o'clock was striking as Piers Porter passed under the great doorway into the lofty chill of Westminster Abbey. Enoch Baxter was standing in his usual spot at Poets' Corner, having a particular penchant for the memorial to Ben Johnson. Piers had never enquired into the reason for this. There was, of course, the theatrical connection, but even so it seemed an unlikely choice for the slightly 'spivvy' figure cut by Baxter with his chequered jacket, slick-backed hair and polyester tie. But he was, after all, only a middle-man, one that transferred information – at a price ... though just how involved Baxter was, Porter couldn't quite be sure.

Feigning interest in the almost over-familiar, crowded little corner of the Abbey, Piers made a point of 'accidentally' bumping into Baxter (literally) to draw attention to his own presence.

'I do beg your pardon ... '

Baxter swung round and immediately stepped back and into his old profession – that of actor.

'Well, if it isn't old Porter!' Baxter clapped him on the back with hideous familiarity.

If the truth were told, Porter found Baxter's habit of surprising one with a different voice and persona each time they met a little trying. But he was a reliable contact, and useful, too. It was amazing what and whom he knew.

In the course of the brief exchange that followed – an exchange witnessed only by a small group of Japanese tourists with their immaculately dressed female guide – Baxter managed to pass a large envelope to the Private D. who, for his part, was already savouring the moment when he would open it and see what Baxter had offered him this time.

It was just before they parted that Piers Porter became aware of a shadowy figure a yard or two to their left, apparently scrutinising one of the inscriptions minutely but who must have witnessed what had taken place between Baxter and himself. A glance established that the figure was European, male, dressed in a long dark overcoat and carrying a hat. The figure did not look at them directly, but Piers was sure the man was aware of their presence, despite his apparent absorption in an inscription. Porter brought the encounter with Baxter to a close as rapidly as possible, then walked off a little way into the Abbey while keeping the dark over-coated figure in view. The light was fading and at some moments the figure seemed to be nothing but an emanation from the Abbey's own shadows. Piers was almost convinced his imagination was playing tricks on him when, looking towards the doorway, he saw, silhouetted against the wintry half-light, a figure of medium build in a long, dark overcoat, settling an old-fashioned trilby hat upon his head and making purposefully out towards the street. Piers tried to hurry after him, but his way was blocked by the same group of Japanese encountered at Poets' Corner and, by the time he had managed to excuse-me his way past them, the figure was nowhere to be seen.

7

The Chief C. sat resignedly behind a desk whose chaos of papers seemed but a reflection of his own distraught looks.

'So, it's been taken out of our hands. It's not just London any more. But how have they done it? There's money behind this, believe you me, Porter. How else could so many of those Mills and Boons in the country's libraries have the inside ripped out and replaced with bits of some novel called *Anna Ka-something-or-other* by some foreign bloke? How could people switch on for *Coronation Street* and find all they could get was bloody *Hamlet*!!? And now they've even got Buck Palace!'

Porter straightened in his chair. 'What happened there, then?'

'Oh, graffiti, of course.' The Chief C. pushed a report towards the Private D. which detailed the offensive words painted on two separate walls of the palace. '*Hunger is the best sauce in the world*' was one. The other was, '*There are only two families in the world ... the Haves and the Have-Nots.*'

Piers recognised them immediately, and smiled. 'Ah, Cervantes!'

'Sir who?' The Chief C. ran his fingers through his neglected hair.

'The Spanish writer Cervantes. They're both from *Don Quixote*.' Piers pronounced it lightly, in the correct Spanish fashion – Key-ho-tey.

'I don't care who bloody wrote any of it. I just wish people would stop daubing it on every available space that takes their fancy.'

'But people have always used graffiti as a way of protesting when they feel disempowered.' Piers was watching the Chief C., his pity laced with the stirrings of contempt – not an emotion he was often taken with, and certainly not one he liked to acknowledge in himself.

The Chief C. pushed back his chair irritably. 'Give me a good old-fashioned 'fuck' or 'cunt' from the bust-stop crew any day. You know where you are with that.'

'*Da steh' ich nun, ich armer Tor! Ind bin so klug als wie zuvor*,' murmured Piers.

The Chief C. looked at him accusingly.

'Goethe,' said Piers, to save the Chief C. from asking. '*Faust*.

"There I am, a poor fool, and am no wiser than I was before".'

The Chief C. grunted. 'I think we'll all be a little wiser soon. They're bringing in Eusebius Eddington.'

Had Porter been in the habit of blanching, the mention of Eusebius Eddington would have elicited such a response from him now. Normally, Eddington was only called in for serious espionage cases – cases in which the security of the State was felt to be at risk. Perhaps those proverbial 'Powers That Be', thought Porter, weren't quite as obtuse as they sometimes seemed. Perhaps they were aware of the possible long-term implications of what was going on. After all, if every Mills and Boon reader switched to Tolstoy ...If Forster's '*Only connect*' stared from walls instead of 'Fuck' (or 'fukc') ... If Shakespeare were to replace ... just think! ... *King Lear* above all. Subversive. Definitely subversive. No, it wasn't surprising at all that they were calling in Eusebius Eddington – he whose very name linked him with the stars, with the grandeur of the universe ... He was a relation of the illustrious Sir Stanley Eddington, astronomer and physicist who, as every school-child ought to know, is famous for his research on the motion, internal constitution and luminosity of stars and for his elucidation of the Theory of Relativity. Eusebius shared his relative's perspicacity of mind but not, as far as Piers recalled, his breadth of spirit. Cold, clinical analysis was his method. Scientist, military man and technical expert on the weapons of the world, his outward appearance was as devoid of charm as his manner. His clipped speech and chilly eyes did not make him a pleasant colleague and Piers spent a moody evening trying to steel himself for his encounter with Eddington the next day by listening to some particularly fine recordings of Bach's Forty-Eight Preludes and Fugues.

Despite the calming effect the abstract complexities of the music always had upon him, Piers Porter's sleep was troubled by non-sensical dreams in which the letters A to G seemed to dance with doubles of themselves to a motley little orchestra conducted mechanically by none other than Eusebius himself. Piers was glad when a cold dawn finally broke and the musical letters danced back into the murky realms of his subconscious.

8

The media had, of course, been focussing on the story for several days now. Hapless library users had been harassed regarding their opinions about the 'substitutions' and 'messages'. Producers of various TV soap operas had been asked for reactions to finding their emissions hi-jacked by 'the Bard', and advertisers to fully express the anger they felt when '*Don't waste your time and money on this rubbish*' and other such trade-damaging devices would flash onto the screen in the middle of a major promotional campaign.

The media wanted anger, outrage. Hordes of reporters roamed the country for vox pop material. But the majority of library users had confessed they were grateful for the substitutions, which had introduced them to authors they would otherwise never have tried – and they'd found them a good deal better than their usual reading diet. One little lady (recently retired from her office cleaning job) became quite eloquent about George Eliot, while a company director spoke of having rapidly become a Balzac addict owing to the substitution of *Le Père Goriot* for one of the ill-written spy stories he usually consumed for 'relaxation'. The TV soap producers, for their part, could see the funny side. 'Let's face it,' said one, 'the family quarrels we give them pale into insignificance compared with what goes on in *Richard III*, *King Lear*, or *Hamlet*. Given a choice, that's what we'd rather be directing – but there's only room for a handful at the top, and the rest of us have to earn a living somehow.'

Most of the interview footage was, therefore, unusable. It didn't work the whole situation up into the froth of a crisis and a confrontation as the media people wanted. As one little old man succinctly put it, ' It's great! After all, what would *you* rather see sprayed all over your local bus shelter, *Only connect* or *F∗∗∗off?*'

However, now that Eusebius Eddington had been called in there was, at last, a 'story'. This meant it was serious, and they managed to fill some tele-time with shots of Eddington emerging from a Rolls Royce, hurrying up some steps, and disappearing through the illustrious doors of 'Headquarters'. But that's all they would get. Eddington was not a media man.

In a room on the other side of the doors through which the cameras had watched Eddington disappear there waited a somewhat agitated Piers Porter, knowing he would be expected to pass on all the information he had accrued so far about the case.

It was several hours later that Piers emerged, pale, exhausted, waving the cameras and microphones aside as he all but collapsed into the waiting car. He just wanted to get home to Laetitia, to his music and his books, to the safe cocoon that protected him from such characters as Eddington.

But this time the cocoon was not strong enough. The knock on the door came in the middle of the night.

9

'Let's call it the case of the Double Quincunx.' Eddington was not smiling.

'The double *what?*' The Chief C. was somewhat baffled to find himself arrested and placed in a well-guarded room along with the Private D., three odd-balls called Baxter, Feinster, and Gombrich, and a number of equally baffled police officers who'd been called in to witness the brilliance of Eddington's solution.

Eddington made use of a convenient flip-chart and felt pen to elucidate his meaning for the Chief C. and others present.

The 'Big D' Gang

'A quincunx is an arrangement of five objects, four marking the corners of a rectangle, the fifth in the centre – so.' He marked five dots, well spaced, on the upper half of the large white expanse of paper, then repeated it on the lower half. 'As I said, a *double* quincunx.' He then began to mark letters beside the dots – by the top left dot a 'B', by the top right a 'C', a 'D' in the centre, 'F' lower right, and 'G' lower left. He repeated this for the lower quincunx, but this time he added whole names – Botticelli, Cervantes, Dante, Forster, Goethe.

Piers could feel the icy eyes of Eddington upon him, waiting to pounce on the least flicker of reaction, but was determined not to give him that pleasure. He stared, non-commitally, at names which, at any other time, would have stirred a pleasant facial response.

When Porter failed to show any reaction, Eddington turned away and began to fill in names on the upper quincunx – Baxter, Chief C. ... he hesitated over the central D, left it blank, and moved on to the F for Feinster and, finally, G for Gombrich.

'Neat, isn't it?' snapped Eddington. 'A piece of cleverly constructed polyphony.'

It was only at this point that Porter showed any response. A pained look passed across his face. He could scarcely bear to think that such a creature as Eddington should even know that musical term, let alone utter it (even if its use were not strictly correct, 'poly' meaning 'many', while there were only two interweaving elements here).

'It may be "neat",' offered the Chief C., emboldened by a confusion more extreme than he had ever known before, 'but what does it mean?'

'Quite simple,' came the clipped reply, and Eddington proceeded to unravel the mystery before the astonished eyes of all present, captives and captors alike. 'You will notice that the letters of each quincunx comprise the first five consonants of the alphabet.'

'What about the vowels?' interrupted Baxter.

'Please don't interrupt,' responded Eddington. 'All will be made plain if only you will exercise a little self-control and listen! Think of the meanings of the word "consonant" – think of its musical associations.' He allowed his gaze to rest momentarily on Porter, while reaching for a dictionary from which he went on to read the following definition: 'Harmonious in tone or sound; being characterised by the presence of æsthetically pleasing sensation or perception associated with the intervals of the octave, the perfect fourth and fifth, the major and minor third and sixth, and chords based on these intervals.' He clapped the dictionary shut. 'Musical harmony ... the letters A to G upon which musical notation is built. At the centre of this 'mystery' is a person closely associated with music – and that person is none other than ... ' here he took up the felt marker-pen again and wrote before the central 'D' of the upper quincunx the word 'Private'. There was a gasp as all eyes turned towards Piers Porter, Private Detective – commonly known as 'the Private D'.

'But that's ... '

'No, not ridiculous, Chief Constable, any more than your own part in this. But let's take a good look at the constituents of this pretty little pattern. We have Baxter, an out of work actor who refused to do voice-overs for lager ads. He wanted to act Shakespeare.

Baxter gritted his teeth at the sneer in Eddington's voice. Images of the gouging out of eyes formed vividly in his mind, though he was not, by nature, a violent man.

'He wasn't content to scrape a living like most of his tribe, so he was ripe for recruitment to this particular brand of social subversion. He believed that if he could help get everyone "into" Shakespeare, there'd be more openings for people like him. So that deals with B. Now C – the Chief Constable himself, whose bumbling ignorance and obtuseness fuelled the fire of crusading zeal among people like the Private D. here – who is behind the whole thing.

Piers stared steadily back at him.

'And, of course, there's the "old boys" network – Porter's old school friend here, Max Feinster, the gentleman publisher ... '

Max lowered his head before the sneering accusation that the term implied from Eddington's thin lips. He was, he knew, one of the last giant pandas, relic of a distant past in which one could lack aggression and still survive in the world of books. Eddington ruthlessly refused him the dignity of silent shame, poking at him with specially sharpened words.

'Business getting tougher and tougher in the world of *belles lettres*, eh, Max? Can't stand up to a bit of healthy competition from TV tie-ins and celebrity autobiographies, can you, "old boy". And as for Gombrich here, apparently just a misdirected old fool ... '

The man in question turned a worrying shade of purplish-red. Even the police officer guarding him looked a little concerned and was, perhaps, trying to recall some detail of his First Aid training.

'He willingly agreed to his shop being used "for cultural purposes". Having been approached by agents of the "gang", he was gulled into a false position. Gombrich is one of those creatures most dangerous to the State – the uncultured person who wants to be cultured ... someone with ambitions, possessed of a certain native wit who, once he rubs shoulders with "learning", becomes politicised and an automatic threat to the *status quo*.'

It was difficult to say who was looking more bewildered at this point, Gombrich or the Chief C., both of whom were still half a sentence behind in following the twists and turns of the argument (added to which, the Chief C. couldn't quite remember what '*status quo*' meant).

'Mr Gombrich didn't realise that allowing his shop to be

used "for cultural purposes" meant having insulting quotations from Dante daubed on his innocent windows – windows selling goods to keep the masses happy, to make them feel they are not masses at all. And it was you, Private D.,' he all but spat the name, 'you, Mr Piers Porter – who should have known better – it was *you* who tried to "harmonise" all these elements – pretending to be something you're not. Your whole life is a tissue of lies; how else could you have brought yourself to marry a woman called Laetitia?'

'WHAT??!!'

'And we see how neatly the letters are reflected in the second quincunx,' Eddington continued. 'B for Botticelli. Funny how the head of his Venus appeared in all those hairdressing establishments. Quite a little network of helpers you had among those who sweep up the hair. Then there's Cervantes. Must have been a bit tricky getting that on Buckingham Palace. A little easier getting the Dante quotes on the napkins and tablecloths in those restaurants. And if Forster had been alive, I'm sure he'd have appreciated the "Only connect" joke – not so much the Ritz, but Simpson's, of course.'

Piers Porter suddenly felt overcome by despair. In order to have made that last comment, Eusebius Eddington must have known Forster's *Howards End* pretty well – must have known the scene set in Simpson's. And if he did know the book well and yet had not been 'modified' by it, what hope was there, after all?

'The pattern is complete – though I think we can now bring in those excluded vowels. First A. In fact, let's make it a double A to fit in with the doubling of the other letters.' He inscribed two As at the top of the page, above the double quincunx. 'AA, for Artistic Authority – or, more to the point, Absolute Authority ... which is what I have and what you want. I Eusebius Eddington ... ' He wrote his own name between the upper and lower quincunx and circled the initial letters, 'I have that authority.'

It seemed to Piers that suddenly, behind him, he could feel presences, many presences, powerful and encouraging. He spoke.

'Authority you may have, but *artistic* authority, NEVER!'

'You, Private D., are a naïve little worm. Science and military power, in the hands of government, have power over all things.'

'But true science is not the enemy of Art,' began Piers, urged on by Voltaire, Diderot and one or two others. 'Both represent the quest of the human spirit for its own fulfilment.'

'Balderdash!' yelled Eddington, with such a vigorous wave of his arms that he scared away the presences Porter had felt coming to his aid. 'Charge them with public nuisance offences,' he ordered. 'Bail if you like. They're quite harmless really. We'll gradually round up all the others, the small fry "helpers". They'll not give us any more trouble once they're ... helped to understand the consequences.'

'But there's so much that doesn't fit your "pattern",' yelled Piers as they took him away. 'What about the S for Shakespeare and Scriabin, and ... and ... what about the man in the Abbey ...?'

Porter's last view of Eddington was of him shaking his head, as if with a cold kind of pity for the presence of such lunacy in the world.

10

Laetitia set down a small silver tray on which two glasses of sherry were kept apart by a porcelain dish of lightly salted cashew nuts. Piers lay back on the *chaise longue*, his eyes closed, lost in the spaces of Sibelius's Second Symphony played at perfect volume.

'Poor love,' murmured Laetitia.

Piers opened his tired eyes and smiled a little wearily. 'I was just imagining,' he murmured, sleepily, 'that at this very moment a little old lady in Sidcup might be reading Tolstoy for the first time and thinking how very much better it was than ... '

'Try not to think about all that now, dear. You've had a hard time.'

'Not as hard as Eddington's going to have. Piers chuckled as he took the first sip of sherry. 'With all this turning the schools and universities over to technology and business and vocational courses, there are going to be plenty of out-of-work and disgruntled Arts lecturers who can't get jobs and who'll try and turn things around ... take up the torch ... '

'But people like that are so law-abiding.' Laetitia sat on the low stool next to the open log fire, her long, slim legs tucked elegantly to the side.

'Don't you believe it! Some of the best and most radical graffiti I've ever seen was on the walls around Oxford and Cambridge – and in the loos. I always remember the time Max came up to visit. We were ... '

But suddenly the door-bell rang.

'Ignore it,' said Letitia. 'It's probably some blasted newspaper man again. You're not expecting anyone are you?'

Piers shook his head. 'I've had enough of other people – except you, of course.' They both smiled the smiles of a perfectly contented couple. Sibelius's Second Symphony soared to its climax.

'I'll just check the *ratatouille*,' said Laetitia. She unfolded herself, stood up with her usual grace, and went off towards the kitchen.

Piers got up, too, stretched and yawned, then wandered over to the window of their third-floor flat which overlooked the deserted Kensington street below. From the entrance to the solid old building a figure emerged into the misty night, swathed in a long dark coat and old-fashioned trilby hat. The figure paused and seemed to look around, then, from a large bag, pulled out some implement that could have been a large paintbrush, dipped it into something in the bag, then busied himself with the wall. Wide awake now, Piers struggled to open the security locks of the window to get a better view and to call out to the man ... who looked vaguely familiar. But by the time he had opened the window the figure was moving off into the fog, whistling a tune which, at least as it came to Piers Porter, sounded remarkably like the *Marseillaise*.

II

I LIKED MY BIBLE BECAUSE IT HAD A LILAC COVER

… and judged it by that (which is normal for nine). With its pages thin as old skin and gilt-edged, it just asked to be touched, to be opened.

I always turned first to the back for the maps. Diluted blue seas, all limpid and calm. Pale-butter-coloured countries called Cush, Phut, and Lud. Made-up sounding names – Edom, Moab, Uz, and Gad. Tongue-twisting Cæsarea Philippi. (Tongue-twisting at ten, anyway.)

The pictures were a first encounter with 'difference'. A grown-up woman on a donkey (and it was no seaside ride). Men who wore table-cloths on their heads – the grandmotherly tasselled kind. Men with long hair. People without shoes – as if it were normal. Feet of ancient times.

Though some things were familiar: the scenery looked a bit like the Lake District, only not so rained-on green. Jesus calming a storm on the waters made me think of that rough Suffolk holiday when we watched the life-boat go out into terrible seas. And Joseph looked weary – as fathers often did.

It was a very considerate Bible. The Crucifixion was not pictured. There was no Mary upset.

And enough punctuation to last a life-time. It suggested generosity.

Its repetitions satisfied. 'And God said, Let ... and it was so.' Over and over. Reassuring.

It even had rhythms for the body. You could waltz at the start of Numbers 1,5: 'And these are the names of the men that will stand with you ... '

And you could spot whole alphabets of new words to embroider the tongue with – alabaster ... bondage ... covenant ... dwelt ... epistle ... firmament ... gird ... howbeit ... iniquity ... jubilee ... kindred ... loins ... Though it was a shame the 'p' of 'psalm' had to be silent.

I played with the words like new toys, juggled them, bright shapes without the shadows of meaning – 'anoint an ass' – 'brethren beget bondage' – 'the balm of a psalm' – and some went spinning off and caught hold of non-Bible words – 'quench a wench' – 'bribe a scribe' – 'epistle-gristle'.

So you can imagine my disappointment when, in a dull and secondary classroom, we were dragged through what it all actually *said*. I already knew the Christmas stuff, of course. Christmas and Crucifixion. And a few miracles. Loaves and fishes. But all that 'old men' stuff and God wobbling his angry beard and taking things out on people, and sick jokes like telling people to kill their children and changing His mind at the last minute. And fancy any father taking notice of a God that'd even suggest such a thing. And if I'd been Job, quite frankly I'd have given Him the finger and gone the other way. Or Jonah. Though it wasn't till later I learnt the right word for all that. Sadistic.

And the women given such a hard time – or *blamed* for everything. (I was growing up curious as Eve.) And *I* think they made

I liked my Bible because it had a lilac cover

that up about Salome and the head on the plate. There was a man behind that: a woman would never think up something like that. She'd think, 'Somebody's child', and not go through with it.

All that – it really put me off my Bible for a while. But luckily you forget a lot of what you learn at high school.

Now I can remember my Bible and know what it *really* taught me – the loveliness of lilac, otherness – Phut, Uz, Cæsarea Philippi … maps of lands diluted by sunshine …

And words … words …

equity – hearken – plenteousness – replenish – vineyard – yieldeth – Zion.

'WHERE DID YOU PUT MY KHAKI SHORTS?'

Your khaki shorts?
Yes, my khaki shorts.

What do you want those old things for? You haven't worn them for ages – must be three years at least.
Just tell me where you've put them.

I haven't 'put' them anywhere.
Where are they, then?

I don't know. Why should *I* know where they are? They're your shorts, aren't they?
But you're the one who does the washing and ironing and organises everything.

And I'm expected to use up brain-space remembering where I put a frayed old pair of shorts that haven't been worn for about five years.
You've thrown them away, haven't you.

Not as far as I remember – no. Why would I do that?
Because you're completely unsentimental about other people's things – like when you gave away Tom's first little bicycle to that woman up the road.

Who couldn't afford one for her own little boy. Anyway, Tom'd just passed his driving test.
You must have some idea where they might be.

'Where did you put my khaki shorts?'

Have you looked through both wardrobes – *properly*?
Yes.

With your eyes open? You know what you're like.
I know what *you're* like.

I'll pretend you didn't say that. You've got at least four other pairs of shorts. I've washed and ironed *two* pairs just this week. Wear those.
I don't want to. I want the khaki ones.

They probably won't even fit you. You're not the same shape you were ten years ago, you know.
Nor are you, come to that.

But I'm not the one looking for some frayed old bit of clothing that's been knocking around for fifteen years.
How do you know they're frayed if you haven't seen them?

I *don't* know. I'm guessing.
You've used them for dusters, haven't you.

I have *not* used them for dusters.
I bet you have.

Look – why've you suddenly got this thing about your khaki shorts? Have they got some special association I don't know about? – someone in the past? – something you *did* wearing those shorts?
No!!

You say 'no', but why should I believe someone insane enough to have a sudden and totally unaccountable obsession with an old pair of shorts?
I have not got an obsession with them. I simply want to know where they are.

But *WHY*, for Christ's sake?!
I was just thinking I might ... look nice in them, again.

What on earth gave you that idea?
You don't have to be so unpleasant.

I am *not* being unpleasant. I simply can't imagine why you should suddenly think you'd like nice in something you'll scarcely be able to squeeze into and which are probably frayed and faded anyway.
It was just a picture I saw.

A picture in a gallery?!
No. In a magazine.

Oh, for goodness sake! Okay – which magazine?
This one.

Show me the picture.
Look. There. Don't they look nice, those khaki shorts?

They look 'nice' because they're on a model – size 10 I'd guess, and I doubt she's more than twenty. You, my dear, are size 14, according to your labels, and a professional woman of 49. ... And now you've made me burn the pizza.
Sorry, Josh.

Besides, that's not khaki – it's mustard.

HELLO, INDIGO

Adventures and metamorphoses.

Searching among some old hermit's bric-a-brac for a tale of wolves, lost sisters, jewels, wishes … Searching and searching by the white of the moon.

Mad light stops play.

Imagination can only gawp at the iron-shoed Hitler-witch closing the oven door. How wrangle over metaphors after that? How rhyme? … How? … How? … How?

Sounds as if we've found that tale of wolves – their misery by moonlight.

But that's not exactly what I meant, not what I meant at all. Not just the *sound* of wolves, lost sisters, jewels, wishes. 'Adventure' carries a future. 'Metamorphosis' takes time. The old adventures just won't do. (Futures are problematic, now.) No, they will not do – not after the twentieth century, cutting itself like some crafty, demented teenager.

Repeating the old adventures is chewing gravel.

Feel around for the light-switch of an unfamiliar room. There's no quick fix, no click of a fixture to light up where we are, where to go, what stories to tell. Wanting the old tales, knowing they won't do. Eyes, for the moment, have to get used to this dark kind of light. It's not so unpleasant after all – full of unseen perhapses.

This is where we are. Might as well welcome it.

Hello, indigo.

THE MEANING OF GERANIUM

Suburban bus-shelter – approaching it on a misty morning and seeing a figure topped with ... yes, geranium.

My hope – its unquellable energy – predicts a punk pitching rebellion against the local beige. My taste is for extraordinary hair, liking it shaved against the big-wigs, long and straight against all things prinked and prim, and brilliant geranium against the pursed lips of beige.

Abandoning good intentions of walking to the station (in favour of geranium-haired companionship at the bus stop) seems less a defeat than a radical choice.

It turns out to be only a hat.

A geranium hat. Something like a beret but a touch more flamboyant. It clings, at a precarious angle, to a mess of darkly greying hair on a wonderfully whiskered woman – face all folds and tucks, the squishy end of a roll-your-own fermenting in the corner of her mouth. A local have-not with a greasy haversack. One of the cranks that have always nestled in the nooks and crannies of the world. An Old English 'cranc', a Middle Low German 'krunke', a Dutch 'krinkel'. A crinkle in the smooth suburban table-cloth.

The word 'Jumbly' comes. She's a Jumbly – a geranium Jumbly (remember them? – 'Far and few, far and few are the lands where the Jumblies live. Their heads are green and ... '). A real live Jumbly in our midst ... in the mist ... glowing geranium through the damp white morning. A beacon. Showing the way? – or a danger signal? (Mad. Avoid ... Avoid ...)

Too late.

Her name? Pamela. An extremely silly name for a face like that. Tucked. Folded. Hanging in dollops. Hairs little bunches

The meaning of geranium

of limp springs. Silly for a body all sacks of flour and potatoes pushed into old trousers and a bobbly jumper. Old-fashioned November 'Guy'.

Trouble with her teeth bringing her out on such a foul morning. Showing it. Yes – that upper molar did look as if it … could be causing problems. And now a conducted tour of her mouth, with entire dental history.

Rabelais' muse.

But after the dentist it's the library. 'They want my Rimbaud back.'

Hot water from a tap marked blue. *Rimbaud*!

'Bloody nuisance. I've had it out two years. Renewed it every three weeks. "Recalled for another reader." Some local kid started their A levels, I suppose. Or someone fancies themselves a bit of a rebel – "raging against the multiple forms of contemporary repression".' (A quote from the editor's introduction?) 'We can all do *that*.'

'Can but don't – very often,' I say.

'Ah, well – each to their own.' (Subtext: don't be so judgemental …)

'Is it a … French edition? – or do you read him in translation?'

'Bit o' both … bit o' both. See … ' (rummaging in the greasy haversack, bringing out Rimbaud in a protective wrapping of fragile, much-crumpled tissue paper, removing it with a deference usually reserved for the world's holy books, checking the cleanliness of her right hand, then opening the book at random.) 'See … the poetry's in French, but it's got a non-poetry translation at the bottom – that small writing. See? I've still got a bit of the old frog-talk up there … ' (tapping the side of her head) 'from ages ago. Over there a bit as a youngster, y'know. But I need the translation for the more complicated stuff.'

'Any special favourites?' (I'm walking on marshmallow, bemused.)

'Not too taken with *Un Saison en enfer* – we can all do that stuff, can't we.' (At which point the last spitally fragment of the roll-your-own detaches itself from her lower lip and lands on the pavement. She kicks it aside.)

'*Le Bateau ivre* – now that *is* good. Nice idea ... this boat breaking away from its moorings, going off into the unknown. Changing stuff. Changing the way you see stuff. I like that.'

A roughly torn piece of paper marks a place about two-thirds of the way through the volume. 'Woops – better take that out before I go to "returns".' She sniffs loudly. 'This weather – really makes y'nose drip, don't it.' Rummaging in the haversack again – for a handkerchief, hopefully. The book on the bus-shelter bench, the ragged book-mark on top. She blows her nose copiously.

The writing on the piece-of-paper book-mark is round, clear, almost childish. '*Intro. p.ix a utopian liberation from the limitations of the self p.xiii language's potential to free the imagination from reality.* And, underneath – much larger and underlined – *JE est un autre* (no page reference).

'That's better.' Stuffing the dampened handkerchief up her sleeve. (I imagine it moist against the wrist.) She consults a large, masculine watch. 'Bloody buses.' She scratches her head, up under the geranium beret which, like the cigarette, can cling to its precarious moorings no longer and falls to the pavement. She retrieves it and holds it on her left knee.

'Lovely colour.'

'What?'

'Your hat. Lovely colour. Geranium.'

'My fogat.'

'Sorry?'

'Fog-'at. The 'at. I wear it when it's foggy. So people can see me coming.'

She pulls a hair-clip out (a hank of greyish-black hair detaches itself from the rest) and refastens the beret as best she can. An even dafter angle than before – that is, looking at it

The meaning of geranium

with an eye to the socially acceptable.

But what the hell! With a colour like that – glowing from the inside (have you seen geraniums at dawn or twilight?), singing of all the window-boxes and warm stone steps of southern Europe, hurling itself through English mist – you can get away with anything.

Sitting beside her, suddenly believing beige days are numbered. Believing in The Revolution ... A fiercely gentle revolution ...

Watch out! Here it comes! – *geranium* ...

GERONIMO ... *!!*

IN THE BRUISE-COLOURED NIGHT

Wake to the suffocating dark. It's something like three. If there are noises now, it's usually some kind of violence – the sex of cats or hedgehogs, the hatred of humans, alarms. The time when those once in love punch out their disappointments, rip at their frustrations, grind away at their despair. The hurting night.

A woman of sixty wakes weeping from dreams of a dead mother. Mothers wake sweating from nightmares of their children drowned. Children cry from the teeth of the fairy-tale wolf, are sick in their beds, develop alarming temperatures, have asthma attacks. Day's blue counterpane, embroidered with white clouds and gold threads of sunshine, is drawn back and the naked body of the hideous night is exposed. The empty, cold, and silent universe. Those seeming points of light that laser the mind with their distances.

Or think of it as the mind swabbed of the dazzling day by that Quasimodo with a dirty mop you saw once: a limping, eyes-to-the-floor life that still haunts the dim corridors of your night-times – those dingy passageways scabbed with sad old photos that might have been bearable once. And the singing – the distant, heart-rending song (though not words, exactly), twined with some deep and throaty joy (though is it joy, exactly?) that pulls you on, tempts you to continue rather than crouch down on the dusty floor, arms over your head, spine curved against the dark, in a declaration of utter submission to ... nothingness.

In the bruise-coloured night

And you know the dark spiders are out and about. You fear them ... yet feel for them and their lonely life in dusty corners. The older and bigger they grow, the harder to hide. You wish you were a tiny one, with all its webs still to weave. Or, better, just a spider egg, pure white and glossy with possibilities – luminous as the moon, but not so mad-faced and cold.

But as it is, you stand in an empty, mirror-lined room. In front and behind, your repeated self stretches away in those mirrors of infinite regress, diminishing into past and future from where you are now, in the room – though which is before, which after?

Closing your eyes is no escape: night churns up the grey silt at the bottom of memory – your first dead cat at the side of the road; the snake basking across your cliff-side path; the sound of your grandfather's heart attack ...

A bench of clay men clasp their sides with stifled laughter at you – you in the corner there, just when you thought you were invisible, in the dark. Only a child thinks closing your eyes makes you invisible. Only a child believes in dreamland and twinkle stars. Others know the violent ways of the night.

The only comfort: the bruising tends to fade when morning comes.

Yes – when morning comes.

And it always does.

COME BACK LAPIS LAZULI, ALL IS FORGIVEN

Lapis Lazuli. A blue sea lapping lazily.
Which made it impossible to live with.

That unbelievable blue – Mediterranean, Adriatic, Aegean ... the ultramarine sky over Greece ...
That's the point. It was unbelievable. Too good to be true ...
And thought far too much of itself. Tin-pot god.

The blue of those gold-stellationed heavens spread on the curved vaults of old basilicas ...
Little stencilled stars on patchy blue distemper.

True lapis lazuli with its specks of gold ... see the constellations in the deep blue firmament ...
Gold?! Huh! Little bits of pyrite. Spare us the fanciful comparisons, can't you?

From the valley of the Kokcha, tributary of the Oxus ... Marco Polo visited those lapis lazuli mines ...
So?

Its genealogy so exotic. Lazuli. From 'lazulum', from the Arabic 'lazaward', from the Persian 'lazhuward' ...
The origins of which are extremely obscure. Unknown. Very *illuminating*! And 'lapis' only means stone, anyway.

That's the kind of thing you would know.
You mean 'the truth'?

I wouldn't say that in company if I were you: you make yourself sound so old-fashioned.

The Age of Reason isn't dead, you know. It's only just beginning. We know the universe …

We do?

… as a vast nothingness speckled with hot stones swirling in galaxies … bath-water down a plug-hole, grains of sand suspended, whirled, sucked into a black hole …

I see you are not opposed to metaphor, then.

Sorry?

Your metaphor – for a galaxy. I find it very … enriching. I was back, at once, in those childhood seaside holidays that seem to have been much longer than two weeks of the year … the tingle of sunburn in the bath, salt on the lips and dulling the hair, the sand you didn't realise was still stuck to you until it came to emptying the bath and the gritty residue was streaked along the bottom and had to be sluiced towards the plughole, watching the sand-grains whirl for a moment before … 'Oh dark, dark, dark – they all go into the dark' … (You do know Eliot, I take it? T.S.?) … thinking how sad for those little grains of sand, after aeons of being rock, then aeons more of the grinding to sand, aeons of the oceans washing over you, then warm dry beach with the sun so glorious on you … so long … so long … only to lodge between some meat-eater's sticky toes and end up washed down into a stinking drain …

Sometimes I wonder how you manage to get through the day, you and your imagination.

Sometimes I wonder how you get by without one.

Perfectly.

Good for you.

You don't mean that. You're making fun of me.

No I'm not. It's very up-to-date. Very 'with-it', 'in tune with the times', 'à la mode', 'dans le vent', 'on the cusp of the zeitgeist' ...
So where does that leave you?

On the cusp of the next zeitgeist – the next wave, *'la nouvelle vague'* ...
Would you care to describe it to me, this 'wave'?

No problem. It's heavenly. It's lapis lazuli ...
Oh *bollocks* to you and your lapis lazuli!

It's not my lapis lazuli. Anyone can have it.
No-one with any sense would touch it with a barge-pole.

It must be very hard for you, always worshipping where the old glass has been completely bombed out and replaced with the clear stuff. You can never have those sudden surprises of a coloured glow on stone – the shiftingness of it with the changing angles of the sun as the seasons turn and ...
Spare me your 'spirituality'!

Oh, I wouldn't call it that. I just think we need to ...
... see things as they really are – stop constructing comforting little myths and worshipping our own constructions in buildings that are more about power-games than ...

Exactly.
What do you mean 'exactly'? You were disagreeing with me just now. Don't tell me your lapis lazuli tide has turned.

Not at all. I'm simply in favour of seeing things as they really are. Incredible. Amazing. Overwhelming. Marvellous. Excruciating. All the rapture and the don't-know-what-to-make-of-it. Incomprehensible. It's beyond reason.
You're beyond reason.

Come back Lapis Lazuli, all is forgiven

Won't you join me? It's very pleasant here.
  You have to be joking.

Probably.
  What kind of answer is that?

As near as I can get to being 'truthful'. I believe in fun and uncertainty, you see. Call it 'Negative Capability' if you like.
  I don't like.

That's your look-out. But you don't mind if I go now, do you? I feel as though I've acquired diving boots when I've been with you for a while – dragging me down into murky water. I can't *breathe*. I'm out of my element.
  Please yourself.

Goodbye, then.
  Goodbye.

I'll try not to think about you – worry about you.
  There's no need.

You won't accept my offer of lazuli?
  No.

I don't like to think of you living a maggot-coloured life.
  Then don't.

All right. I won't.
  I'm fine.
  Perfectly fine.
  I don't mind the maggots ... really.
  Not really.
  Not really.
  Not really ...

THE HIDDEN LIFE OF CARMINE

carmine ('ka:main) *n.* **1.** a vivid red colour, sometimes with a purplish tinge. **2.** a pigment of this colour obtained from cochineal.

cochineal ('kotʃI,ni:l) *n.* **1.** also called **cochineal insect**. A Mexican homopterous insect, *Dactylopius coccus*, that feeds on cacti. **2.** *a.* crimson substance obtained from the crushed bodies of these insects, used for colouring food and for dyeing **3.** the colour of this dye.

Cochineal. That stained little bottle of food colouring – there at the back of the cupboard ... there for years and years because you only need half a drip to ice a little girl's whole birthday cake rose-pink. Suddenly sinister. The kind of fact you can't forget. The crushed bodies of insects. A lurid essence. How many insects to make that bottle? How big are the insects? Are they beautiful?

Massacres to keep nice little girls in pink icing. (So what's new?)

Ghosts of those crushed lives haunting all the pretty birthday cakes. When the candles won't light – when the candles *refuse* to light – that's them doing their voodoo. Or their voodon't. And when the candles refuse to be blown out, too.

I want to know more. The old *Enc. Brit.* ...

> **COCHINEAL**, *a natural dyestuff ... the dry pulverised bodies of the females of* Dactylopius coccus *... the male is half the size of the female and, unlike it, is devoid of nutritive apparatus;*

The hidden life of carmine

it has long white wings and a body of a deep red colour, terminated by two diverging setae. The female is wingless and has a dark-brown plano-convex body; it is found in the proportion of 150-200 to 1 of the male insect. The dead body of the mother insect serves as a protection for the eggs until they are hatched ... the insects are carefully brushed from *the branches of the cactus into bags and then killed by immersion in hot water or by exposure to the sun, steam, or the heat of an oven ... The dried insect has the form of irregular fluted and concave grains, of which about 70,000 go to a pound. The best crop is the first of the season, which consists of the unimpregnated females.*

(So, there you have it.)

Lipsticks, of course, give them their sweet revenge. It isn't just cups it comes off on. We're talking shirts. With the spiky spite from cactus-eating, a carmine kiss is indelible on a white collar. A fleeting Judas, it betrays (by tradition) the truth to a wife who'd suspected anyway.

> Little narrative: carmine on shirt – wronged wife – knife in male chest (or maybe bullet) – chest leaks carmine. Revenge of those females. Wingless, they never stood a chance.

Cochineal. Lurking in lipsticks that sweat greasily in handbags. Lipsticks that smirk at your wishes, your secrets, when you fish them out (in the 'Ladies') for that quick flick of red (flashing 'bed'), renewing the glossy temptation, the lurid lure. Wound up from its tube like a sudden erection, it sniggers at you: '*Animal.*'

Or is its red a sisterly warning of what that bed might bring? 'The dead body of the mother insect serves as ... ' Whichever, they won't let you forget, won't let you be easy, those carmine, those cochineal furies.

Talking it over with Genghis Khan

Though such secret spite *can* be ambushed into love.

Paris. The tomb of Oscar Wilde. After many defacements, a notice appears: we are not to deface the monument. So a new ritual established itself: the lower part of the flying-Sphynx tomb stippled with kisses. Defacement? No. A loving subversion by lavishly carmined lips.

Dactylopius coccus might be all in favour of that.

REMEMBERING SAFFRON

A grey place and a grey day. Maybe not everyone's dressed in dark, but it certainly seems so. That kind of thing seeps into your mind, your mood – even if you start out sunny.

Some delay. The cross-city bus so long in coming. I imagine it bleeding its red into some roadside drain to arrive plain metallic so it'll fit in with the day.

After a grey while, a dull-coloured coach draws to the curb some way ahead, draws alongside a place dim with the grind of a grey day starting in stolid buildings under valiumed skies. A few half-hearted hootings at the inconvenience of a coach stopping just where it has. No appetite for real aggression though: too much effort on such a day.

The door hisses open. The bored driver – propped by forearms on the steering wheel – stares ahead. And then it started ...

A river of laughing saffron spilling out into the grey – and grey giving space to it partly from shock, partly from soft deference, perhaps.

A party of laughing Tibetan monks in their saffron robes – each with one bare shoulder. And party's the right word. They're having a *good* time.

Some of the grey faces around me wither to mouldy masks: disapproval – the gathered black lines of envy's pursed lips. But other grey faces sprout tiny daffodil-yellow smiles, dulled eyes suddenly singing sky blue. (We're all either Marthas or Marys, maybe). And when those daffodil smiles open to speak, bright little birds fly out from their throats, trilling sunshine.

That saffron stream collects to a pool, bubbles of bronzed baldness playing on the surface. Saffron spreading, made way for by grey. The coach has emptied itself and pulled away.

Drivers and cyclists turn to look. There are nearly accidents – luckily just 'nearly'. A bronze arm raised from a bare shoulder, leading the saffron pool trickling off in a luminous stream through silt, considerately single file not to inconvenience the surrounding grey too much.

I'm sorry when those saffron robes don't file past me – they go the other way.

And wherever they're going (heaven only knows – in this place, at this time), I wish I was going with them – wish I was a bobbing head, a sprightly glance, was sandal-footed, saffron-robed, laughing in their company.

Bright fresco on the memory.

Saffron: use for flavouring long grey days.

THE SHOCK OF PINK GRAPEFRUIT

It's the same every time. The same every time. Even now.

Reverse of that sweet birthday cake with its pink icing over yellow marzipan, suspicious and not matching and drawing such attention to itself. Suspiciously yellow and under the pink.

With those grapefruits, it's the pink that's startling. We're used to cutting and finding yellow.

Generations and generations of ordinary grapefruits you've seen – the outer grapefruit mirrors the inner and both conform to the proper idea of grapefruitness. Then, that never-to-be-forgotten shock of the first time, the not-far-off-water-melon-flesh pink that hit the retina, the optic spasm that skewed the brain. *What??!!*

It's the dirty joke your grandmother tells.

It's the school swot turned prostitute.

It's your first squashed rabbit.

A red ambulance blanket.

First sex.

The mind squirms away from it – squirms like a pink worm on a yellow leaf.

'Pink grapefruit' is what I thought on the bus that time it swarmed with the Wonders of the World.

It began at the bus stop. I was re-reading *Nausea* – reviving an old acquaintance because my daughter was studying Sartre and, though I couldn't hope to match her on *Being and Nothingness*, I didn't want to let myself down on his novels when she came home for the weekend. It was supposed to be my field.

One other person joins me at the bus stop. She's dying to talk, I can sense it. But I put up the magic barrier of book-absorption, hoping she'll see the title, think it's a horror story, and comprehend my reluctance to leave it at a suspenseful point. I've just got to that 'existential moment' about the root when her friend turns up.

'Ow-allo. Bin meaninter poprand an'xplain bout them pears.'
'Ow-saright. I gotemoff Pat.'
'Yer*got*em!?'
'Yeh! Didn'Jim tellyer?'
'Ow, yu-know what Jimis.'
'Bu-ow di-they endup on Eye-leen's doorstep?'

Her friend explains how they ended up on Eileen's doorstep and the intricacies of how Eileen discovered who this Tesco bag of windfall pears was really meant for. It was, indeed, a very complicated story, by all accounts. I'm lost after the first five minutes – partly because the teller keeps remembering extra little details and going back over it all to fit them in. And the monologue of the bag of pears is so insistent that no matter how many times I read it, I can't get beyond *Nausea*'s '*I scraped my heel against that black claw: I should have liked to peel off a bit of the bark. For no particular reason, out of defiance, to make the absurd pink of an abrasion appear ...* ' Over and over I read it until the words lose their habitual meaning – just like Roquentin's root.

The bus arrives just in time to prevent me yelling in their faces, 'For Christ's sake shut up about those silly fucking pears!'

The shock of pink grapefruit

A rapid scan of the bus shows me the wisest seat to sit in. A spare 'double' with subdued non-talkers in front and behind. But just after I sit down – and while the pear-sharers are still sorting out their fares – the person behind me changes seats to be nearer the front ... which leaves a free double right behind me.

Yes, of course they do ...

After a further five minutes (I've given up on Sartre – keep the book open for form's sake, but the black marks on the page might as well be Sanskrit), the pear saga seems finally to have exhausted itself. Unlike the teller of it.

'D'you see tha' programme las'night?'

'Wha' programme?'

'Tha' one'bout them fish.'

'No – atcherly ... yes! We don' norm'ly'av tha'sor'astuff on, but Chas was ou' and I sa' there an' couldn't be arsed t'ge up 'n turn over an' I could'n reach the wha's'it thing. Mazin', weren't they, them fish. Th'way they *communicate* ov'rall them miles of ocean.'

'Jim reckons they're cleverer'n us humans – animals.'

'And the size ev them sting-ray things!'

'D'you know, I love the way they move, them sting-rays. Them ripply skir'things. Marvellous, 'nt they.'

'An' what'bout them ones wiv their littl'babies.'

'Weren't they lovely?! Sometimes y'forget, don'tya, all the 'mazin' stuff in the wowld.'

'Yeh. 'Sfulla wonders, init. *The Wonders of the Wowld!* Huh! Listen to wus goin' on. Nex one'smine. Mind owyego, Gwen.'

'Anyou. No leavin' no more pears on the wrong doorstep!'

'Yeh. My brain! One of the wonders of the wowld, it is.'

'Seeya.'

She gets off the bus – which suddenly fills with heaving ocean. A vast aquarium. Humbled, I watch from under a rock as the great whales turn their vast circles and plunge, communicating through their incredible technology ... This salt-water element pushes against me, my hair lifting and drifting as undersea fronds ...

... and the huge sting-rays, alien and strong, ride the currents, rippling and floating, the amazing taper of their tails undulating past me ...

... and the laughter-faced dolphins nudging their babies to the surface to breathe – to breathe ...

Don't be fooled by yellow skins. More grapefruits are pink than we think, it seems. It makes you want to look inside every one – just to see.

It makes you look at lemons differently.

(Personally, I'm just waiting for that blue banana.)

THE LAVENDER BRIDE

Here she comes, the lavender bride!

Not simpering in someone else's colourless notion of loveliness – not silly white – but glorious in her own idea of herself. Ready, in her lavender sheath, to be all things. There's red and blue in lavender – hot and cold, sex and saintliness, danger and a picture-book sky. Look how she smiles her possibilities.

No veil: she doesn't pretend to be demure. No need for tears – no fear she's being sacrificed on that altar. She's taken what she wants from the idea of 'wedding', and the rest is – lavender.

Such a hot day! But while the dutifully hatted and handbagged mop their proverbial brows, she's cool as a lavender cucumber.

Did you note the twinkle in that little girl's eye? She's thinking what colour bride to be. Right now she's toying with scarlet. That leggy nymphet – 'Wedding? Not likely!' – is beginning to reconsider the matter. In a dress of live sunflowers ... a possibility ...

The tyranny of white is over. Flags are out for the rainbow.

And the wedding-cake is ...

chocolate!

CERISE: YES

The passing of G. Mendoza-Jones will be deeply mourned by only a handful, perhaps, of enthusiasts and visionaries. It is not a name to trail the glory of literary prizes and honours, but to those who know the *œuvre* of this idiosyncratic writer, the knowledge that there will be no more of those tantalising collections of mini-narratives will make life the sadder. If only a little.

Mendoza-Jones' first volume of 'short short stories' – *Shaggy Ant Stories* – slipped by without attracting the attention of any major critic, but the second collection – *White dwarfs / Dark stars* – was enthusiastically reviewed by the more enlightened of literary commentators who perceived the possible influence of Borges and Beckett, one even claiming to have found the natural successor to them both (a claim Mendoza-Jones would no doubt have dismissed with that typical self-effacing and ironic smile). The book briefly achieved cult status and could no doubt have become even trendier had its author not spurned the kind of media circus that has helped promote lesser talents.

The title of the third collection – *Daisies on the oak tree* – goes some way to encapsulating the slight grace and elusiveness of the tiny narratives that can scarcely conceal the weight and solidity of what they are actually proposing. The category of 'narratives' for these very short prose pieces has been challenged more than once: Julio Escamodio, for example, claims they have more in common with the spirit of the essay – though in a highly evolved condition, perhaps well-suited to the twenty-first century's impatience with the sustained, investigatory text. Interestingly, there is a connection with Montaigne (credited with having invented the essay form) in that, like him,

Cerise: yes

Mendoza-Jones had a 'medal' struck bearing a personal motto: not Montaigne's famous *Que scais-je?* but *Do it differently*. And Mendoza-Jones certainly did – though not for the sake of being different, but in order to refresh the thinking of readers and, one suspects, of writers, too.

Epsilons of the Moment puzzled some critics with its resort to a singularly old-fashioned epigraph – a quotation from E. M. Forster's 1910 novel, *Howards End*: 'You meant to keep proportion, and that's heroic.' In a rare interview given to a post-graduate student (who clearly touched the altruistic side of the writer so often closed to the critical establishment), Mendoza-Jones claimed the Forster epigraph didn't have any particular connection with the texts that followed. But one can scarcely take such a proposition at face value, given the tone and method of the texts themselves.

But how to talk about those texts? I've spoken to many people who share my enthusiasm for them – especially for the *Epsilons* collection – and every single reader claimed a different piece as their favourite or as representative of the work as a whole. So I will take the easy way out and simply talk about my own favourites, hoping they will provoke those as yet unfamiliar with this literary outsider to rush off and seek out every available copy. Give them as birthday presents! Give them for Valentine's Day! Take them to dinner parties instead of flowers or wine ...

Here is the seventh 'Epsilon' from *Epsilons of the Moment*:

> *Acapulco is a funny name. And Sausalito. And so is Timbuctoo. I was in a distant country where men asked me my mother's name. 'Susan,' I said. One laughed so much they had to fetch the shaman to administer curative herbs and exorcise the threatening tooth-spirit from his mouth.*

And here is the nineteenth 'Epsilon'.

In The Lexicon of Madness, *the man who thought he was a tulip was among the greatest curiosities – until the revised edition, which featured a woman convinced her yellow-rubber-gloved hands were daffodils and thus unable to wash the dishes.*

Then, of course, there are the even more elusive 'cherry texts' (twentieth to twenty-fifth 'epsilons'). My personal favourite is the first of the sequence.

A cheerful singing-class of children: 'Cherry ripe – cherry ripe – ripe – I – cry — ' Oddly old-fashioned. But maybe their singing teacher was old. Children'll sing anything. Jesus wants me for a sunbeam. Humpty-Dumpty sat on a wall. London's burning. It's all the same to them.

The terse, thought-provoking twenty-fifth – the last of the sequence – has proved an irresistible magnet for dissertation writers, the reverberations of its four simple words provoking a veritable rainbow of interpretations.

Cherry: no. Cerise: yes.

Perhaps the most illuminating of the commentaries comes from an S. Bender who, apparently, plucked up courage to ask the author directly what was meant by the four-word narrative in the context of the whole sequence. The tantalising answer was, 'We have to work at our humanity'. A request for clarification produced a somewhat irritable, 'Have you never seen a sculptor constructing a portrait out of clay? We're not *born* with bright souls, you know. We have to build them, glob by blob.'

Bender then explores how this might explain the whole significance of that vital shift from 'cherry' – that physical, squashy, finger-staining (with what appears to be blood?) product of the earth – to 'cerise', which is simply the French word for 'cherry' but which we have adopted for the *colour* of cherries, an 'idea' refined, if you like, out of the purely physical entity. Bender goes on to relate this to the references in *White Dwarfs/Dark Stars* dealing with the gaps between Man and Nature, in both a positive and negative sense, culminating in the piece called 'Head to head'. Although Bender may be guilty of some oversimplification in reading this text as 'an embodiment of that fundamental gap between man and animals – the capacity to imagine another's sufferings and to celebrate another's joy', this does capture something of its essential spirit. Link this with Mendoza-Jones' singularly unsentimental view of children in *Deceptive windows* and the cherry sequence begins to make total sense.

Had Bender delved a little deeper, illuminating links could have been made with Mendoza-Jones' educational theories – quite unique, though with a light spicing of Ivan Ilych and A. S. Neil. While most educational theorists deal with the perennial problem of how to turn a human animal with the capacity for speech into a full moral being, Mendoza-Jones takes nothing for granted about what the term 'full moral being' consists of. However, there will no doubt be some illuminating obituaries in the educational press dealing with the subject.

My present purpose is to mark the passing of one of the most original writers to emerge from these islands – original in terms of work as well as personality. From a purely selfish point of view, I am inconsolably saddened that there are no more Mendoza-Jones texts to come and that the world I inhabit no longer contains her wit and broad humanity.

CAMPAIGN FOR MORE TOPAZ

'What do we want?'

'Topaz!'

'When do we want it?'

'NOW!'

'What do we want?'

'Topaz!'

'When do we ... '

Come on. Join *in*! Don't be so in*hib*ited. World's not going to get better if you keep your mealy mouth shut. Open it up and shout for topaz!

That snowy owl with the topaz eye is watching you. Better be wise. Better go for topaz.

No, madam, it's not more *tow-paths* we're shouting for – though that wouldn't be a bad idea. No, nor for toe-pads or toothpaste. What we want is that wise-gold jazz of ... topaz.

Nobody knows the topaz I've seen – that old iguana with the topaz eye, glowing hearts of countless common flowers, topaz lichen lighting roofs and rocks – and Gaugin, now *he* was something of a topaz man. Think deep yellows in stained-glass windows. And everyone knows, everyone knows the tree-frog has topaz jelly for toes.

But I'm talking topaz of the spirit. *That*'s what we're after.

You don't know what the hell I'm on about, do you. So listen. Be wise. Remember that owl with the topaz eyes.

Campaign for more topaz

Basics first. In case you didn't know, gem minerals come colourless in their pure state (most do, anyway). Colour only comes with impurities. So *pure* topaz – the colourless kind – isn't worth the cost of cutting. Only the *impure* is precious – that unmistakeable gem sunshine tinged with wine.

Forget those screeching diamond sopranos and those rumbling old gypsum basses. Just sway to the human topaz jazz.

Pulp all the patriarchs.
Shred the fundamentalists.
Recycle the supremacists.
But hang on to that sweet ol' pick 'n' mix man – his children all colours of the ethnic rainbow and every sweet-toothed tint between.

(Some say Diana was carrying a topaz child.)

You wanna do something after all? Okay. Be a topaz prophet. Stride about the world in a great topaz robe that billows in the breeze of your speed, if you must, but why not just topaz shorts and sandals? Open your arms and preach against the Seven New Deadly Sins:
 Ob-ed-i-ence
 Cer-tain-ty
 Pur-i-ty
 Inn-o-cence
 Sing-le – mind-ed-ness
 Hu-mil-i-ty
 Chast-i-ty

When you preach against burnt-black Obedience, try parables of armies, führers, orders from on high, and how obeying orders is no longer an excuse. Ob-ed-i-ence: the sin of letting others think for you. Yes, man – it's easy, so easy ...

When you come to that royal-blue sin of Certainty, suggest a campaign to re-canonise Doubting Thomas – this time for his doubt.

And as for that supreme white sin of Pur-i-ty ... well, for God's sweet sake, we all know what *cleansing* means these days. Verily, verily I say unto you, it's better to kick up a stink.

Pink innocence is simple-minded. Declaim its dangers. Announce an absolute duty to *know*. Recite how Innocence begat Ignorance, that begat Stupidity, that begat Excuses. That owl has its topaz eye fixed on pink. (Tell them they've been warned.)

When you get on to blood-red Single-Mindedness, you can lower your prophetic arms and quietly remind the crowd that every loathed dictator has, in-deed, been single-minded as a winding sheet – that the most beloved among us have been many-minded, their patchwork souls spread wide (cite da Vinci, here – his painting, poetry, planes ...)

Struggle (tell them) to free the spirit from that grime-grey Humility that comes from being forced to one's knees by such heavy heavens. Don't feel dwarfed by the stars: size isn't everything. Even in our faulty biology, each of us is more than Jupiter. Look. Com-plex-i-ty. Poss-ib-il-i-ty. Ca-pac-i-ty for com-pass-ion. *Con-scious-ness*. What else do you want, for Christ's sake, to make you feel good about yourself as a form of life!

Chastity? Of the body, if it pleases them, let it go. But that moon-shine Chastity of the *mind* – that's the deadliest of the Deadly Seven. Whores and lechers of the intellect, that's what we want – at it with everyone and everywhere, at it all the time ... penetrating and being penetrated by all the otherness offering itself on all the corners of the world. (That should get them going!)

Campaign for more topaz

Before leaving them with the topaz benediction of an easy wave and a smile, remind them of those deadly colours – burnt black, royal blue, odourless white, sugar pink, blood red, grime grey, moon-shine. Remind them what lovely life awaits them with tolerant topaz – its sunshine, wine, sweet pick 'n' mix, jazz ...

Sshh. Don't look now, but ... they're behind you. Swarming. New sins conjure new devils to serve them. Yes, there they are, those spruce-looking spirits in clay-grey designer wear. See those designer labels – Lucifer, Satan, Be-elzebub, Mephistopheles ... Tight little bottoms and a cat-walk look.

But there are angels, too. There. Don't laugh at the angels. They can't help it. They're too busy to groom their wings. Okay, so they're shedding feathers here, there, and everywhere – but it thrills the children to find them. Instead of 'Glorias', they sing a sound like sea-gulls – courage for wild, unpredictable places (not sticky little Sunday-school hymns). Okay, so they're shambolic – wrapping themselves in bits of saffron silk and old ruby woollies. But they're angels just the same.

Oh, if you can't see them, you can't see them. But you can still join the campaign.

You're not sure you wanna com*mit* yourself?!

Okay, let's talk about it some more. I know a nice little jazz café. We'll leave the others to it for a while. I'll treat you to a nice cold topaz beer.

Here comes the waiter.

What do we want? Topaz ... times two.

BUT IS IT *PERIWINKLE*?

Eighteen and in France. So it mattered. But which novel was it in? So many that year – in English, in French – searching ... searching ... The way you do, then.

(Only *then*?)

Was it such an idyllic day the girl was having? You were too innocent for irony back then. Especially irony in French.

Pervenche. Periwinkle. The sky was periwinkle blue, it said.

Didn't actually know what colour that was – not *precisely*. Just that it seemed to gather into its blueness all that living should be. Oh, happy day!

How had the girl in the novel made mundane day-to-dayness gather to that kind of contentment?

Of course one looked it up in the dictionary: yes, a light purplish-blue. But *how* light? Just what degree of purplishness? And exactly which *kind* of blue was in there with the purple? – aquamarine azure cerulean cobalt electric indigo kingfisher *lapis lazuli* navy Prussian royal sapphire turquoise ultramarine or *woad*-blue?

Or maybe you just don't get that colour sky over England.

Oh, to go back ... to go back ... Especially now: blossom by blossom the spring beginning ...

Waking with the words 'felicitous mahatmas' in your mouth suggests you have either come through some very strange – if

But is it periwinkle?

unremembered – dreams, or that you have finally arrived at some kind of contentment: a reserved smile and a loin-cloth, perhaps. About as far as wisdom goes.

It feels as if that's where you might be. At last. It's taken you twice as long as the girl in the unrememberable novel to reach what was summed up in her 'periwinkle sky'.

At least you *think* it's happiness. Especially on days like today – the almond flowers perfect and stock still against a cloudless heaven ...

Though even now – and maybe for ever – the question breezes in over your shoulder: beautiful blue, maybe – ah, but is it *periwinkle*?

Being grown-up means learning to live with uncertainty.

But you want to keep looking?

Oh, very well. If you must. Grab that passport. Try South.

A MOTH-COLOURED NAP

Not deeply asleep – just the brown softness, the little dying, the reminder of eternal night brushing against the mind. Ghost of the butterfly day-time – no patterns to speak of: distillation of dullness. Just leaves a little brown dust from its wings. Tells of all that we are not, all we have failed to fulfil, with night coming on already.

Beige. Buff. Pale mushroomish.

You'll hear people say 'Red Admiral', 'Cabbage White', 'Small Blue'. But a moth is a moth is a moth. 'Death's Head' the only one to fake a big name for itself.

All the technicolour of the tango – the tangle and go of sex – gives a wing-tip brush with explosive reality. Then we snooze it away to just a fistful of dust.

Even when we're most alive we're half napping. 'How else bear it all?' you might say. How else play out our perverse, obligatory plot of dust and soul to an audience of eyes staring out from other clay? What else can we do but spend our light heroically fiddling in the Park of Idols at the heart of Dream City? That, and other benign (mainly) perversities. 'Look at me now and here I am.' The old tune. (Nothing to be done?)

We could try remembering that water is altogether astonishing and difficult. And not forgetting the wonder of six little spoons – the tiny roses worked on each narrow handle. These and other such rare devices. (Make a list and read it out if you feel yourself nodding off ...)

A moth-coloured nap

We could all be Purple Emperors. Mostly we just stay moths – wings pinned for eternity.

'*Watchet auf*' ... (see Bach).

['Sleepers, wake' – J. S. Bach's cantata BWV 140 (1731) – '*Watchet auf, ruft uns die Stimme*' (Sleepers, wake. The voice is calling us.)]

REASONS TO BE PURPLE

Be, purple people.

Be *purple*, people.

Be purple *people*.

So, when you've nothing else to play with, you play with words – or merely with their punctuation. Not such a bad game. Lots more words to own than 'Monopoly' properties. A better game. *Infinite* possibilities …

Well, it's better than going on about 'Humanity with all its fears' – its 'still sad music' and 'wearisome condition', and how none of us can bear very much reality. Where does that get anybody? Just stating the bloody obvious.

Certain molluscs (*Purpura haemastoma* and *Murex brandaris*, so I'm told) have cysts adjacent to their heads. These cysts produce a pus-like matter which, when spread on textiles in the sun (see the cloth laid out under blue Roman skies), will turn the material a reddish purple.

From 'yuk' to beauty with the help of a star (though ninety-three million miles away). That's what we are.

Two-thirds just water: how *do* we do it? – discover the galaxies; make dictionaries of each other's languages; work out how to knit gloves and dance on our toes. We've discovered within us the patience to make exquisite mosaics and to find (chipping grain by grain) the miraculous Pietà at the heart of the block of marble.

Reasons to be purple

We've made organisations that try to stop wars; made laws so that life might be less nasty, brutish, and bought; sacrificed ourselves by the million for an ideal of freedom; and turned wood, cat-gut and horse-hair into Bach's Cello Suites.

Unable to get into each other's heads, of course – not completely – but we dream and weep with Chopin, smile with Satie, and pledge ourselves to the Universal Brotherhood of Beethoven's Ninth.

We've found out how to preserve the seed-head of a dandelion in a glass paper-weight, and how to splint the broken leg of a baby hedgehog – and we do it.

Scavengers of evil? Of course we are. And the longer we live, the more we know it. But in the superb schizophrenia of our evolved state (to date), we're also emperors swirling in purple.

Water and a few other bits and bobs: that's us. Yet look … look …

Purple: be sure to wear – especially when old.

AN INTERVIEW WITH THE AUTHOR

The first thing that stands out about the collection is that it's flooded with colour. There are only a handful of stories that don't feature colour in an important way and many of them use colour in the title.

The stories are hugely varied in form and length, but colour provides a unifying element. The few that don't use colour directly are nevertheless linked to the colour element and what it stands for in the other stories. For example, 'Looking for Little Miss Universe' pits joy and humour against the sadness of human mortality, and that's very much in line with some of what I'm trying to do elsewhere in the more obviously 'colour-full' stories.

Quite a number of the colours you use aren't what I'd call 'straightforward' ones. They're very specific tones – like 'reseda', 'magenta', 'saffron', 'periwinkle'.

I've always been fascinated by the names of colours. It must go back to seeing the names on my grandfather's oil paints when I was a child. I use this detail very directly in 'After uranium' where they're in contrast to the stories the old man tells the little girl about war. Thematically, it's part of my attempt to foreground the different, the rich, and the unexpected, and making the tales visually interesting, too – and more precise than, say, 'red' or 'green' or 'blue', which would be a bit boring. And, of course, in 'A grandmother's green should be reseda', the contrast between the two different shades of green is very significant – the granddaughter wanting her to be a dignified 'reseda' while the

225

grandmother's real character and her hidden past is expressed through her preference for 'emerald' – which the girl comes to understand in the course of the story. The colour names are also linked with my love of playing with the sounds of words.

Perhaps we can talk about the 'playing with the sounds of words' in a minute. But I wonder if you'd like to say a bit more about the way colour – and even individual colours – functions in the stories.

For me, colour – along with music – is one of the greatest sources of joy in life and, even in sad or serious stories, I usually try to retrieve or create something positive: I hope the foregrounding of colour helps to achieve this. In 'The colour of '33', we go with the narrator and the man she loves to an exhibition of Kandinsky's work. Among all the wonderfully coloured paintings, there's one small, uncoloured one called 'Grim situation' – which only makes sense when you read the date, 1933, and know it was the year Hitler became Chancellor. His regime persecuted the Bauhaus artists, of which Kandinsky was one. This stands for the whole history of that ghastly period, and the narrator can only escape it by 'entering' a painting that's full of healing colour. In 'One magenta sock' the colour becomes an enrichment of life and is associated with a creative and unusual person. In some stories, colour is set against 'no colour': in 'Come back, lapis lazuli, all is forgiven', that rich blue is set against 'maggot-colour'; saffron is set against grey in 'Remembering saffron'; lavender against conventional white in 'The lavender bride', and so on.

Do you have a favourite colour?

Don't laugh – it's actually pale grey ... But maybe partly because against it you can put just about any of the glorious colours that exist and they are both enhanced. In terms of the *sound* of a particular colour, I think maybe 'lapis lazuli' – it has those gentle, lapping 'els' and the zippy, energetic 'z' near the middle.

An interview with the author

The collection ends with a string of little stories that hardly seem stories at all, in the conventional sense.

Ah, but what the reader has to do is construct or be aware of the 'big' stories behind them! 'The lavender bride' isn't just a few lines about a young woman who wears a lavender wedding dress. It suggests the whole history of women being made to conform to certain ideas of 'purity' etc. The young woman in the story defies convention – and in doing so sets a valuable example to others, freeing their imagination to be themselves and not cow-tow to others' ideas of what one should be. These small stories are exercises in 'condensation', if you like, and the reader does sometimes have to work a bit harder at them.

Religion crops up in various stories. The title story actually starts with the sentence, 'When Eva first learned about wars and things, she thought she'd better start going to church – just in case.' She's heard that God is supposed to answer prayers. Yet you're not really a 'believer' in the conventional sense.

No, but I was educated at a wonderful convent school so religion is part of my 'imaginative universe'. What I've tried to do in various stories is recuperate some of the richness of religious imagery and put it to use in a new way, but still with an 'altruistic' intent – a route to a more worldly salvation, if you like. Of course, in the title story the girl's naivety is partly a critique of certain religious attitudes in the face of the overwhelming suffering inflicted by powerful war-mongers, here represented by Genghis Khan and Hitler. At the end of the story, the girl engages the help of two religious statues – man-made 'art works', even if rather 'plastery-looking' ones. They appear to come to life, throw aside the trappings of religious iconography and follow the girl out of the church and into the world – *as statues*. It's tied up with the girl's attempt to start a fashion for replacing the word 'rebirth' with 'Renaissance' – which evokes a blossoming of Humanism and interest in the products of Man's cultural life, as well as 'nicer clothes' than the other option, 'Resurrection', which, as the girl muses, only suggests dusty old blood-stained sheets.

In 'Campaign for more topaz', the speaker takes the idea of the Seven Deadly Sins and proposes seven new ones to replace them. Then, in 'I liked my Bible because it had a lilac cover', I take biblical words out of their original context and turn them into something pleasurable – 'new words to embroider the tongue with' – and finish with a string of them which suggest that a certain approach to life can contribute to social and personal fulfilment. And above all the loveliness of 'otherness'. But I don't want to analyse it to death!

I guess that leads nicely on to your pleasure in playing with the sounds of words.

Even before I could read, my mother used to read poetry to me. One of my favourite poems was John Masefield's 'Cargoes'. It begins, 'Quinquereme of Nineveh from distant Ophir... '. I hadn't the faintest idea what it was about but it was full of the most beautiful-sounding, mysterious words. Then, of course, I studied Anglo-Saxon poetry at university, and I think that also raised my awareness of word-sound. I taught poetry for years, too, and, like many young people with literary ambitions, I started by writing poetry – which focuses the mind like nothing else on the sound qualities of words.

You have to enjoy what you're writing, and, for me, one of the pleasures is 'playing' – if that's the right expression – with words. Thematically, 'playfulness' is important to the collection as it's one of the things – along with colour – that I try to set against the darkness which can so easily overwhelm us. 'The colour of '33' starts by turning the name of the painter Kandinsky into 'sky-candy man', for example. As I said before, the narrator escapes from his one colourless work, and all it stands for, into a 'healing' colour – a sweetness plucked from the sky! And then there's the fun of the gargoyle names in 'Speak, gargoyle'.

As you mentioned, the stories are very varied in form and voice.

I think variety and surprise are important in keeping the reader's interest – and are also a source of pleasure in themselves. As well as conventional first and third person narratives, I also use second person in a couple of stories, which is less usual. It kind of 'implicates' the reader in the story: it's a very direct address. Italo Calvino makes use of it in his novel *If on a winter's night a traveller*, which I use as a reference point for the story 'Mr Davidsbündler comes to call' (hence the story's subtitle). And the odd name of the 'visitor' I've pinched from the composer Robert Schumann's imaginary 'Band of David' – people who would slay the cultural Philistines. But one doesn't have to know that to enjoy the story – I hope!

Other forms I use include a letter ('Say "Hello" to the fairies, Karl'), a monologue (spoken by a gargoyle), a parody detective story, an obituary, a couple of dialogues, one side of an implied dialogue, and I end with something that could be described as a weird kind of little secular sermon. Sometimes I am asking the reader to make a big adjustment from one story to the next. But I hope that's part of the fun!

In many of the stories it feels as if the actual endings are not that important in terms of what the story is really 'about'. Is that a fair comment?

Oh, yes. But then I think that's often the case with short stories as well as novels – apart from some detective fiction where the whole point seems to be to find out, at the end, 'who done it' – though I undermine this in my spoof detective story. Yes, I think it's very much what happens in the course of the stories that really counts ... though there are a few exceptions – including two where the whole point comes in the last few words (but I'm not going to tell you which ones!) and which may just catch the reader out ...

It's always interesting to know how much a writer has taken directly from their own life. You've already mentioned your grandfather's paints, but are there any other significant incidents or characters you've lifted straight from life?

Oh, definitely – though sometimes the unexpected things, like the oldish woman in 'The meaning of geranium' – she's a 'local character' and I've described her exactly as she is. The incident at the centre of 'A grandmother's green should be reseda' is an adapted version of something that happened in my childhood (I still have some of the postcards referred to). Despite the 'fantasy' element of 'Pictures for an exhibition', the kernel comes from the fact that my grandfather – who, while still a teenager, fought in the First World War – would only ever copy other people's paintings. 'Looking for Little Miss Universe' was triggered by an old photo I found of my grandmother soon after she died, in her nineties: she was just a little girl in a fancy-dress costume of stars and moons. 'One magenta sock' stems from the fascination my children had for the lurex socks worn by a visiting friend – a poet. 'The colour of '33' came from a visit to an actual Kandinsky exhibition – though the two young Americans are invented – I think! Sometimes, when you've been involved with writing an incident for longer than you took to experience it, the edges begin to blur between what actually happened and one's own shaping of it into a story. That's happened to me more than once! Then there are little details, like the Bible with the lilac cover – which I still have. There are some images from 'In the bruise-coloured night' that originate from the opening exhibition at Tate Modern. The conversations in 'The shock of pink grapefruit' I did actually experience and 'The lavender bride' is my beautiful daughter-in-law. The starting point for

An interview with the author

'Campaign for more topaz' was a local demonstration against a proposed new road that would have cut through the best part of the nearby town – including the convent school where I'd been a pupil and where I was teaching at the time. Even the nuns were out there demonstrating, yelling for all they were worth. And so was I. Then I caught sight of my neighbour, a devout Catholic – on the pavement, just watching. I called to her to come and join in but she 'didn't like to' ... as if it were something against her religion! Anyway, that was the feeling behind 'Topaz' – though for some reason I hear it in a slightly African-American voice. And when I was eleven or twelve I had a school friend with whom I used to discuss whether or not animals had souls – used in 'After uranium' ... along with the three-legged dog I remember from a Cornish holiday when I was six.

But, then, of course, there is obviously lots of material in the collection that cannot possibly be taken directly from life – though one cannot write about anything that's not 'in your own head' in some form or other, even when it emerges as extreme fantasy – as in 'Pink' or 'Speak, gargoyle'. I must say, I do have a great affection for my gargoyle – and its wish to say everything before it's too late. In essence, you might say he's an aging writer ...

The title. Why did you choose that particular story to be the title of the whole collection?

Actually, I did consider one or two others, including 'Speak, gargoyle' – which is a reference to Nabokov's autobiographical *Speak, Memory* – a book a I love. But in the end I decided that 'Talking it over with Genghis Khan' did several useful jobs at once – which, ideally, you want from a title. I think – hope – it's intriguing because a bit unusual, and it suggests the coming together of two totally opposite 'things' ... a sort of resolving of an impossibility. The idea of 'talking it over' is of civilised, personal dialogue undertaken to sort out some fairly small problem, whereas the association of Genghis Khan is with large-scale, unstoppable violence and cruelty. In the face of such awfulness, literary creation can only be on the scale of 'talking it over'. But I think the title does alert the reader to the fact that the stories, though light-hearted in many ways, do engage with our darker, more destructive side as well as our puzzlement over our own natures as sentient beings in a vast, detached universe. In one sense, the whole collection is 'talking it over' with ... yes, Genghis Khan!

Even though a number of the stories deal with very dark subjects, you've also spoken a lot about fun and pleasure.

If there is no delight in either the writing or the reading of stories, why bother with them? But at the same time, I don't think you can be a worthwhile or useful writer unless you tackle the darkest or most troubling sides of human life – even if you're doing it in quite miniature works. You don't have to write a *War and Peace* in order to make people think. And you can wrest some joy and beauty from the terror and strangeness of existence on a small scale and maybe bring about some little transformations in the process ... perhaps.

Heather Reyes is a writer and creator of the *city-pick* urban anthology series. She has published both fiction and non-fiction: *Zade*, *Miranda Road*, *Perfectly Fine ...* , *National Christmas*, *An Everywhere: a little book about reading* and *Book-worms, Dog-ears, and Squashy Big Armchairs: A Book Lover's Alphabet*. Her short stories have appeared in a wide range of publications in the UK and USA, along with articles on the work of avant-garde writer Christine Brooke-Rose, the subject of her PhD.

She has worked as an English teacher and editor, and lives near London.

Perfect gems of city writing

city-pick

Discover some of the best writing on our favourite world cities with the **city-pick** series.

Berlin
Paris
New York
Istanbul
Venice

St Petersburg
Amsterdam
London
Dublin

'Brilliant ... the best way to get under the skin of a city. The perfect read for travellers and book lovers of all ages.' Kate Mosse

'Superb ... it's like having your own Kindle loaded with different tomes, except only the best passages.'
The Times

'A different point of view. Tired of the usual guides? Can't be bothered with apps? Meet the alternative.'
Wanderlust

'What a great idea! A sublime introduction.'
The Sydney Morning Herald

'The beauty of this clever series is the breadth and reach of its contributors.' *Real Travel Magazine*

'We love the city-pick books. They're right up our street!' *Lonely Planet Traveller*

Available from all good bookshops
www.oxygenbooks.co.uk

'A brilliant guide to the city of books ... I love Heather's passion for reading and the blend of erudition and intimacy.'
Helen Dunmore

Heather Reyes
AN EVERYWHERE
a little book about reading

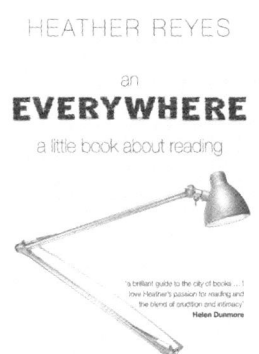

During several months of treatment for a serious illness, the writer decides to turn a necessary evil into an opportunity: the luxury of reading whatever takes her fancy.

An Everywhere: a little book about reading is a quietly passionate and witty defence of the joys and consolations of reading in both the difficult and day-to-day aspects of our lives.

'*An Everywhere* is an extended love letter to the joys of reading and a celebration of the book as physical object. An illuminating and often moving guide to an individual's relationship with the written word.'
W. B. Gooderham, *The Guardian*

978 0 992636 40 1   Paperback original   £8.99
978 0 992636 43 2   e-book

Available from all good bookshops
Oxygen Books
www.oxygenbooks.co.uk

'A delightful gift for a fellow book lover ... This informative compendium of thought-provoking facts and anecdotes, written with wit, style and erudition.'
The Bookseller

Heather Reyes

BOOKWORMS, DOG-EARS, AND SQUASHY BIG ARMCHAIRS

A BOOK LOVER'S ALPHABET

A hugely entertaining, original and informative A–Z of everything you ever wanted to know about books – the ideal gift for anyone who's passionate about books and reading.

'Curl up by the fire and luxuriate in a book that dissects all the ways the written word enchants us ... It not only celebrates the sense of curiosity that book lovers already have, but – thanks to its kindly, welcoming tone – helps to further it.'
Reader's Digest Book of the Month

'Heather Reyes is an Ambassador for the cause of reading.'
Lovereading

'Full of winning anecdotes ... a book to dip in and out of.'
The Simple Things

978 0 99263 64 3   Paperback original   £8.99
978 0 992636 47 0   e-book

Available from all good bookshops

Oxygen Books
www.oxygenbooks.co.uk

'Rich, poetic, painterly, wise and tender.'
Maggie Gee

Miranda Road
Heather Reyes

From London's Archway to Paris, a bitter-sweet and wonderfully witty meditation on love, on being a mother and a daughter, and on the difficulties of freeing ourselves from the past.

'Hugely readable and quietly profound ... lyrical and deeply moving.' Beatrice Colin

'Leafy Archway street inspires magical story ... rich and witty ... poetic, light and politically insightful.' *Ham and High*

'Beautifully written ... from the moment I started it I got hooked ... The tones of that mum, the images, the two voices coming and going. After reading, I savoured the echoes of the lovely voices in my head. This novel is a jewel.'
UK Amazon ***** review

978 0 99263641 8   Paperback original   £8.99
978 0 9926364 4 9   e-book

Available from all good bookshops
Oxygen Books
www.oxygenbooks.co.uk

Forthcoming from Oxygen Books

DON'T MENTION IT
The A–Z of Modern Bullshit

Malcolm Burgess

The hilarious new title that does for modern bullshit what the author's bestselling *I Hate the Office* did for office life.

From *business consultant* ('someone who is paid a small fortune and gets to wear a Prada suit for saying what you and your colleagues have been saying for years in the office kitchen') and *glamping* ('sleeping in a tent on a Cath Kidston lilo') to *Christmas bestseller* ('a book you would never dream of buying for yourself but it is somehow felt to be suitable for relatives and people you don't like very much'), come hundreds of rapier-sharp entries in subject order.

Malcolm Burgess has written for *Metro*, *The Times*, *The Daily Mail*, *ES* and many other newspapers, and his Radio 4 comedies include *Fear and Loathing in Crouch End*.

'Genuinely laugh-out aloud funny.'
City AM on *I Hate the Office*
'Hilarious ... cynically examines the angst of modern office life.'
XFM on *I Hate the Office*
'Laugh-aloud funny.'
Caroline Raphael, Head of BBC Radio 4 Comedy

978 0 9926364 5 6   Paperback original   £8.99
978 0 9932997 2 8   e-book
Published 22 October 2015

www.oxygenbooks.co.uk

Forthcoming from Oxygen Books

National Christmas
Heather Reyes

Trafalgar Square. London's National Gallery. Night falls on 23 December. For the next three days the Gallery is closed to visitors. But there's plenty going on behind those closed doors as the paintings take their annual holiday and step out of their frames. This year, however, four intruders throw the usual celebrations into chaos as the painted world tries to foil the criminals' plans and administer suitable punishments ...

A perfect Christmas novel – as superbly entertaining as it is thought-provoking – where love, generosity and kindness finally triumph.

978 0 9926 36 4   e-book
Published 29 October 2015

www.oxygenbooks.co.uk